Henry's Law

HOLLY J. MARTIN

ISBN: 9798720700454

Above all, love each other deeply,
because love covers over a multitude of sins.

1 Peter 4:8

Other books by Holly J. Martin

The Johnson Family Series:
Princess
Harmony
Heaven
Sweet Love
Forgiven
Brilliant Captive
Stolen Valor
The Wiseguy's Daughter

Also by Holly J. Martin
Divine Risk
The Incarnation of Grace

The Johnson Family

David Johnson   Elsie Johnson
Marcus
Henry
Theodore (Teddy)
Mason (Bear)
Garrett
Bobby and Ty
Davey
Caleb
Jack

Prologue

Sophia began to regret wearing the pretty summer dress with multicolored flowers. It probably wasn't the attire one wore when one engaged in criminal activity such as drug trafficking.

The stale, hot air in the two-seater single engine Cessna airplane was making her nauseous. Well, the heat and her nerves, which had been on high alert for far too long.

It was hard to believe it had been only three days since she received the desperate call from her brother, Santiago.

He had just finished college and was excited to make a name for himself in the computer-programming world. Sophia was so proud of her younger brother.

It hadn't been easy for Santiago when their parents had died in a car accident when he was thirteen. He was angry and had turned to the gang that plagued their small town of La Victoria in the Republic of Colombia.

And Mateo Sanchez, the leader of the pack of thugs, had been all too happy to provide Santiago with a new "family."

More than once Sophia and Mateo had clashed over her brother. Sophia was determined to raise her brother in the church just as her parents would have wanted. Just like she had been raised.

There hadn't always been animosity between Sophia and Mateo. They had grown up together and played together as children. They attended church together, and at one time, Sophia would have said that Mateo was her closest confidant.

All that changed when they were twelve. It had been rumored that Mateo's father and only living parent had gotten in trouble with gambling and owed a drug lord in Bogotá thousands of pesos.

Mateo's father was killed for his debts, and instead of turning to the church and friends who loved Mateo, he turned to the very people who had ruined his life. He stopped coming to school and church. No matter how many times Sophia reached out to Mateo, he lashed out at her.

Her father forbade her to have any contact with Mateo, which wasn't hard to do since he would have nothing to do with her. But that changed when they turned sixteen.

But then, a lot of things changed for Sophia when she turned sixteen. She had been a late bloomer, but by her sixteenth birthday she had developed curves that she would forever consider her curse.

Mateo noticed and began to show up wherever Sophia went. At first she was glad that she had her friend back in her life, but she soon saw the look in his eye and knew that he had forever changed. He became obsessed with her. Her father, on more than one occasion, had angry words with Mateo.

It stopped when she attended university. And, when she returned home, she had more important things to worry about. Her parents had died, and she had the responsibility of raising her brother.

The war over her brother began and Sophia won very few battles. But she had thought her brother would get away from the gang life when he went away to university. And, for a time, he did—or so she thought.

Santiago did very well in school, but what Sophia didn't know was he had gotten into drugs. She also didn't know that Mateo was the supplier of those drugs, and he all but owned her brother.

Sophia had spent the last eight years trying to help Santiago get away from Mateo. She realized only three days ago just how indebted her brother was. It was more than she would ever be able to pay back on her modest teacher's salary.

When she received the call from Santiago, she could hear him begging for his life. She had never been so afraid. Mateo took over the call and instructed Sophia to meet him at an abandoned warehouse just outside of town.

After saying a quick prayer, Sophia drove to the location. It was twilight and the red howler monkeys and cicadas sang loudly.

Sophia entered the warehouse to find her brother on the ground, badly beaten. Mateo sat calmly in a wooden chair, watching Sophia try and tend to her brother. Santiago was crying, babbling about being sorry.

"Why do you put up with him?" Mateo asked, disgusted.

Sophia glared at Mateo. "He's my family. Family takes care of one another."

"I'm afraid even you can't help your brother now, Sophia," Mateo said softly.

Fear washed over her. She tenderly brushed the blood-matted hair out of Santiago's face.

"What have you done, *hermano?*" she whispered to her brother.

"You thought he had gotten his life together living in Bogotá. He has done nothing but lie to you, *mi corazón,*" Mateo said tenderly.

"Don't call me that! Santiago may have stumbled, but it's been you who has been there to encourage him. Why can't you just leave him alone, Mateo? Please . . . for me?"

Sophia saw Mateo clench his jaw. He sat forward and looked at her bitterly.

"He is weak, Sophia. It's easy for you to blame me for his failings. I am guilty of many things, *amor*, but your brother's character is not one of them."

Sophia took a deep breath. "Tell me what I can do to help my brother."

Mateo shook his head and leaned back in the chair. He crossed his legs and clasped his hands in his lap. "The stakes are too high this time, Sophia. There is nothing you can do to help him. I let him call you so *you* could say goodbye. This is a courtesy for you and not one I have ever extended before." Mateo stood. He took one last look at Sophia and began to walk away.

A sob escaped Sophia as she stood and ran in front of Mateo, preventing him from moving forward with her hands on his chest.

"No! You cannot do this! I will do anything to save my brother."

Mateo narrowed his eyes and smiled. "Anything, *mi corazón?*"

Sophia removed her hands and swallowed. She nodded.

Mateo stood and appeared to think for a moment before he spoke.

"I will give you two choices, *mi reina*. You may wipe out your brother's debt by becoming my wife today."

"And what is the second choice?" Sophia whispered.

Mateo smiled. "You *will* be my queen, Sophia, make no mistake, but if you choose for that day to not be today, then you can deliver a shipment of goods into the United States for me."

Sophia turned white. "Drugs."

"What's in the shipment is not your concern. I only need you to deliver the goods, and I think a woman with your particular charms will be able to accomplish this with no problems."

Mateo handed her a slip of paper. "In three days, at this very time, meet me at this location. It's an airstrip. I will give you your instructions then. And bring Santiago with you. He will be in my custody until you have completed the task."

Mateo and his goons left and she was able to get her brother home and take care of his broken body.

****

Sophia sat in her car and cried before she met with the school principal and told him that she would need several weeks' leave to take care of some unexpected business. It broke her heart to leave her children. She loved being a kindergarten teacher.

She and her brother arrived at the airstrip at the instructed time. Santiago assured her, between his apologies, that he would be fine until she returned, and from this time forward, he would straighten his life out and make her proud.

She hugged him and walked with her backpack to Mateo, who stood at the small plane. He almost looked sad for Sophia, she thought.

"You don't have to do this, Sophia. Just turn around and walk away."

Sophia shook her head. "I can't."

"What about your godly fiancé? Have you told him about your plan? I've heard that even he doesn't care for your beloved brother."

Sophia sighed. "My fiancé, as you well know, is a missionary and has been doing God's work for the past year. He will be home soon and we will be married. I will be home long before he comes back. He doesn't have to know anything about this."

"Not the best way to begin a marriage, is it?" Mateo chided.

Sophia did feel a twinge of guilt at the planned omission, but she pushed it aside.

"Let me worry about my fiancé, Mateo. What are your instructions?"

Chapter 1

The plane landed in a field. Sophia had no idea where she was, but wherever it was, it was cold.

She hadn't accounted for that. Her thin cotton dress was wholly inadequate. But little did she know, thankfully, that the cold would be the least of her worries.

When the plane made a bumpy landing and stopped, she asked the pilot in Spanish, who had been silent for the entire trip, if they were in Canada.

"No comprende," he said.

A little surprised, she asked him again in English.

He shook his head. "No, we've crossed the Canadian border. We're in Maine."

She didn't know where that was. She tried to remember her geography, but for the life of her, she couldn't remember a State of Maine.

"How far is Boston from here?" she asked.

From the one sheet of paper Mateo had given her, an address in Boston was her destination.

The pilot shrugged. "It will probably take you five hours to leave Maine and another three hours to get to Boston."

A white van was parked not far from where the pilot had set the plane down. He began to unload the merchandise (drugs) into the van. She felt a little bad about not helping, as was her nature, but really, she had enough to answer for when she said her prayers.

There wasn't a soul around besides herself and the pilot. And, once he finished loading the drugs, which were thankfully in sealed boxes, he got in his plane and started the engine.

She tried to holler to him, but he never acknowledged her. And then he was gone. She walked to the van and opened the driver's door. The keys were in the ignition and a map lay on the passenger seat.

It was dark with almost no traffic on the road. Sophia saw movement from the side of the road, so she stopped the van. In the moonlight, the biggest animal she had ever seen walked onto the road in front of her van.

The beast stood at least six feet tall and must have weighed a thousand pounds. But that wasn't the most spectacular thing about him. His massive antlers spread at least five feet across. The sight took Sophia's breath away. A moose. She had read about them but she never in her wildest dreams thought she would see one standing before her.

The moose slowly walked in front of the van and stopped, looking directly at her for a moment before sauntering across the road and disappearing into the dense woods.

Sophia said a quick prayer of thanks for the sight and reiterated her prayer for safety and forgiveness for delivering the drugs. She asked that the drugs never find the hands of anyone, but that they be destroyed.

She had been traveling for about two hours when in her rearview mirror she saw blue lights. She began to panic as she drove to the side of the road and stopped.

It looked like a truck with lights that stopped behind her van. Two men got out wearing a dark green uniform. The patch on their chest read Border Patrol.

The two officers flanked the van and the officer closest to the driver's door motioned for her to roll down the window. They both shined a light into the front of the van.

"Step out of the van," the officer demanded.

Sophia slowly opened the door and stepped out.

The officer roughly turned her around and pushed her against the van. By this time, the other officer was standing beside her as well.

"Well, look what we have here. A fine-looking chica," one officer said.

"I think we need a cavity search to be sure the chica isn't concealing a weapon," the other officer said, laughing.

The first officer stood behind her and raised her hands above her head. He kicked her feet apart, almost making her fall to the ground. He caught her under her arms and then covered her breasts. He squeezed hard.

Sophia gasped as silent tears fell down her face.

"Any *comprende*, chica?" he whispered in her ear as his hands continued down her body until he reached her ankles and he began to move his hands upward under her dress.

Sophia held her breath as he touched her private parts. Just before his hands dipped into her panties, the other officer pushed him out of the way.

"I'm the senior officer, fucknuts. I'll be the one checking for concealed weapons. You open the van and make sure the product is there."

As the senior officer began touching her breasts, the other officer slid open the van door.

"Well, look at that. I believe we have approximately sixteen pounds of a schedule W drug."

As the senior officer started up her bare legs, he said, "I think we have time to have a little fun before we torch the van."

The other officer laughed and began to load the drugs into his truck. A set of headlights could be seen in the distance, but the men didn't pay them any mind. And, again, just as the senior officer began to pull her panties down, the headlights stopped behind the officers' truck.

"Move the fuck along," the officer hollered at the headlights as he loaded the drugs.

Two men got out of the vehicle and the two border patrol officers drew their guns.

"Easy there, fellas, state police. What's going on?" the large state police officer inquired as he flashed his light on the senior border patrol officer.

He put his gun away and crossed his arms. "We got a tip that a white van had crossed the Canadian border on its way to Boston carrying schedule W drugs. We were bringing her and the drugs in."

"We'll take over now. Our report will acknowledge border patrol's initial search and seizure."

The state police stepped forward to take the drugs and take Sophia into custody. There was a tense moment before the border patrol officers stepped away.

The large state police officer turned her around and placed her in handcuffs and led her to their SUV.

Once she was settled in the vehicle, he went back and spoke with the border patrol officers. Sophia was afraid for the state police officers, but after they finished speaking, they shook hands and loaded the drugs into the SUV.

Once they were on the road, the smaller state police officer turned around in the passenger seat and addressed her.

"Can you understand English?" he asked.

Sophia didn't say a word. She just stared at him.

He turned back around, and they drove for about an hour until they reached a building called Somerset County Jail.

The officers brought her to a room and took her picture and fingerprints. A woman officer brought her to a room for her to undress and put on an orange jumpsuit. The woman officer saw that Sophia was shivering and gave her a white, long-sleeved shirt to put on under the jumpsuit.

Once Sophia was searched by the woman officer and dressed, she was led to an empty cell. Sophia walked in and the door clanged shut. She felt like an elephant was sitting on her chest. She couldn't take a full breath as the tears began to fall.

She lay on the cot in the corner and curled herself into a ball, trying to make herself as small as she could. As she shivered and cried, surprisingly, she fell into a terror-filled sleep.

Chapter 2

Henry tried to breeze by his secretary's desk without being stopped.

"Henry, I need to talk to you," she said.

His hand was on his doorknob when he was busted. He sighed. "Charlie, I've got court, I don't have time. Whatever it is, just handle it," he said very authoritatively.

"Henry Johnson, you do not have court today. Do you forget I set your schedule for you? You have been avoiding me all week," Charlie said quietly.

The hurt in her voice stabbed Henry. He hung his head and sighed as he walked back to Charlie's desk.

She looked beautiful as usual, but even more so these days. She reminded Henry of a young Nicole Kidman with reddish corkscrew curls running down her back. She was tall and thin, well, usually thin. She now sported a big belly that looked like she'd swallowed a soccer ball.

Henry sat in the waiting chair in front of her desk.

"Well, as you know, how long have you been with me, again?" he asked.

Charlie smirked. "Ten years."

Henry smiled and nodded. "Ten years. Wow. As I was saying, in the last ten years you have gotten to know me and you know very well that if I don't like something, I refuse to acknowledge it."

Charlie nodded in acknowledgement. "I know all too well. But"—she pointed to her belly—"this cannot be ignored away."

Henry crossed his legs and held up his tie to study it. "Yeah, about that, why did you have to go and get pregnant? It's like you drove a wedge between us on purpose."

Charlie laughed. "Henry, you were the one who footed the bill for IVF treatments. This is a dream come true for me and Josh."

Henry looked up and scowled. "Josh. Why did you have to marry him? Look what he's done to you. Why do I have to suffer for your bad life choices?"

Charlie looked at him like he was an errant child. "You introduced us. Now be serious for a minute. Today is my last day until my maternity leave is over. You have to let me know which applicant you want from the list I sent you."

"Why can't we just go with my plan? I will supply you with a full nursery right here. We can knock a few walls down. Simple. You take a couple of days off to actually have the little bane of my existence and then come right back to work."

Henry could see tears start to form in Charlie's eyes. He jumped up and knelt in front of her and took her hands in his.

"You know I love you, right?" he asked.

The tears glistened in her eyes. She nodded.

"I want nothing but the best for you and Josh. You take as much time as you need. I trust you to hire somebody to sit here temporarily. Notice I didn't say *replace* because nobody could ever replace you, Charlie."

Charlie wiped a tear away. "Thank you, Henry."

"But, just for the record, I'm not happy about any of this. And make sure you don't get some lovesick woman in here who tries to sleep with me and trap me into marriage."

Charlie laughed. "Duly noted. Tell me, how come your rule about not sleeping or dating women in the company doesn't apply to the women on the opposite side of the courtroom, like the district attorneys? Aren't they coworkers?"

Henry stood and walked to his office door. "They are not coworkers. Besides, how am I going to win the case if I don't make them fall in love with me?"

"Oh, I almost forgot. You actually do have court in about two hours. Lilly called to ask if you could fill in for her at the Skowhegan District Court. She said she's not feeling well and she is on the roster for in-custody arraignments."

Henry looked at his watch. "Well, I better get moving. I'll check on Lilly after court. If I don't see you before you leave," he said, kissing the top of Charlie's head, "break a leg. And, if you need anything, don't hesitate to call. I'll check in on you to make sure Josh is measuring up."

Charlie laughed. "I don't think *break a leg* is the proper encouragement in this instance, but I get your sentiment. And no more gifts! The giant teddy bear that was delivered yesterday is bigger than me!"

Henry strode out of the office with a wave of his hand.

"Say hello to Lilly for me," Charlie hollered after him.

He made the thumbs-up sign and proceeded to the elevator.

****

In the morning, Sophia was taken to a bathroom and then to another holding cell. This cell smelled like sweat and urine. And it wasn't empty.

There were three men and two women sitting in the holding cell when Sophia was directed in. The female officer with the name tag M.E. Landry instructed the male officer outside the cell to watch the inmates.

The moment the door closed, the men began to make noises with their mouths and say foul things to Sophia. The benches were not full, but no one would move so she could sit down. She moved to the back of the small cell, slid down the wall, and sat on the floor.

One man began to speak to her and make sucking noises. She ignored him, which made him angry. He knelt in front of her and grabbed her hair.

"Don't ignore me, you fucking piece of Mexican shit. I'll fuck you right here."

She had had enough. She began to fight and punched him in the eye. This fed his rage and he in turn punched her in the face, pushed her to the floor, and ripped her jumpsuit open.

The men in the holding cell were cheering him on and the women sat silently. An alarm went off before the door was thrown open and two officers in full combat gear entered and pulled the man off her.

The female officer named Landry helped Sophia up and brought her to an empty room. The whole time the nice female officer was swearing and cursing about the no-good officer who was supposed to be watching. She got Sophia another jumpsuit that also was miles too big.

"Sorry about that. He's a dickhead. Doug, the inmate. Well, the officer is, too, but that's just between you and me. I'm afraid we don't have anything that fits you. You're a tiny thing, aren't you? Well, tiny in most places."

With shaky hands, Sophia buttoned the jumpsuit up.

"You probably don't understand a thing I'm saying, but there will be an interpreter at the court. I'd like to know your story. You don't strike me as a drug trafficker. I'll help you out as much as I can while you're in here. But hopefully you'll get bail and go home today."

Officer Landry led Sophia back to the holding cell where everyone was getting hand and leg cuffs to go across the street to the courthouse.

She could feel her eye swelling as she shuffled across the street with the other inmates. The pain in her face was nothing compared to the humiliation of the leg shackles. She tried to remember that she was doing this to save her brother's life. A thought occurred to her as she entered the holding cell at the court. If she was granted bail today, the border patrol agents might be waiting for her. There was no doubt in her mind that they intended to rape her. They must be working for Mateo. No, her best bet would be to stay in jail.

Chapter 3

"Hello, ladies," Henry said, addressing the court clerks at the window to the district court.

Behind the glass, the clerks smiled and gathered around to talk to him. Any attorney worth his salt knew that if you made the clerks in the court happy, your life would be easier. And who didn't like easy? Besides, each and every one of them were delights, but his rule of no sleeping with those he worked with included the clerks.

"I thought it was Lilly's day?" Susan, the head clerk, asked.

Henry nodded. "It was, but I heard she's not feeling well, so here I am, Johnny-on-the-spot."

Susan gave him the list for the day along with their prior records and buzzed him into the lobby outside the holding cell. There was a table and two chairs.

"Oh, I'm glad it's you," Officer Landry said as Henry sat down.

He was intent on reading the paperwork, but answered just the same without looking up. "That's not what you usually say. Are you finally ready to use those handcuffs on me?"

A ball of paper hit him in the head and he looked up.

"No, asshat, I'm glad you're the Lawyer of the Day," Officer Landry said.

Henry smiled. She was always fun to tease. Although there *was* a time that he would have broken his hard-and-fast rule of no fraternization with Officer Mary Ellen Landry. She was a badass and hot as hell. There wasn't an officer in the entire county who wasn't a little afraid of her. She was a good cop.

Before she met her policeman husband, Henry had tried like hell to get her to go on a date with him, but she always said, "I don't date players.

I'm looking for a good guy who I can settle down with and start a family." He always appreciated her honesty, but he had still wanted to bed her.

"Well, anytime you tire of Officer Whatever-his-name-is, you just call me. Now, what's up with this Jane Doe and the biggest drug bust in Maine's history?"

"Yeah, something is off with that. She is definitely not the usual customer. I don't think she'd say shit if she had a mouthful of it. The rest are the same old repeat customers."

Henry was intrigued. He trusted Officer Landry's gut instinct. More than once he had asked her opinion in regard to prisoners.

"So, are we thinking maybe she's a prostitute for the drug lord? Girlfriend of the drug lord? We don't get many drug lords here in Maine. Does she have any teeth?" Henry asked, beginning to read the paperwork again.

"Oh, she's got teeth and a whole lot more."

Again, Henry looked up to see Officer Landry smirking.

"What's that supposed to mean? Can she speak English?"

Officer Landry was serious again. "I don't think she can understand or speak English. An interpreter is expected any minute. I'll have you talk to her last. Just so you know, there was an incident in the holding cell before we came across the street. Fucknuts Trask was supposed to be watching."

"Who attacked her?"

"Dalton Kimball," Officer Landry said disgustedly.

"Jesus, what a waste of space. He's in here for assaulting his girlfriend last night. Is there a complaint coming from this new assault?"

Officer Landry nodded. "I have to write it up this afternoon."

"All right, send Kimball out first," Henry said.

Dalton Kimball sauntered to the table and sat down.

Henry looked up to see his eye and smirked.

Dalton smiled like a fucking idiot. "She's a spitfire, that one. But, my girl, Lori, is here in gen pop in the female ward. She's not gonna like the Mexicali taking a swing at her big daddy."

Henry just stared at Dalton. "You're a vile human being, aren't you, Dalton."

Dalton just continued to smile. "Yup, but you work for me, bub. So, I suggest that you get me out of this hellhole today."

Henry just smiled calmly. "All right, let's see what we can do."

****

When Henry had interviewed everyone but Jane Doe, he took a moment to speak to the interpreter before he asked Officer Landry to bring her out.

Henry was making some notes when he heard the door open and he looked up. He felt like he'd been kicked in the gut.

She was the most beautiful woman he'd ever seen. Black eye and all. He couldn't explain the anger that overtook him when he looked at her swollen eye. Her long dark hair was disheveled and hung down her back. Her dark eyes were like black pools that threatened to suck him in if he looked into them too long. Her full lips were slightly parted, showing perfectly white teeth.

She sat down and he hadn't been aware that he was holding his breath or hadn't looked at anything but her for several long minutes.

"Hola," the interpreter said.

That got Henry out of his stupor. He didn't need a friggin' interpreter, he could speak some Spanish and now wished he had sent her home.

"Hola," Henry repeated.

Jane Doe sat there looking down at her hands, not answering.

Henry began to go over the initial evidence for the bail hearing, but stopped to ask her a question.

"Can you hear? Are you deaf?" he asks loudly.

Jane Doe lifted her head in surprise as if he was an idiot for asking loudly if she was deaf. He smiled at her for his stupidity and, for one brief moment, Henry knew that she understood him. She looked right back down at her hands.

When their eyes had met, it was as if he were in a trance. Henry shook his head to clear it. If she didn't give him something, she was going to have to stay in jail, and for some strange reason, that was not in any way acceptable.

Try as he might, he couldn't get her to speak.

11

They were told that the judge was ready for them. Henry told Officer Landry to make sure Kimball went first and that he was well away from Jane Doe.

Henry went into the courtroom to speak to the DA regarding what she was asking for bail. He was not happy with the discussion.

The judge called Dalton Kimball and asked how he pled to the charge of domestic assault.

"Not guilty," Kimball said.

"Counsel, the State is asking for ten thousand dollars cash bail. Can your client come up with that?" the judge asked.

"No, Your Honor," Henry answered.

The judge asked the State to go over Kimball's prior history, which was extensive.

"Counsel, tell me what your client can make for bail and then tell me why I should lower his bail," the judge said.

"Well, Your Honor, Mr. Kimball isn't missing any work because he has no job. But he has told me that he gives his assurances that he will not skip bail."

The judge and the DA just looked at him like he was having some sort of fit.

Henry just stared at the judge.

"I'm setting bail at five hundred dollars and, Mr. Kimball, if you should be able to make bail, I'm holding you to your assurances that you are not a flight risk."

They went through the rest of the inmates until it was Jane Doe's turn. When he watched her shuffle to stand beside him with her leg shackles and black eye, he wanted to put Dalton Kimball through the fucking window.

The judge inquired of her plea.

Henry answered and said not guilty.

The judge turned to the DA and asked her what she was asking for bail.

"Your Honor, in light of her not telling us her name and the fact that she was transporting eighteen pounds of heroin with a street value in excess of two million dollars, the State is asking for two hundred and fifty thousand dollars cash bail."

Henry felt Jane Doe wince when the DA was pointing out what she was transporting. He looked at her and her eyes were closed and she looked like she was fighting back tears.

He was angry for the high bail, but he had nothing to work with. However, he wasn't giving up.

"Your Honor, that is excessive bail for anybody in Maine. Why don't we have her moved to a hospital setting and have her evaluated? She doesn't seem to be able to understand what is being asked of her. It's also clear that she doesn't belong in a jail cell . . ."

"Your Honor, may I speak?" Sophia asked in English, but with a strong Spanish accent.

The entire courtroom fell silent.

The judge nodded. "Please."

"My name is Sophia Garcia Rodriguez. I'm from Colombia. I am not asking for bail at this time."

Henry just stared at her.

"Counsel?" the judge asked.

"Your Honor, in light of Miss Rodriguez's addressing the court and speaking English, very well, I might add, I think we can safely say that she understands the severity of the charges and will not pose a flight risk," Henry argued.

The DA stood.

"Your Honor, Miss Rodriguez's statement indicates that she is the very definition of a flight risk. She has no ties here in Maine. There's absolutely nothing to keep her from fleeing Maine to go back to Colombia."

"Your Honor . . ." Henry began in a heated voice.

Sophia gently raised her hand. "Your Honor, I repeat, I am not asking for bail at this time. I would like to go back to the jail, please."

The judge himself looked like he didn't want to send her back to jail, but he sighed and nodded.

"Very well, you are remanded back to the custody of the Somerset County Jail."

Chapter 4

When they got back to the jail, Officer Landry escorted her to a cell. Before she unlocked the cell, Sophia spoke softly.

"Officer Landry, thank you for your kindness to me. I'm sorry I didn't speak before. I was scared."

Officer Landry nodded. "It's all good. I'll try and watch out for you, but I'm not here all the time . . . so just watch yourself. And, stay away from a woman named Lori. She's a nasty one."

Sophia nodded and entered the cell. She heard the door clang shut and she winced.

The smell of body odor, sweat, and urine permeated the whole female ward. She could only imagine what the male ward smelled like.

Taking a quick look around, she could see someone on the top bunk, but they must have been sleeping because there was no movement. There was a metal toilet in the back of the cell and a small counter and chair to serve as a writing desk.

Sophia quietly lay on the bottom bunk and silently prayed for strength and comfort.

She could feel that she was being watched so she turned over and saw a woman hanging from the top bunk. Her blonde hair hung down. She didn't speak, just stared.

"Hola," Sophia whispered.

Suddenly a big smile appeared on the woman's face. "Hi, they sure were right, you're quite a looker."

Sophia didn't know how to respond.

"Who's they?" she asked.

The woman jumped down from the top bunk and sat in the chair across from the bottom bunk. "They, as in everybody in here. Word travels fast."

Sophia sat up and crossed her legs, facing her new roommate. She was petite like Sophia but not quite as endowed. She was very pretty in a rough sort of way. One side of her long blonde hair was flipped to one side and the other side was shaved. Her blue eyes held strength and curiosity. She had a good, kind face.

"I'm Maggie Stevens. Well, I might as well tell you right now, you're going to find out anyway, my real name is Magdalene, but I prefer Maggie, obviously. Most of the inmates refer to me as 'whore' because, you know, Mary Magdalene in the Bible."

Sophia smiled and nodded. "I'm Sophia Rodriguez. I think Magdalene is a wonderful name. You know, it's a myth that Mary Magdalene was a prostitute. She was by most historical and biblical accounts a woman of great beauty and wealth. But more important than that, she was loved by Jesus more than all the rest of the apostles. Apart from Jesus's mother, Mary Magdalene was of very high importance."

Maggie stared at Sophia before she laughed. "No shit? I like that. But all that aside, I'm pretty sure my mother was pissed that she was pregnant and decided to make my life hell by naming me after a whore. Where you from?"

"I'm from Colombia."

"Cool. If you don't mind me saying, you don't look like any drug trafficker I've ever seen."

Sophia smiled. "Thank you, I think. But you're right—I'm a kindergarten teacher. I did something very bad to save my brother. I'm very ashamed."

Maggie shrugged. "Hey, we all do stupid shit sometimes. Especially for those we love."

Sophia's heart swelled with compassion for her new friend. She had never met a more humble nonjudgmental person.

"Do you mind if I ask you what put you in here?" Sophia asked.

"I stabbed a man," Maggie said casually.

Sophia's eyes must have gotten big because Maggie laughed. "Don't be shocked. The bastard used me for a punching bag for years. One day, I'd just had enough. I didn't kill him, but I'm not sure I would have cared if I had. And, to be truthful, it would be safer for me if I had killed him. When I get out of here, he's probably going to be waiting for me."

"Maggie, that's awful! You will have to protect yourself. Can you leave town?"

Again, Maggie shrugged like it was just an everyday occurrence that someone was waiting to harm her.

Officer Landry appeared at their cell and announced it was time for lunch. Maggie and Sophia walked to a medium-size cafeteria that was in full swing serving lunch.

Maggie walked to the other side of the room so Sophia got in line for food. She could hear those around her talking about her like she wasn't there. She was being referred to as the drug trafficker, the one that punched Dalton, the pretty one, and the Mexican.

Lunch was a plop of mashed potatoes with turkey and gravy on top, carrots, and a dinner roll. Sophia was walking to an empty table when she was shoved from behind, making her dump her tray and land face-first on the floor.

Just as she was starting to get up, a foot kicked her in the stomach, taking her breath away. Sophia fell back to the floor. Someone then put a knee in her back, grabbed her hair and pulled her head off the floor, banging it back down hard. Blackness closed in all around her.

****

Henry paced back and forth across the old camp linoleum.

"Would you please sit the fuck down? You're making me dizzy," Garrett admonished.

Henry had been so discombobulated after court that he didn't bother to go back to Portland. He was staying at the family camp in Harmony. It was just ten miles or so from the jail.

His brother Garrett and his wife, Lilly, were staying at camp until their house was finished. They'd built a house down by the pond. He had also come to camp to check on Lilly. She said it was just the sniffles and nothing to worry about.

Henry was one of nine boys. He also had one sister. He was next to the oldest with Marcus being the eldest Johnson child. He loved having a big family.

Henry sat down on the kitchen stool and took a pull of his beer that Garrett had set on the counter for him.

"So, when can you move into the house?" Henry asked.

"We plan to move this week. Since you're here, maybe tomorrow we can move some stuff," Garrett said, waggling his eyebrows.

"Sure," Henry said absentmindedly.

Garrett snapped his fingers in front of Henry's face. "Earth to Henry? What the fuck is wrong with you today?"

Henry shook his head. "I had this arraignment today that I can't get out of my mind."

"Didn't go your way?" Garrett asked, smirking.

It was well known in the Johnson family, and probably far beyond, that Henry Johnson did not like to lose. Thankfully, it didn't happen very often.

"No, it didn't, but it wasn't anything that I did wrong. She wouldn't help me in any way. I was trying to have a reasonable bail set for her, but she told the judge that she didn't want bail set. She wanted to go back to the jail. Who the fuck wants to stay in jail? And, she had just got attacked by another inmate before court. She was sporting a pretty good black eye."

"Why, indeed. Which case was it?" Garrett asked.

Garrett used to own a magazine in New York, but in the last year he had sold it and started a local paper.

"She's charged with drug trafficking."

"What, like the biggest drug bust in Maine history? The word on the street is she is an illegal immigrant," Garrett said.

"Who fucking cares if she is an immigrant? She still deserves a reasonable bail and last time I checked, *all* people in the United States were presumed innocent until proven guilty," Henry spat.

Garrett held up his hands. "Whoa, calm the fuck down, Dershowitz. I said that was the word on the street. *My* paper referred to her as Jane Doe. What did they end up setting the bail at before she declined?"

"Two hundred and fifty thousand," Henry growled.

"Jesus, that's a little high."

"No shit," Henry said. "Listen, I'm going to use the office for a while. I have a shit ton of emails to go through since I didn't go back to the office this afternoon."

Garrett patted Henry on the back. "No problem, bud. See you in the morning."

Henry started to walk to the office when he turned. "Are you sure Lilly is okay?"

Garrett just looked at Henry before a huge grin broke out on his face and he nodded.

Henry smiled. "You fucker. Congrats."

So, another brother married and expecting a child. Henry was happy for all of his siblings, but that wasn't for him. He was in his forties and had always been adamant that he would not get seriously involved with a woman. He and his brothers referred to it as *Henry's Law*. He had had to stand by and watch as his father fell apart after their mom died of a brain aneurysm when he was fourteen. He vowed that if that was what love did to you, he wanted no part of it.

And he was happy to say that he was very successful. He loved all women and they loved him. They had fun and then he left. No hard feelings. No drama. He always woke up in his own bed alone in the morning.

And, as far as kids went, he loved them. He had oodles of nieces and nephews whom he loved with all his heart. Since he believed that children should have a mother and a father who are married, because he was old-fashioned like that, kids were off the table for him, period.

Henry opened his computer, but hadn't read even one email. All he could see was Sophia Garcia Rodriguez's scared face and that fucking black eye. He really wanted to punch something. Something like Dalton Kimball's face.

Chapter 5

After the third load of heavy furniture was delivered to Garrett and Lilly's new house, Henry decided to go to the jail and see Sophia Rodriguez. He had slept like shit and the day had gotten no better.

He just couldn't get her out of his mind. Why wouldn't she want to get out of that shithole? Why was she driving a van full of heroin? He couldn't shake the feeling that there was way more to Sophia Rodriguez than met the eye.

He had to know. He jumped in his truck and headed to Skowhegan. He was about halfway there when he looked down at his old Levi's, work boots, camp T-shirt, and flannel shirt. He probably should have changed.

He turned the heat on in the truck. It was fall and there was a chill to the air. *If she is from Colombia, she must be freezing her ass off.* He hoped they had given her enough blankets.

Henry rolled his eyes at himself. What the fuck was wrong with him? He was just going to talk with her and see if he could get any more information from her. He had filed an official attorney of record with the court after the arraignment. Whether she liked it or not, Sophia Rodriguez had an attorney. And a damn good one if he had to say so himself, and he did.

For the rest of the trip, Henry convinced himself that this was strictly a lawyer/client situation. He would check on any of his clients. Had he ever gone to check on any client after only meeting them once? No.

The dispatcher buzzed him into the waiting room. Not five minutes later, Officer Mary Ellen Landry appeared.

She looked him up and down and smirked. "Casual day, Counsel?"

"Um, it's Saturday, Officer. I've been helping my brother move. Listen, I know it's not visiting hours, but I thought you would let me meet with Miss Rodriguez for a minute," Henry asked, giving his best puppy-dog face. It had never let him down yet.

The smirk disappeared instantly. "I would, Henry, but she's in the infirmary."

Henry's concern spiked immediately. "What? Is she sick?"

Officer Landry looked uncomfortable. "No, there was an incident at lunch yesterday."

His concern was replaced with anger. "What the fuck, Mary Ellen? What happened?"

"Dalton Kimball's girlfriend, Lori, is what happened. But don't worry, Maggie Stevens beat the shit out of Lori. She's not in the infirmary, she's in the hospital."

"How bad is Sophia?" Henry asked, trying to sound calm.

"Not bad. She has an egg on her head where Lori slammed it on the floor. But Lori didn't get a chance to do much else, thank God. She's just under observation for today. She will be back in her cell tomorrow."

"Who's her cellmate?" Henry asked.

"Maggie Stevens. Nobody will bother Sophia anymore after they saw what she did to Lori."

"Does Maggie need an attorney now?" Henry inquired.

Officer Landry smiled. "No, I was the officer on duty and I didn't see a thing. No charges will be filed. But I can't be everywhere, Henry. If an inmate is bent on hurting someone, there's only so much the jail staff can do. She needs to get out of here. I really don't believe she would run."

Henry nodded, deep in thought. "I'll come back tomorrow. Are you on duty?"

Officer Landry shook her head. "No, I'm off, but I'll put you on the list to see her as her attorney of record."

Henry started to leave but turned around. "Is she warm enough?"

Officer Landry tilted her head and looked thoughtful. "I'll make sure she gets an extra blanket."

Henry left feeling, what, he wasn't sure, but he didn't like it. If he was honest with himself, he would admit that he did know what the feeling was. It was the same feeling he had as a teenager and witnessed his mother fall to the ground and die. And the same feeling he had as he watched his father sink further down the rabbit hole of grief and despair. It was helplessness and it fucking sucked.

****

Her head throbbed. She had woken up in the jail infirmary yesterday, but now she was back in her jail cell with Maggie, fresh from the shower.

Sophia sat as Maggie combed and braided her hair. She picked up the Bible she had requested from the jail library.

"Tell me your favorite story in the Bible," Maggie requested.

Sophia smiled. "Have you heard of the Book of Ruth?"

"No, I haven't read the Bible. My mother wasn't really the religious sort."

"I'm sorry. You seem like you had a very difficult childhood, Maggie."

"Oh, don't be sorry, you know what they say, if it don't kill you, it makes you stronger."

Sophia laughed. "I see what you're saying, and I believe you, but I like to think of it as everything you've gone through has brought you to be where you are today, a survivor. And I'm glad you're here or I never would have met you and called you my friend."

"Yeah, I don't think I would have wanted to miss that either," Maggie said quietly.

"So, the story of Ruth . . ." Sofia began. "I was a young girl when I first heard it and I think it was the beginning of my dreaming of a love like theirs. My mother used to tell me that I was in love with love. I think she was afraid I would fall in love with the first boy I met and run away with him. Of course, I didn't, and as I got older, I became more practical, but I still love the story of Ruth.

"There was a woman named Naomi who moved with her husband and two sons to a foreign land. The woman's husband died. Her two sons married women from the foreign land and then they died. Naomi decided she had nothing left, so she was going to move back to her homeland. She told her two daughters-in-law that they should go back to their families since their husbands—her sons—were dead.

"One daughter-in-law, Ruth, said no. She said wherever Naomi went she would follow, and Naomi's God would be her God. This was, how do you say, a big deal. Ruth had grown up in a country with different gods and values. But Ruth loved her mother-in-law and wouldn't leave her side. They both traveled back to Bethlehem, Naomi's homeland."

"Bethlehem, like where Jesus was born?" Maggie asked as she finished Sophia's hair.

Sophia turned around and sat crossed-legged, facing Maggie. She smiled and nodded. "Exactly, the place Jesus was born. See, you know more than you think. So, when they got home, the people of the village talked about Naomi and her horrible luck and about her foreign daughter-in-law.

"Naomi was quite poor, so Ruth went to the fields where they gathered the harvest to glean. To glean means when the workers gathered the harvest, some would fall to the ground and the poor could gather it, glean, what was left behind. It was a way to provide for the poor.

"Ruth was gleaning in the field and the owner of the land came around. His name was Boaz. He was a very wealthy landowner. He saw Ruth and he asked his men who that woman was. They told him she was Naomi's widowed daughter-in-law. Boaz told his men to let extra wheat fall to the ground so she would have plenty. He also told Ruth to not glean in any other fields but his and she would have his protection.

"I like to think he was immediately smitten with her and she him. When Ruth went home to Naomi with a good portion of wheat, Naomi asked her how she had gotten so much and in what field she had gleaned. Ruth told her it was Boaz's land. Naomi knew that Boaz was a kinsman of her late husband. A kinsman was a man from the husband's family. If there was tragedy that befell the family, the kinsman would help the widows and orphans.

"Ruth continued to glean in Boaz's fields. There was a night that Boaz was needed on the threshing floor and Naomi told Ruth to wait until Boaz had eaten and drank and went to bed so she could lie at his feet and uncover them. It was a way for Ruth to let Boaz know that she was interested in him and if he was also interested, then he could choose to wed her as her kinsman. Ruth did as Naomi instructed and Boaz found her and sent her home so no one would see that she stayed the night with him. It was all very innocent. There was one man who was next in line as kinsman to Naomi's husband's family. Boaz went to him and asked him if he intended to redeem and purchase Naomi's dead son's lands and wed Ruth. The kinsman closest to Naomi said if he was to redeem Naomi's dead son's land, it would interfere with his own inheritance. The man then declined and Boaz became the redeemer and married Ruth."

"That is so romantic," Maggie whispered.

Sophia smiled. "Yes, but that's not the best part. Because of Ruth's loyalty and faith by following Naomi and worshipping her God, the one true God, she was not only rewarded by God and was blessed with love, marriage, and protection, but Ruth had a son with Boaz. His name was Obed. Obed had a son named Jesse and Jesse had a son named David. King David. God loved David more than all the other kings in history. God said David had a heart after his. King David's lineage gave birth to Jesus. God's only son.

"God loved Ruth. A woman not born unto God's chosen people and made her the mother of Jesus's lineage. Apart from Jesus's mother, Mary, Ruth was blessed above all women."

"Wow, and she had no idea what was in store for her when she met Naomi," Maggie said wondrously.

"That's right, Maggie. None of us knows what the future holds."

The officer on duty opened the cell door and told Sophia that she was to meet with Attorney Johnson.

Sophia looked at Maggie, uncertain.

Maggie touched Sophia's shoulder. "It's okay. Attorney Johnson is one of the good guys. You can trust him."

Sophia nodded and smiled. She followed the officer to the room where Attorney Johnson waited.

Henry stood when Sophia entered the room and remained standing, just staring at her.

Sophia could feel the heat rise to her face. She stood there until the attorney cleared his throat and apologized and asked her to sit down.

"I'm sorry you were hurt," the attorney said.

Sophia's eyes flew up to his. She had heard the genuine concern in his voice. She unconsciously touched the egg on her head.

"You have nothing to be sorry for. This wasn't your fault. I'm the sorry one, Attorney Johnson. I let you think I didn't understand English. I was scared."

"Henry. Please call me Henry. I totally understand that you were scared and no apology necessary. Do you mind if I ask you, Miss Rodriguez, why you don't want to be bailed?"

"You can call me Sophia. I'm safer here in jail," Sophia said, looking down at her hands in her lap.

"Can you tell me why you're not safe outside of jail?" Henry asked.

"I cannot. If I told you then you would not be safe. Please don't ask that of me, Attorney . . . Henry."

Henry sat back in his metal chair and sighed. "Okay, for now, but I will need more information eventually to prepare a defense for you."

Sophia nodded. "I understand. We can run across that bridge later."

Henry narrowed his eyes and smirked. "You mean cross that bridge when we come to it?"

Sophia tilted her head. "*Sí*, that's what I said."

****

Sophia saw Henry almost every day. He would check on her and sometimes bring her a strong cup of coffee. She did miss her strong Colombian coffee. She found she looked forward to his visits and was sad when he didn't come. She also was curious about the butterflies in her stomach when she thought about Attorney Henry Johnson.

She did try very hard to not think about Henry. She had a fiancé back in Colombia, but for the life of her, every time she closed her eyes, it was Henry Johnson that she dreamed of.

Chapter 6

It had been a couple of weeks, but he was getting used to his new temporary secretary. His name was Kent and he was almost as efficient as Charlie. Although, Henry would never tell her that.

He did mention to Charlie when he visited her in the hospital after giving birth to a son that he thought that Kent sometimes stared at his ass.

Charlie almost fell out of the hospital bed, she was laughing so hard. All she could say, eventually, was *it is a great ass*, to which Henry thoroughly agreed. Josh, Charlie's husband and a fellow attorney, just scowled at Henry.

Henry was antsy. The board meeting was taking way the fuck too long. He hadn't seen Sophia yesterday and he was anxious to talk with her. He really enjoyed their talks. They would talk about her home in Colombia and her childhood. He in turn regaled her with stories of his and his siblings' adventures.

He told himself that he visited her because she was his client, but in truth, he enjoyed his time with her. She was almost calming, which was fucked up because she was the one in jail.

Henry did some research on the Colombian drug cartel and didn't like what he learned. How the hell did sweet Sophia get involved with the cartel? He didn't want to, but he needed to press her for information. The case against her was proceeding and he had nothing to run with.

There was another reason for Henry wanting to press Sophia for information. He wanted her out of jail. He hadn't had a decent night's sleep since he met her. He was constantly thinking about her safety and well-being. So much so that he hadn't gone out with a woman since he laid eyes on Sophia. What the hell that meant, he didn't even want to analyze.

"Do you want to tell me what the hell is wrong with you?" his brother Marcus asked after the board meeting.

Henry sank down in the plush chair in Marcus's office and sighed.

"I need to go to Skowhegan for a few days. A court case," Henry said.

"You've been doing a lot more criminal work lately," Marcus pointed out.

Henry shrugged. "I guess. I think the corporate law thing isn't challenging enough. I've been doing it for a long time. I think it's time to expand my horizons," Henry said, grinning.

He knew this would get Marcus going. And it did.

"Um, I'd just like to point out that this is *your* company too, Henry. The company needs you here. I need you here."

Henry rolled his eyes at the eldest of the Johnson clan.

Marcus grinned. "So, who's the latest swimsuit model you're dating? Or is it a lingerie model?"

Anger spiked in Henry. "Do you really think I'm that shallow?"

Marcus looked confused at his tone. "Yes? It's your own law, Henry. No serious relationships. Just fun. And, if I'm not mistaken, it was about three weeks ago when you dated an underwear model."

Henry didn't look happy. "She wasn't a full-time underwear model. She had her picture taken in her underwear *once*, but she was a professional volleyball player."

"A professional volleyball player. I rest my case. Don't bite my head off if you're miserable dating supermodels. It's your law, which means you have the power to break it. What you need is to fall in love with a good woman. A woman who keeps you on your toes."

Henry scrubbed his hands over his face. "Just because all my siblings but one have broken the Johnson relationship law doesn't mean I will succumb. Caleb and I will have to stand by our bachelor code to keep the Johnson name in good standing."

****

Later that day, Henry decided to take a trip to the Skowhegan jail. He told Kent to cancel his appointments for the next couple of days and to tell the legal staff, which Henry was in charge of, to handle any court hearings.

Henry stood as Sophia was shown to the visiting room. There were several other inmates visiting with their families that day. He watched as several of the inmates asked her over to introduce her to their families. She seemed to radiate light and everyone felt it.

Sophia smiled shyly as she sat down. "Hola, Henry."

Henry grinned. "Hola, Sophia. How are you?"

"I'm fine. I've missed talking to you," Sophia said softly.

"Sophia, you say that if you were let out of jail, you wouldn't be safe. Is that right?"

Sophia nodded. "Sí."

"What if I told you, I could keep you safe. Would you agree to be released from jail?" Henry asked.

"Henry, why are you helping me? I cannot afford to pay you and I will not accept an attorney that the taxpayers of the people of Maine are paying for. I'm guilty of what they have charged me with. I accept that."

Henry leaned toward her. "I don't want to hear you say you're guilty again. That's not good for any defense I argue. I know what you're saying, but please, let me handle the legal end of things. As for paying me, by letting me take your case, you *are* helping me."

Sophia looked unconvinced. "Henry, I know that you have a golden heart, but you cannot work for free."

Henry narrowed his eyes. "You mean I have a heart of gold."

Sophia nodded. "Sí, that's what I said."

Henry couldn't stop the smile. He should write these incorrect idioms down.

"Hear me out, please. Most attorneys with any moral compass donate their time to handle cases pro bono a couple times a year. Meaning we work for free. You will be my first of the year and since it's autumn, I need this case to make my quota," Henry argued.

Sophia nodded. "Fine, I will not go down that bunny hole."

Henry paused. "Rabbit hole. You won't go down that rabbit hole."

"Sí, that is what I said," Sophia said a little impatiently.

She was fucking adorable. Henry put his hands on the table. "All right, now back to keeping you safe once you get out of jail."

27

Sophia held up her hands. "Henry, I'm sure you could keep me safe, but my bail is so high that it is not even worth arguing about. Instead, tell me about your camp. I love it when you talk about the small town of Harmony. It reminds me of my hometown of La Victoria."

Henry was just about to tell her about the campfires and s'mores when there was a commotion at the far side of the room. It was Lori, one of Dalton Kimball's girlfriends, shouting at the woman visiting her.

Lori jumped up to leave the room, but spied Sophia. She walked to their table and put her meaty hands in front of Sophia and leaned in.

"Well, well, I've been waiting to see you, little whore. If you think Maggie is going to save your ass again, you're wrong. Just know that I'm after you, bitch."

Henry watched Sophia. She didn't look the least bit scared. Which was weird because he was a little scared of Lori.

"Lori, I'm not afraid of you. I forgive you for hurting me. You must be in a great deal of pain. I will pray for you," Sophia said softly.

Henry thought Lori's head was going to explode. She was practically frothing at the mouth, she was so angry.

"Save your prayers for yourself, whore. You're going to be the one in pain and that little bump on the head is nothing compared to the beating I'm going to rain down on you," Lori said and stomped out of the dayroom.

Sophia turned to Henry and very calmly said, "She has some anger problems."

The guards announced to the room that visiting hours were over.

Sophia stood and held out her hand. "Thank you, Henry, for visiting me. It's always the best part of my day."

Henry wanted to pull Sophia to him. Holding her hand wasn't enough, but he held on to her hand with both of his until the officer walked to them and said no touching.

That pissed Henry off even more than Lori's threats. He wanted to hug her. He had never wanted to hug anybody as much as he did right now.

Sophia pulled her hand away and smiled shyly as she walked out of the dayroom. She looked back at him with a look so sweet and innocent that it made Henry want to protect her from all the Loris of the world. And he intended to start right now.

Henry walked to the jail lobby but instead of leaving, he rang the buzzer. An officer asked him what he wanted. Henry tossed his bank card on the counter.

"I'm here to bail Sophia Rodriguez," Henry instructed.

The officer keyed in the name and looked back at him. "It's two hundred and fifty thousand dollars cash bail."

Henry looked bored. "I'm aware. Is there a problem? I've given you my bank card. Call the bank and withdraw the funds. And, I want her watched from this second until she walks through that door. There's been a threat made against her."

Henry began to pace back and forth. Patience was not his strong suit. He wouldn't breathe easy until Sophia was standing before him.

Chapter 7

Sophia had just gotten back to her cell when an officer unlocked the door and motioned for her to come. The officer told her that she had been bailed.

Sophia turned to Maggie. "I will visit you as soon as I can. If you get out before my trial, I will let you know where I'm staying. Please be careful and watch out for Lori," she pleaded.

Maggie smiled and hugged Sophia.

"Don't worry about me. I've only got a few months left and then I'm going to do what we talked about. I'm going to leave town and get a job," Maggie said with tears in her eyes.

They hugged one last time before Sophia followed the guard to a room with her backpack and the clothes she wore into the jail. She changed into the same summer dress and flats and was led to the lobby.

The door opened and Henry stood waiting for her. Sophia smiled and couldn't help herself as her feet carried her to Henry and she jumped into his arms and hugged him tight.

Henry's hug was the sweetest, most comforting thing she had ever experienced. He was warm and smelled of outdoors and a manly scent that was only Henry's. She inhaled deeply before slowly pulling away.

She instantly felt a little embarrassed. He was her attorney and doing his job. She had to remember this.

"But, how?" Sophia whispered as if at any moment the guards would realize she was leaving and grab her and take her back to her cell.

Henry looked at the officer who had just completed the transaction and shrugged. "I pulled a few strings. The law is a very complex thing. Now, I need you to sign the bail papers and we will be off."

Sophia walked to the counter and took the pen Henry held for her. He had his hand covering most of the paper.

"It just says that you will not leave the state and blah, blah, blah," he said, pointing to the line for her to sign.

Sophia would have liked to read the paper, but she got the impression that Henry just wanted her to sign it, so she did. She trusted Henry. She shivered as she signed the bail document.

"Is this all you have for clothes? Do you have a jacket?" Henry asked.

Sophia shook her head.

Henry pulled his sweatshirt over his head. It was yellow and black and had the word Bruins on the front. It looked very old and well loved.

"Here, put this on. We'll see about getting you some warm clothes tomorrow," he said, pulling the big sweatshirt over her head.

It hung almost to her knees. He rolled up the sleeves to her wrists and smiled. "Better?"

The sweatshirt was warm and smelled like Henry. Her heart fluttered and she could feel her face heat up. She nodded. "Sí, gracias."

Henry ushered her out the door and to a big black truck. He opened the passenger door and helped her into the massive truck.

He climbed in and started the engine. "How would you like to visit Harmony, Maine?"

Sophia smiled and nodded.

Henry turned the heat on and reached around her to grab the seatbelt. His face was so close to hers. Their eyes met and Sophia felt her world spin on its axis. She wanted to kiss him. She had been kissed before, but she had never felt like this. This feeling stole her breath away and made her heart thump against her chest.

After a few seconds that felt like long minutes, Henry clicked the seatbelt and put the car in gear. He mumbled something about it being the law that everyone must wear a seatbelt.

Sophia took a deep breath to get her wits about her and watched out the window. The town gave way to forests and fields and the trees had the afternoon sun, which highlighted the brilliant yellows, reds, and oranges. It was beautiful.

As they drove farther away from the jail, Sophia couldn't help but worry about her brother. If Mateo found out she had left the jail, he might think she had run away and he would harm Santiago.

"Penny for your thoughts," Henry asked quietly.

Sophia smiled. "You have a beautiful state."

Henry nodded. "My mother loved the autumn in Maine. But I think it's a tad cold for what you're used to."

Sophia laughed. "True. It is colder than anything I have ever experienced but I can tell you that I used to dream about visiting America. Specifically, New England. In fact, some of my favorite books were written by authors living in New England: Nathaniel Hawthorne, *The Scarlet Letter*; Harriet Beecher Stowe, *Uncle Tom's Cabin*; and my kindergarten class's favorite, *Charlotte's Web* by E. B. White."

Henry laughed. "Ah, yes, *Charlotte's Web*. A favorite of mine as well. I used to read it to my sister and now I read it to my nieces and nephews. I like to identify with Templeton. He was my favorite."

Sophia laughed. "No! I would never think of you as Templeton, the rat. You are more like Charlotte. A very special friend," Sophia said quietly and quickly became embarrassed.

Henry was quiet for a moment before he said, "I like that, but I'm pretty sure most everyone who knows me would say I was definitely Templeton."

Henry slowed down the truck and turned onto a dirt road. They traveled a short distance and stopped in front of a large carved totem depicting wildlife.

"That's beautiful," Sophia whispered.

"Yeah, it was carved with a chainsaw. I'll take you to see the man who carved it and maybe he will give us a demonstration. This is camp. Sophia. You'll be safe here. Many years ago, my father put the camp in a blind trust that can't be traced to any of us kids. When we're here, no one knows where we are. And that's the way we like it. As long as you are here, you're safe."

"Henry, I can never repay your kindness, but I thank you from the bottom of my heart."

Henry shut the engine off. "You're welcome. I'm glad I am here to help. Now, stay put until I come around, please."

He got out of the truck, opened the passenger side door, and helped her down. Her stomach filled with butterflies when he took her hand. He was such a gentleman. She hadn't met a man with such manners since her father.

The camp was a huge building with another large building attached. It was green with white trim. It was majestic, sitting among the tall pine trees.

Henry unlocked the front door and waved his arm. "Sophia Rodriguez, welcome to camp."

Sophia smiled. "Thank you, Sir Henry of Harmony. It is a great honor and blessing."

Henry stared at her for a moment before taking her hand and leading her through each room and giving a little tour. He led her to his childhood room and told her she could sleep there and he would crash in one of his brothers' rooms.

She only had enough time to set her backpack on the bed before he pulled her to the sitting room and began to build a fire in the woodstove.

"I'll get you warmed up and then I'll see what I can scrounge up for dinner," he said, crumpling up newspaper and stuffing it into the stove.

It got dark early. The woodstove warmed her thoroughly, and with her belly full from the cheese omelet that Henry made for them, Sophia could hardly keep her eyes open. She had asked to help clean the kitchen, but he insisted that she sit by the fire on the couch. She never saw him come back from the kitchen. She felt like a kitten, curled up and purring. She fell fast asleep.

Chapter 8

Henry sat on the coffee table and watched Sophia sleep. He felt like some sort of voyeur, but he couldn't help himself. He just couldn't tear his eyes away from looking at her. She was perfect. And, somehow, her sweetness and innocence radiated from her, even in sleep.

When she had walked into the lobby, his legs almost buckled. She was drop-dead gorgeous. She was petite, but she had curves that you could even see even in the modest dress she wore.

Since he had met Sophia, he felt like he had an angel on one shoulder and a devil on the other. He and the devil got on great. They always had. It was the angel who plagued him. He didn't like these new feelings of protectiveness and wanting to be her white knight. Henry loved women and he enjoyed their company, as well the carnal pleasures. His life ran relatively smoothly.

And the little devil was assuring him that once he had sex with Sophia, this spell she had over him would be broken. He would still help her with her legal troubles and win, but his thoughts and his life would be his own again.

Henry picked Sophia up from the couch and carried her to his childhood bedroom. He smiled, thinking about what teenage Henry would have thought about such a hottie sleeping in his bed. A bed that had never seen a smidgen of action except for his own fantasies.

He laid her down and covered her up with the homemade quilt that his mother had made him so many years ago. As he left the room, he looked back and studied her beatific face. He could almost see the angel on his shoulder smirking. Bastard.

Sleep didn't come easily. It never had. As a matter of fact, some of his most brilliant closing arguments had come in the middle of the night when he couldn't sleep.

He woke to the sun just coming up. He had slept in his brother Bear's room. He had the biggest bed in the house. Henry wasn't small by any means, but Bear was a brute.

He showered and in Garrett's bureau he found a pair of old jeans that fit him, along with a white button-down shirt. It wasn't his usual camp attire, but he didn't want to subject Sophia to some of the vulgar T-shirts that they wore. He had a little class. Actually, he had no class at camp, but he could pretend. After all, he was a lawyer.

He threw some bacon on the griddle and whipped up some pancakes. Henry looked up from the griddle to see freshly showered Sophia shyly walk into the kitchen. She wore another summery dress with little flats. How was it that she was hands-down the most beautiful and sexiest woman he had ever come across, and she didn't have a vain bone in her body? Not a lick of makeup and as unpretentious as they came.

Most of the women he dated gussied themselves up to the nines. And, what was worse is he thought he liked that.

"Good morning. How'd you sleep?" he asked.

Sophia smiled. "Very well, thank you," she said and laid down his sweatshirt that she had been wearing on the stool. It was folded perfectly.

Henry stepped away from the counter and handed her another sweatshirt he had found in his sister Jack's closet.

"Here this should fit you a little better. I would have tried some other clothes, but they're mostly summer clothes and she's almost six feet tall. But we will be rectifying that today. I'm taking you shopping."

"Henry, you don't have to do that. I'm sure I can make do. You've been too kind already," Sophia said quietly.

"Nonsense, it will be fun. It will be like *Pretty Woman*," Henry teased.

Sophia looked confused.

"What, you've never seen the movie *Pretty Woman*?"

Sophia smiled and shook her head. "We didn't have a television. We read books and played outside."

Henry looked horrified. "What a horrible childhood you must have had! No *Scooby-Doo*, no *Jonny Quest*, no *Lord of the Rings*? We will have to rectify that. But, to be completely honest with you, we don't have a working television here at camp either. On a really good day, we may be able to get a ball game on the old console in the den, but usually one of us has to get on the roof and adjust the antenna. My parents were adamant that camp was for family time and the good ol' outdoors."

Sophia smiled. "They sound a lot like my parents. My brother and I never would have complained to our parents that we were bored. That would have given us a household task, to be sure."

"That would have gotten us a swift kick in the ass," Henry said, chuckling. "Now the most important question of the day: do you want rainbow sprinkles on your pancakes?"

"Um, I don't know what that is, but I'm going to say no," Sophia replied, taking the plate of pancakes and bacon he handed her.

"Rainbow sprinkles are what they call a staple in the Johnson house nowadays. The kids love them."

Sophia smiled. "From all you have told me about your nieces and nephews, they sound lovely. The same age as my kindergarten class," she said as a shadow passed across her face.

"Hey, you're going to be in your classroom teaching again before you know it," Henry reassured her.

Sophia nodded and tried to smile. "I miss them."

****

After breakfast they loaded into the truck and headed to Freeport. There was just one place they needed to go for warm clothes: L.L. Bean. His best friend's sister worked there and had agreed, when Henry called her, to meet them there and help Sophia get everything she needed.

It was about a two-hour drive from camp. On the way, Sophia asked him to tell her about his siblings. He had shown her around the camp and pointed out pictures of each of them.

"Okay, Marcus is the oldest and he took over running the family business from my father. He's married to Zena and they have five kids.

"I'm next in the lineup and they should have stopped with me, but they continued."

Sophia smiled.

"Teddy is next and he's literally a rocket scientist. He used to work for NASA, but now he runs a school for genius kids in upstate New York with his wife, Emma.

"Bear is next and he's in the military, along with his wife, Kate. They no longer go off on missions, thank god. They live in California and we just found out that Kate is expecting triplets.

"Then there's Garrett. He used to own a magazine in New York, but he sold it and moved back here to Maine. He lives just down the road from camp, actually. He started a local newspaper and he's married to Lilly, who's an attorney. I just found out days ago that they're expecting.

"Next is Bobby. He's a twin. He's a surgeon and his wife, Ava, is a psychiatrist. They live down the road from camp toward town.

"Ty is the other half of the twins. He was a professional baseball player for a hot minute, but an accident ruined that. He now manages the farm teams for the Boston Red Sox. His wife, Riley, runs a cupcake shop in the Old Port in Portland. They just had a baby girl.

"Then there's Davey. He's a professional chef and owns a restaurant in New York. His wife, MacKenzie, is the pastry chef and co-owner. They have twins.

"Next is Caleb. He takes care of the advertising end of the family business. He's kind of a pretty boy. The women act like he's a friggin' member of the Beatles. He's single like me. We're a dying breed in the Johnson clan.

"And last, but certainly not least, is my baby sister, Jack. She's . . . well, she's a lot of things. A mother of quints, a supermodel, music mogul, and tougher than all us boys combined. She's married to Jared, who grew up with us. They split their time between Maine and New York."

By the time Henry had finished, they had arrived at L.L. Bean.

"Now, there will be a test when we get home," Henry joked as he opened the passenger door for Sophia.

She laughed. "I hope I can meet them someday."

Weirdly, Henry wanted that very much. Another smirk from the angel on his shoulder.

As they walked in, Will's younger sister waved to them. Henry hugged her.

"Hey there, kiddo. How've you been? Will said you've left a trail of broken hearts when you left a few weeks ago for college."

The girl rolled her eyes. "Will thinks he knows everything."

"Jenny, this is Sophia. Sophia—Jenny. Jenny is going to help you find everything you need. And, if you can't find it here, Jenny knows where you *can* find it. I'm going to meet her older brother, my best friend, for a cup of coffee. Jenny knows where we'll be, so take your time and meet us when you're finished," Henry said, handing over his bank card to Jenny.

Jenny smiled and took the card. "This is going to be epic. Henry tells me you're Colombian? she asked Sophia.

Sophia smiled and nodded. "Sí."

And in Spanish, Jenny asked Sophia if they could converse in Spanish. It would help her brush up as she was majoring in Spanish.

It was Henry's turn to roll his eyes and in perfect Spanish replied to Jenny, "What in the world can you do with a major in Spanish?"

"You sound like my parents!" Jenny said and took Sophia by the arm, whisking her away. Sophia looked over her shoulder at him and smiled.

This time the little devil on his shoulder perked up.

Henry walked across the street to the coffee shop where Will was waiting for him.

Will Hayes had been Henry's best friend since kindergarten. They played ice hockey together, went on double dates together, and even attended law school together. There were no secrets between him and Will. Will also adhered to Henry's Law. Actually, it was Will who actually coined the phrase. They vowed to never get involved in a relationship. A sort of bachelor's creed.

Will had just recently been nominated for the district court bench. Henry was beyond proud of him.

"Your Honor," Henry teased.

Will stood and hugged Henry. "Don't be an ass clown. How ya been?"

Henry grinned. "Living the dream, my friend."

Will shook his head and sat back down. "You're full of shit. I took the liberty of getting your coffee."

"Thanks."

"So, what's this I hear . . . Jenny is clothes-shopping for a *friend* of yours. Since when did you start dressing your dates?" Will teased.

Henry felt his temper rise. He sat back in the chair and crossed his arms and shrugged. "I'm being a friend. Have you read the papers? The big drug bust up north?"

Will nodded. "Sure."

Henry just stared at Will.

"No fucking way, Henry. Are you her attorney? And you're shopping for her?"

Henry's temper really began to rise. "Calm the fuck down, Judge. Yes, I'm her attorney and yes, I'm getting her some warm clothes. So what?" he asked with an edge to his voice.

Will stared at Henry. He knew Henry almost as well as his siblings did. He held up his hands. "Okay, man. You know what you're doing. I'd say she's one lucky woman to land you as an attorney and even luckier to land you as a *friend*."

"Fuck you. Not everything is sexual. I'm capable of being a nice guy and helping out my fellow woman, in this case."

Will nodded. "Absolutely. I never thought anything different. You're the most philanthropic person I know."

Henry smirked. "Smartass. Now tell me about that hit-and-run case you heard last week."

He and Will talked and drank coffee for a couple of hours. Henry was wired when Jenny and Sophia walked in the coffee shop with multiple bags. Sophia was dressed in skinny jeans, Bean boots, white long-sleeved shirt, red-checkered flannel shirt, and a winter parka with the hood trimmed in faux fur. She looked like she just stepped out of a L.L. Bean catalogue. And those jeans . . .

Will saw Sophia enter with his sister and just stared. "Yup, you're the most philanthropic fucking person I've ever met."

The little devil on Henry's shoulder smiled and nodded his head vigorously.

Fuck me.

Chapter 9

Sophia was overwhelmed, but she was warm. Jenny was delightful but she had piled so many clothes on the counter that the clerk almost couldn't be seen. Sophia gently told Jenny and the clerk that she would only require half of what was on the counter.

Jenny sighed and carefully picked out the essentials and a few more items before they left the store. Jenny took her to a store that specialized in undergarments and again, stacked the items high. And again, Sophia told Jenny and the clerk that she would only require a few things. She could wash them often.

By the time they arrived at the coffee shop, Sophia was exhausted. Jenny had insisted that she put her dress in the bag and wear the skinny jeans, a white top, a flannel shirt, and boots that Jenny referred to as Bean boots. Jenny insisted that she looked like a college student.

She linked her arm with Sophia's and walked to the counter with Henry's bank card to purchase coffee and a snack.

Jenny got her coffee and muffin to go, and once they reached the table, Will stood to leave with his sister. Jenny made the introductions to her brother in Spanish.

"Will, I'd like you to meet Sophia. Sophia, this is Will Hayes, my brother. Will and Henry have been friends since kindergarten."

Sophia smiled and took the hand Will held out to her. "It is very nice to meet you, Mr. Hayes."

Will smiled and held on to her hand. "Please call me Will. And I, too, am very happy to meet you."

Henry stood and scowled. "All right, everybody is very happy. Didn't you say you had some briefs to read over today, Judge?"

Will smiled and let go of Sophia's hand. "Did I? Oh, yes, now I remember. Sophia, may I call you that? Will you be coming to the ice arena on Sunday with Henry? You can watch him get the stuffing beat out of him."

Sophia looked at Henry, questioning. "Please call me Sophia, and yes, I would very much like to watch you play ice hockey. But I would like Henry's stuffing to remain where it is, thank you."

Will laughed as Henry smirked. "Duly noted. I'll try to go easy on him for you," Will said as he walked to the door.

"However, she didn't say anything about me not beating the stuffing out of you, bud!" Henry hollered after Will.

Will lifted his hand in acknowledgment as he walked out.

Henry and Sophia sat down and she nibbled on her muffin and drank her coffee. The coffee shop actually had Colombian coffee and it wasn't bad. Not as strong as her coffee at home, but close.

"So, it looks like you made out okay shopping," Henry said, looking at the multiple bags.

Guilt washed over Sophia. "Henry, you didn't have to do this . . ."

Henry touched Sophia's hand. "Hey, I wanted to. Besides, I can't have my client freezing to death before we make it to trial."

At the mention of her trial, Sophia lost her appetite. She put the muffin back in the bag. Worry for her brother engulfed her even as her belly fluttered from Henry's touch. "Shall we go?" she asked.

Henry held her gaze before sighing and nodding. He gathered her bags up and ushered her out the door.

As they walked along the sidewalk to the parking lot, a woman hollered to Henry and jumped into his arms.

"Where have you been? You promised me you would call," the woman whined.

Looking uncomfortable, Henry set her aside, pulled Sophia to his side, and kept his arm around her.

The woman then noticed Sophia and blanched.

"Kitty, I'd like you to meet Sophia. Sophia, this is Kitty, a *friend*," Henry murmured.

"It is nice to meet you," Sophia said, trying to casually move away from Henry. She couldn't think when she was close to him, and anger filled her heart toward the girl. Was she jealous?

But Henry wouldn't let her budge.

Kitty had a sour look on her face. "A girlfriend, Henry? This is a first, and might I add that you're breaking your own rule. No, not rule . . . *law*. Henry's Law, I believe it's called."

Sophia looked up at Henry, confused.

Henry shook his head. "Kitty is always kidding around. We've got to go. It was nice to see you, Kitty," Henry said as he whisked Sophia to the truck.

Once they were situated in the truck and driving down the road, Sophia asked the question that seemed to linger in the air.

"What's Henry's Law?"

Henry looked at her and shrugged. "It's something stupid Will and I came up with in law school and it spread like wildfire. Me and my buddies made a vow that we would never have a serious relationship. We would date and enjoy women's company without any drama. There would be no one to say we couldn't play hockey or watch sports. It was dumb and most of the guys have gotten married and started families."

"But not you or Will. You're both free to live your lives unimpeded," she said, smiling.

Henry looked at her as if to see if she was joking or rebuking him.

"Henry, I'm pulling your foot. You may live your life as you wish."

Henry smiled. "Leg. You're pulling my leg."

"Sí, that's what I said." Her gaze was captivated by the beautifully colored leaves.

Henry pulled into a dirt parking lot in front of a lunch truck. "I'll be right back."

Sophia watched him order something and pay for it. She was glad for the moment to gather her thoughts. So, Henry never wanted to get married or have a family. That made her sad, but she didn't know why. Maybe because that was all she had ever dreamed about. Falling in love and having a grand wedding and having babies. Maybe she was sad for herself.

She was already thirty and it hadn't happened yet. She was engaged, but she hadn't seen her fiancé since he proposed a year ago.

Henry climbed back in the truck with a box. He opened the box for her to see. There were two large lobsters with rubber bands on the claws. They were moving all about the small box.

"Dinner," Henry said, smiling.

Sophia smiled back. His smile took her breath away. "I've never had lobster."

"Well, you're in for a treat," he said and closed the box. They drove back to Harmony in comfortable silence.

Once they got back to camp and Henry had delivered the bags to her room, he took her hand. "Come on. I want to show you the pond."

Henry held her hand as they walked down the gravel road. Part of her knew it was wrong to hold his hand, but the other part of her swooned. He was so handsome in a rugged yet sweet sort of way. His dark hair was almost always disheveled, and his dark eyes held an honesty and curiosity in them. She could get lost in those eyes. For the life of her, she couldn't remember the color of her fiancé's eyes, and that disturbed her greatly. Henry had a dark beard, but it wasn't a normal beard—it had an unusual shape, very much like an evil villain.

Worry for her brother and guilt over not being honest with Henry gnawed at her. He had been so good to her. He deserved to know the whole truth and if he decided to not take her case any longer, she would jump off that cliff when she came to it.

The pond was majestic. The water was like black glass. The tall pine trees stood sentry.

"It's beautiful, Henry."

Henry led Sophia to a small cabin beside the pond. There were summer chairs surrounding a fire pit. He offered her a chair and she sat. Henry proceeded to build a fire.

Once the fire was roaring, Henry sat down beside her. Sophia drew her knees to her chest. "Henry, I need to tell you some things."

Henry turned to her and tilted his head and looked at her with those eyes that melted her heart. "You can tell me anything, Sophia," he said quietly.

Sophia looked into the fire and watched the flames dance. "My brother is in trouble. He's being held captive until I complete my task of delivering the drugs. I'm very afraid for his safety," she whispered, still looking into the fire.

Henry reached for Sophia's hand and held it. "Who's holding your brother?"

Sophia looked at her warm hand in Henry's, and then into his eyes. She told him about Mateo and how they had been childhood friends and how he had chosen a different life. A life inflicting pain and suffering on others.

She confided in Henry about her brother's drug and gambling problems. He wanted a better life than what their small village offered. She told him of all the attempts to help her brother after he would hit bottom from drugs and gambling.

And then, lastly, about the deal she had entered into on behalf of her brother. The offer of marriage or being a drug mule.

"I should have just married Mateo and none of this would have happened," she whispered.

Henry was silent for a moment. "I'm sorry you're in this predicament, but I will tell you that if I were in a similar situation, I would have done the same. I would do anything to save my family, Sophia. There is no shame in that. Your choices tell me a great deal about you. You know that Mateo is in love with you, right?"

Sophia nodded. "Sí. But, part of me doesn't believe that he would harm me or my brother. I don't want to believe it."

"I think you're wrong. I think your brother is in more danger now than ever. I don't mean to scare you, but I think it's time to call Mateo and tell him something to buy us some time until we can figure out what to do."

"Can they trace the phones to our location? Or is that just in the spy thrillers I read?" Sophia asked.

Henry smiled. "No, it's true, but there are ways to call without being traced. Now let's get back to the house so you can tell me every detail about the night you were stopped," he said, standing and snuffing out the fire a bit.

When Sophia stood, Henry put his hands on her shoulders.

"I'm glad you told me, Sophia. Now I can start building a defense for you. Thank you. We will help your brother."

Sophia was lost in Henry's soulful eyes. "I have faith in you, Henry."

Henry dipped his head. She could feel his warm breath on her lips. Sophia's heart was beating out of her chest. Surely, he could hear it thump. Sophia slowly backed away and started walking up the drive. It was a moment before Henry was beside her and they walked the distance in silence.

Sophia knew she should tell Henry about her fiancé, but right now she didn't have the courage. Instead, she would sit with her chaotic emotions for this amazing man beside her and wallow in the guilt over the man she promised to marry.

Chapter 10

Henry had never felt the level of desire that he felt for Sophia. He wanted to kiss her and taste her more than he wanted to breathe. The only saving grace tonight was his mind. His mind was already in high gear as to what he needed to do for Sophia's case. He knew that there would be no sleep for him tonight. And, sadly, he had court in Portland tomorrow. He would push through; he always did.

The lobster pot was boiling but the horrific expression on Sophia's face gave Henry pause.

She started speaking very fast in Spanish. Henry could only catch certain phrases like, "boiled alive," "their little eyes staring at me," "I can't be a part of this . . ."

Henry tried to look as serious as he could and grasped her arms. "Sophia, why don't you go put your new clothes away while I make dinner?"

Sophia wilted from relief. "Sí, sí, gracias," she said and disappeared down the hall.

Henry now looked into the lobsters' beady little eyes. He rolled his eyes as he told them he was sorry and lowered them into the pot.

What was it about this woman that made him question everything? He had never apologized to a lobster before. Nor did he take women shopping or get such a thrill from holding their hands. But he knew deep in his bones that Sophia Rodriguez was different. Special. And that scared the shit out of him.

Instead of making Sophia crack the lobster herself, Henry cracked both lobsters and fished out the tender meat. He melted some butter and went to get her.

She wasn't in his room, so he started searching for her. He found her in the den, standing at the extensive bookcase his father had built into the wall. She was holding a book, reading.

Henry approached and looked at the cover. "Ah, *The Portrait of a Lady*, by my namesake. It was one of my mother's favorites. I believe that's a first edition. A gift from my father."

Sophia gasped, closed the book carefully, and started to put it back on the shelf.

Henry touched her hand. "No, books are meant to be read and loved. That's what my mother always said. She would have been very pleased to see you reading it. I am too."

Sophia blushed and nodded. "Your mother named you after Henry James?"

Henry smiled. "Yes, Henry James Johnson. I'm not sure if my mother thought I would grow up to be Caspar Goodwood, Lord Warburton, or the narcissistic Gilbert Osmond."

"Oh, you are most definitely Caspar Goodwood. Mr. Goodwood is strong and dependable. I believe Isabel loved him, but she was so young that she wanted to experience life a little before marrying. I'm certain after all she went through, she bitterly regretted not marrying Mr. Goodwood when she had the chance."

Henry smiled. "I like that. Dinner is served, my lady," he said offering his arm. They walked arm in arm to the kitchen.

After they had started eating, Sophia gushed, "This is so delicious, Henry! I've never tasted anything like it before."

He had to admit, it was quite good. Every time he ate lobster, he wondered why he didn't have it more. It was known around the globe that Maine lobster was the best and he had it at his fingertips anytime he wanted. But maybe then he wouldn't enjoy it quite so much.

After they cleaned up the kitchen, he asked Sophia to sit down at the table and go over every detail she could remember about the stop. He had his legal pad and furiously wrote down everything she said.

It was late by the time they finished. He asked her if she minded if he worked on the notes he had just taken. She said she didn't mind. She would go to bed and read.

"Oh, I have court tomorrow in Portland and several meetings. It may be late when I get home. Will you feel safe enough here without me?" Henry asked.

Sophia smiled. "Sí, I'm used to being on my own. I feel very safe here, thanks to you. Good night."

Henry watched her leave. He didn't like that she was used to being alone. Was every man in Colombia *loco*? Eunuchs?

Henry went to the office at the back of the camp and studied, making notes from what Sophia told him. He grabbed his phone. He needed to talk to his brother Bear. He was military and had access to information.

"Henry, what's up, bro? It's late. Everything okay?" Bear asked, concerned.

"Hey, bud. Everything is good here. How is Kate feeling?" Henry asked.

"She's good. A little morning sickness but she's about as tough as they come," Bear said.

"Hey, I do have something I want to ask you," Henry began.

"Name it," Bear said.

"I'd like some intel on the Colombian drug cartel. But, specifically on a man named Mateo Sanchez," Henry said.

"Is this for a case or is it personal?" Bear asked.

"Both," Henry replied.

"You got it. I'll get back to you tomorrow."

"I've got court tomorrow, so why don't I call you when I'm on my way back to Harmony?" Henry said.

"Why are you driving from Portland to Harmony?" Bear asked, reasonably.

"I'll fill you in on *that* later. I owe you, bro."

Henry felt better knowing he was going to get some solid intel on this Mateo. He had a bad feeling about him. He made a note to pick up several burner phones tomorrow. He would have Sophia call her brother and maybe Mateo too. It might buy them some time to figure things out.

Henry stared at the legal pad. Something was off about the stop. Why the hell did those border patrol officers choose to chase down this lead? They should have called it in to the state police or the drug task force. Maybe they knew what was in the van. Sophia said the border patrol officers pulled her over and started to put the drugs in their truck when the state police showed up. He needed to go to the district attorney's office and get what little discovery they had. Specifically on the stop. If there were bad cops involved, Sophia could be in more danger than he thought.

His next call was to his brother Garrett, who lived just down the gravel drive. He needed to tell him to keep an eye open.

"Henry, everything all right?" Garrett asked, picking up on the second ring.

"Yeah, everything is fine. I'm sorry to call so late, but I just wanted you to know that I have a guest staying at camp. And, before you get all weird on me, I will bring her to your house soon to introduce you. But what I need is for you to keep an eye open for any cars parked at camp. I'm in court tomorrow and she will be here alone. Can you do that with no questions?" Henry asked.

"Of course, Henry. But seriously? You have a woman stashed at camp? I'm intrigued. This doesn't exactly follow Henry's Law," Garrett teased.

Henry was getting pissed.

"Dude, that stupidness was from law school. For a newspaper guy you sure aren't very current."

"Oh, no, if I recall it was only last month when we played cards that you were crowing about you and Caleb being the only law-abiding studs left," Garrett said, laughing.

"Yeah, well, I don't have time for your stories, fuck nuts. Just watch the camp. Love you," Henry said, disconnecting the call. Why the fuck did his parents have so damn many kids?

Chapter 11

Sophia woke slowly. She was toasty warm under the quilt. She felt like she had been sleeping for days. She couldn't hear any rustling around, so Henry must have gone to work.

She sat on the edge of the bed and really looked around Henry's childhood bedroom. Besides the double bed, there was an old wooden bureau, a nightstand with a lamp made out of milk glass, and a chair with a wooden base and cushions for the back and seat.

Beside the chair sat an acoustic guitar. The windows were beside the chair. Sheer-white curtains hung from the windows with matching tiebacks on each window.

Sophia could imagine a teenage Henry in his old jeans, T-shirt and bare feet playing the guitar. She liked that image.

There were posters on the wall of a man named Jimi Hendrix playing the guitar, the Rolling Stones, a group of men named KISS (they looked scary).

There was one picture on his bureau. It was a five-by-seven snapshot of what must be his mother and father and nine boys. His mother was beautiful and very pregnant. She held the youngest baby boy in her arms. The picture was taken down at the pond. They all looked so happy.

Sophia made her way to the kitchen where Henry had set out the coffee and instructions on how to use the coffeemaker. *Apparently he doesn't think we have coffeemakers in Colombia*, she thought, smiling. And it was a good thing she did know how to make coffee, because his penmanship was awful. She could make out that he would see her tonight.

With her strong, black coffee, Sophia wandered around the camp. There were pictures everywhere of the different kids doing various activities such as waterskiing, pushing each other off the float, driving the boat, and hamming it up on the beach.

Sophia could tell Henry had a wonderful childhood. Well, at least up until when his mother passed away.

Sophia could relate to a child's world falling apart from the loss of a parent or parents. Sophia had just turned eighteen. She wasn't ready to raise her young teenage brother and to try and make ends meet. It had been a real struggle. She loved her brother dearly, but she couldn't help feeling that she had failed him. But, in Sophia's heart, she knew she had done her best.

A pang of guilt hit her as she was pouring her second cup of coffee. She hadn't told Henry everything that had happened during the stop that resulted in her being arrested.

Something told her that it was important, and she should tell him. But another part of her was embarrassed over how the border patrol officers treated her. Not only were they going to rape her, but they may have intended to destroy the van with her inside it!

No, she would tell Henry tonight. If he was going to help her, she needed to be completely honest with him.

Sophia showered and dressed in a warm wool skirt, tights, and a cozy sweater. She made some toast and snuggled down to read her book.

Closer to dinnertime, Sophia searched the cupboards to see what she could make for dinner. It was the least she could do. She found some chicken in the freezer, potatoes, frozen corn, barley, pinto beans. and several spices. She could work with that. She was surprised to learn from Maggie that she thought Colombian food was spicy. That just wasn't true. Quite the opposite, actually. They did, however, like to use spices to flavor their food. Sophia found a large pot and set all the ingredients to slow cook on the stove, and went back to her book.

Some time later, Sophia heard Henry's big truck drive up. She marked her place in the book and waited for him to come in.

He burst through the door and hollered, "Honey, I'm home."

Sophia laughed and joined him in the kitchen. "Hola, how was your day?"

"Oh, the usual thrilling board meetings and paperwork. How was your day and what is that smell?" he asked.

Sophia smiled. "Oh, the usual, cooking and reading," she said shyly.

Henry smiled and went to the stove. He lifted the lid and looked at her questioningly.

"It's kind of a chicken stew. I took the ingredients that I could find and just put them together. Colombians love soups and stews. It will be especially satisfying on such a cold day like this."

"Sophia, I don't expect you to slave over the stove."

"It's no trouble, Henry. I like to cook, and it's been a long time since I had anybody to cook for."

Henry stared at her for a moment. "Well, it smells amazing. There's something I want to discuss with you," he began.

Sophia held up her hand. "I have something I want to tell you as well. Do you mind if I tell you while I have the courage?"

Henry looked worried. "Of course. Let's sit."

They sat on the kitchen stools facing each other.

"You look beautiful. I just wanted to get that out. Go ahead," Henry said.

Sophia could feel her face heat up. "Gracias. Well, when I told you about the stop and my arrest last night, I left a few things out."

Henry looked confused. "Why? I need to know everything, Sophia."

Her face continued to heat up. She nodded. "Sí, I know and that's why, after I thought about it today, I decided to tell you. I'm embarrassed and humiliated to tell you."

Henry took her hand. "Just tell me. I promise I will in no way judge you. But, if I'm going to build a defense, I need *all* the facts."

Sophia took a deep breath. "Both of the border patrol officers checked, intimately, if I had weapons on me, and one of them started to do things to me . . ." she whispered and pulled her hand away.

Henry was silent. Sophia glanced at him. He was angry. She looked away. This was exactly why she didn't want to tell him. She felt the same way with her father. She always felt like it was her fault.

"Sophia, look at me," Henry said quietly.

She turned her head and looked at him.

"Did he rape you?" he asked very calmly.

Sophia shook her head. "He was going to. He told his fellow officer that they would both have 'fun' with me. But there's more. I didn't tell you that after he said that to his partner, he suggested that after they rape me, they would torch the van."

Henry took her hands in his. "You have nothing to be embarrassed about. This is in no way your fault, Sophia. There are a lot of scumbags out there. I'm glad you told me because now I can nail their balls to the wall. I read the report and I know exactly who they are. Is that when the state police showed up?"

Sophia nodded. "Sí. Do you think the border patrol officers were going to steal the drugs?"

Henry shook his head. "No, I think they are working with the man who sent you here. And that's how they knew where you would be traveling and what you were driving. I don't think Mateo ever intended for you to return home."

A chill ran down Sophia's spine. "If Mateo intended to kill me, then Santiago is in danger. Why wouldn't he kill him too?"

Henry got up and rifled through his work bag and pulled out several cell phones. "I bought these so you could call you brother. But I would guess that as long as you and the drugs are in the wind, your brother will remain alive. At least to be used for leverage with you. Call your brother and let's see what's been going on since your arrest."

Sophia took the phone Henry handed her and dialed her brother's cell phone. Santiago answered on the first ring.

"Sophia?" he asked urgently.

Henry put the phone on speaker, but held it up between them. Henry was very close to her. She could smell his aftershave.

"Hola, Santiago. Are you all right?" Sophia asked in quick, urgent Spanish.

"Sí. Are you still in jail? Mateo told me you were arrested. He is very angry with you, Sophia," Santiago said.

"I'm not in jail. I was bailed, but there will be a trial in a few months. Santiago, I could go to jail for a very long time," Sophia said.

"You cannot come home, Sophia. Mateo will kill you."

"Have you been harmed?" Sophia asked.

"No, I have proven to Mateo that I can be very useful to him. I'm creating dummy companies and opening offshore accounts for him. As long as he thinks I'm of use to him, he won't kill me. Where are you?"

Henry put his finger to his lips.

"Santiago, I cannot tell you, but just know that somehow I will try and buy you some time so you can escape. I've got to go. I will call again when I can. I love you."

"Sophia, I'm so sorry. This is all my fault," he said and ended the call.

Sophia fought the tears. She could hear the fear and sadness in his voice.

Henry pulled her into him and embraced her. It felt so good. She cried and he stroked her back and hair.

Eventually, she pulled away and he handed her a clean, white handkerchief. She smiled. Who carried handkerchiefs anymore? An amazing man like Henry Johnson, that's who.

"Gracias. I'm sorry," Sophia said, wiping the tears from her eyelashes.

"You have nothing to be sorry for. You did good. Now there's one more call I want you to make. I want you to call Mateo and tell him that you are out on bail and are trying to locate the drugs. Once you do, you will call him and give him the location."

Sophia looked frightened.

"We're just buying time. If Mateo thinks you're still helping him to save your brother, he won't hurt your brother or send anybody until you give the location of the drugs. Tell him that once you find out where they are storing the drugs, you want him to send a plane to bring you home so you don't have to stand trial here in the United States."

Sophia smiled. "Sí, that is very good!"

Henry grinned and handed Sophia another phone. "That's my job."

Sophia dialed Mateo. Her hand was shaking. Henry took the phone and held it between them like before.

"What," Mateo said menacingly.

"Mateo," Sophia said breathlessly. She wasn't able to take a full breath. She was nervous. She would make a terrible spy.

"Sophia?" Mateo asked. "Where are you? Are you in jail?"

"I've been let out of jail until my trial. I could go to prison for a long time, Mateo!"

"Sophia, you knew the risks when you chose. You should have married me, *bomboncita*. Right now you would be safe and sound under me, where you belong."

Sophia gasped. She could feel her face turn red.

"Sí, I should have chosen to marry you, Mateo. I'm scared, but I think I can try and find out where they are holding the drugs."

That got Mateo's attention real fast. "Sí? Do you think you can do that?"

"Well, you did tell me that I could use my feminine wiles to get myself out of trouble. Maybe I can use them to find your drugs. But, Mateo, when I find them, I want you to send a plane to pick me up and bring me home before my trial."

"Well, *cariño*, you better find my shipment or you will rot in the American prison and your brother will rot in the ground," Mateo said. The line went dead.

Sophia let out a breath and Henry hugged her again. "That was great," he whispered.

They stayed like that for longer than they probably should have. Sophia pulled away.

"Would you like to eat?"

"Yes, I'm starved. But I have to destroy these phones. I'll take them to the barn out back. I'll be right back."

Sophia busied herself with setting the table. She felt like a weight had been lifted from her. She and her brother were safe for the time being. And she was spending time with Henry who was quickly becoming very dear to her heart. She did know how pointless that was, but the heart wants what the heart wants.

Chapter 12

Henry stalked to the barn with a flashlight. He took the phones to the workbench and smashed them with a hammer and kept smashing them.

He had never had so much built-up rage in him before. It almost scared him. He was going to beat the ever-loving shit out of those border patrol officers. And then he was going to take away their badges and disgrace them.

He was practically shaking he was so mad. And to think Sophia was embarrassed! Those fuckers!

Henry threw the hammer down on the old wooden workbench. He grabbed the end of the bench and leaned on it with his head bowed. He needed to calm down. He took several deep breaths.

Henry got the impression that in her past, Sophia had been made to think that unwanted attention from men was her fault. He didn't want to perpetuate that by showing how angry he was. He didn't want her to think that she was to blame for what those assholes did. But he wouldn't forget. And he *would* make them pay.

Henry walked back to the house. The table was set and Sophia was at the stove, stirring the stew. It felt good. It felt right seeing her there. He smiled and washed his hands for dinner.

"This is amazing," Henry said as he finished his second bowl.

Sophia smiled. "Gracias."

"Keep in mind that you don't have to cook, but if you would like to, make a list of ingredients that you need and I'll pick them up on my way home tomorrow night."

Sophia's eyes lit up. "Sí, I would like that."

After dinner, Henry cleaned the kitchen and did the dishes while Sophia made her shopping list.

In the evening, Henry got the woodstove going and they sat and played Scrabble. Sophia usually won, but it was controversial because several of her words were in Spanish. He did enjoy watching her win. Her smile did something to his heart. He found he wanted to make her smile all the time.

****

The two of them fell into a lovely routine. He went to work and before he left work, he would call the landline at camp and ask if she needed anything from the grocery store. She would cook amazing meals and they would talk and play Scrabble in the evenings.

He was getting pressured at work to go to New York for business. He had been sending others, but Marcus felt Henry should be there and since Henry hadn't told his siblings what was going on, he had to humor Marcus.

About two weeks into their playing house, Henry needed to tell Sophia that he would be out of town for a few days.

"Sí, I will be fine. I do not want to disrupt your life, Henry. You have done too much already. I can never repay your kindness."

"I don't expect you to repay anything, Sophia. I hope to correct an injustice. You are the victim in this. Don't forget that. I will have my phone on me. Just use the landline whenever you need to reach me."

He had his secretary in New York schedule every meeting that had to happen, all within two days' time. During the second day's board meeting, Henry's phone vibrated. It was Will.

Henry held up his phone. "I need to take this. Let's grab some lunch and meet back here in thirty minutes.

"Hey, bud, what's up?" Henry asked.

"I've got some news that I think you will want to hear. Nothing is official yet, but word has it that the Colombian government is requesting Sophia be deported to stand trial in Colombia."

Henry's heart dropped to his feet. "What?"

"Like I said, this is way off the books. I just thought you would want to know," Will said quietly.

"Yeah, thanks. I owe you big, man," Henry said distractedly.

"Nothing owed, but watch yourself, Henry. There are some heavy hitters involved with this," Will said.

Henry said he would be careful and when the meeting started up again, he had no fucking idea what was said or agreed to. All he could think about was Sophia and what would happen to her once she was deported. That was never going to happen.

On the jet home, he researched marriage fraud. The penalty of which was up to five years in prison and a $250,000 fine. Not to mention that he would be disbarred. He wasn't really thinking about this, was he?

The more he thought about it, the angrier he got at what Sophia had already suffered. She had been attacked three times since stepping foot in this country and now was charged with a crime that could put her in prison for the rest of her life. And all because she was trying to save her brother. And, given the choice, Henry would do the same for any one of his nine siblings.

No, he thought, *it's about time someone stands up for Sophia*. And he would be that someone. But, in order to make this work, he would have to convince everyone they knew that the marriage was real. That would be no small feat. Henry's Law was going to fuck him until the day he died.

Henry thought of every possible scenario from her running away to her changing her identity. Getting married seemed to be the most logical answer to giving them some more time. It would only be temporary and not real, so what would be the downside? Beside the fact that he had vowed at a very early age to never get married and it was highly illegal. Even though he didn't really want to get married, he did want to protect Sophia. In the end, that was all that really mattered to Henry. And skirting the law seemed like an interesting challenge. Henry never, ever turned down a challenge.

The only small glitch to this brilliant plan was Sophia. How was he going to sell this to her? She already thought he had done too much for her. He started to worry until he mentally forced himself to stop. He was a lawyer for Christ's sake. Convincing people was what he did.

The little angel on his shoulder reminded him that most times he didn't give two shits about what he was arguing other than he always wanted to win. This argument to convince Sophia that she should marry him *did* matter to him. *Shit*.

By the time he made it back to camp, it was late. Sophia had left a little light on in the kitchen for him. He smiled. It was nice to come home to somebody. He shook his head. He needed to stop that shit. This was only a pretense. Eventually, Sophia would be back in her own country and Henry could get back to the life he was used to. Only right this minute, that didn't appeal to him in the slightest.

Henry knocked gently at Sophia's door. There was no response, so Henry slowly opened the door. She was sound asleep with her book on her chest. The bedside lamp was on and it cast a glow over her. She looked like an angel, her long dark hair fanned out on the pillow. Her eyelashes looked impossibly long against her creamy, tanned skin. And those lips were straight out of every man's fantasy. Henry smiled because, below her chin, she wore a flannel nightdress that looked like something his grandmother would have worn. She was a contradiction for sure.

Henry put the book on the nightstand and shut the light out. Otherwise he would have pulled up a chair and stared at her for hours. When did he become so pathetic?

Henry poured himself two fingers of whiskey and sat down with his legal pad to write out the bullet points to convince her to marry him. He would treat this like every other case. He would attack this as if she were the one juror whom he needed to convince to win the case.

By the time the whiskey was gone, he felt like he had a solid argument. She wouldn't know what hit her. She would be praising his brilliance.

Henry trotted to bed feeling pretty sure of himself. He was taking the following morning off and didn't have to be in court in Skowhegan until one in the afternoon. He was looking forward to a nice leisurely morning with Sophia. That night however, his dreams were anything but leisurely. And Sophia wasn't wearing that flannel nightgown. As a matter of fact, she was wearing nothing at all.

Chapter 13

"No, absolutely not," Sophia stated.

They had just finished breakfast. Sophia was finishing her coffee when Henry, out of the blue, stated that he had found out that the Colombian government had requested that she be deported to stand trial in Colombia. Then he told her that he thought they should get married to keep her in the United States.

"What do you mean, no? It's the only way to keep you in the country," Henry argued.

"No."

"Sophia, what do you think will happen when you're brought back to Colombia? And that is assuming the government is who really wants you and not Mateo. I've researched his organization and it's vast, with lots of government corruption."

Very calmly she leaned toward him. "No. I cannot let you sacrifice yourself for me. I make the line. I will deal with Mateo if I must."

"Draw the line," Henry said.

"Sí, that's what I said. Henry, even I know that getting married to stay in the country is illegal. I will not have you get into trouble with the law for me. No."

Henry nodded. "True, it's illegal, but only if people think it's a ruse. If we convince everyone that it is real, then there is no law broken and you remain safe."

"No," Sophia said. She could feel herself getting frustrated.

"Is that all you can say?" Henry asked, sarcastically.

That was all it took. Sophia stood and walked her dishes to the sink and began a tirade in Spanish that would have frightened most American men. She was mild-mannered most of the time, but when she became frustrated and angry, she could go off for a good long time.

When Santiago was a teenager, he wasn't ever scared of her, but when he pushed her too far, he knew better than to continue to press her.

She washed the dishes and ranted in rapid Spanish. She told him he was loco and that she was tired of all the men in her life thinking they knew what was best for her.

When the dishes were done, she turned around and Henry was sitting at the kitchen table with his chair leaned back and his arms crossed. He also wore a grin.

"Impressive. I could only understand about a quarter of that, so in the future, if you want to get the full effect, you need to speak slower. And, I'm not loco."

Sophia glared at him and walked to the bedroom to get dressed. When she came out, Henry was gone. She checked and his truck was also gone. He must have gone to work. She sighed.

It was crazy, what he was suggesting, right? He could get in a lot of trouble. And she was pretty sure Henry didn't want to get married, ever.

She was sorting some laundry when the screen door slammed. Sophia walked to the kitchen to see Henry set some paperwork down on the counter.

"I thought you had gone to work," she said.

Henry looked up from the paperwork. "Yeah, I'm leaving now. I just went to the town office and got us a marriage license. I called city hall and they can perform the ceremony tomorrow afternoon."

Sophia just stared at him. She turned around and began to rant again in Spanish.

Henry followed her and gently pulled her arm to stop and turn her around. "I know this is upsetting you, but I have gone over every possible solution and this is the only one that is certain to keep you safe. Will you please think about it today and we can discuss this further tonight?"

Sophia's heart fluttered. He was so handsome. It was difficult to think when he was looking at her so intently.

"Sí, I will think about it but, Henry, I will not get married in a city hall. If I agreed to this, it would take place in a church and with a minister."

Henry looked confused. "Even if it was not real and only temporary?"

For some unknown reason, this hurt Sophia. She tried to sound casual when she said, "Sí, even though it is not real. I would still require God's blessing."

Henry shrugged. "Fine by me. We'll talk about it more tonight."

Sophia nodded and watched him walk away. The screen door slammed and she heard his truck roar to life.

Sophia paced the length of the camp. She was so conflicted. What about her fiancé, John Williams? Would he still want to marry her after this was over? Would he believe it was a marriage in name only to help save her and her brother? He was a good, godly man, and he would understand. Sophia was certain of that . . . wasn't she?

On her fourth trip from the back of the camp to the kitchen, Sophia spied the phones on the counter that Henry had brought home. He did say she could use them, but to destroy the battery when she finished.

She would call Santiago. She needed to hear a familiar voice. Not exactly the voice of reason, but familiar and loving.

She keyed in her brother's cell number.

"Sophia? What's wrong?" Santiago asked urgently.

"I'm fine, Santiago. I just needed to talk to you about something."

"What is it?"

"Henry, my attorney, has told me that the Colombian government is requesting for me to be deported back to Colombia to stand trial."

"Sí, sí, Sophia, don't let that happen. It's Mateo who is behind the request. Whatever you must do to stay in America, do it."

Sophia's heart sunk. She had suspected Mateo was behind this.

"Maybe Mateo is trying to help me. If he can get me back to Colombia, he can protect me."

"Sophia, do you really think Mateo is doing this so he can protect you? He wants to kill you! As long as you are hiding in the United States, Mateo can't get to you. Trust me, he's trying to find you. Stay where you are. Oh, Mateo is coming. Stay safe, Sophia. I love you."

The connection was broken and Sophia just stared into space for several minutes before she remembered she must destroy the battery. She detached it from the phone, found a hammer in the kitchen drawer, knelt down on the kitchen floor, and smashed it.

Well, it would seem that the decision, providing Henry was still willing to go through with the wedding, had been made.

She went about pulling ingredients from the cupboards. If she was going to recant and seem like a crazy person, she needed to make a nice meal. It seemed perfectly logical.

She had asked Henry if she could use the computer in the office to look up recipes. He had connected her and told her she was welcome to use it anytime, but if she was going to look up porn, to make sure he was around and to show him.

Sometimes it was hard for Sophia to know if he was joking or not. She had been pretty sure that was a joke.

She had looked up a New England favorite, or so it said. Pot roast, baked potato, gravy, and glazed carrots.

Sophia set out the ingredients and watched a video on how to make the meal. It was uncomplicated, but it seemed kind of blah. She would add some of the spices she had had Henry bring home. She set it to slow cook, found her book, and settled down until Henry got home.

She had set the table and was checking on the roast when Henry walked through the door. He gave his usual greeting in fun. "Honey, I'm home."

"Hola, Henry, how was your day?" she replied in her usual greeting.

"Well, I had a defendant charged with manslaughter get ten years instead of twenty years in prison. So, that was good."

"Manslaughter?" Sophia asked.

"Yeah, it was a difficult case. A teenager who had just turned eighteen was drinking and speeding. He went off the road and killed his three teenage passengers."

"That's awful," Sophia exclaimed.

Henry shrugged. "What is that smell?"

Sophia smiled. "It's a surprise. It is a New England favorite."

Henry smirked. "Is it ready? I'm starved. Or would you like to talk first?"

Sophia nodded and sat on the stool. "Sí. I called Santiago today and you were right. Mateo is behind the request for deportation. Santiago says Mateo wants to kill me."

Henry thought on this for a minute. "So, I guess there's no other choice. We have to be married soon."

"Henry, are you sure? You've done so much already."

"Sophia, I wouldn't offer if I didn't think it was our only solution. I'm a big boy. You don't have to watch out for me like you do your brother. Can you let me take care of things? I promise to consult with you about everything before any decisions are made in regard to your case."

Sophia nodded. "Sí. I'm sorry. I've just been so used to taking care of things that it is hard for me to hand control to anyone. I will shoot the bullet and try harder."

Henry's eyes narrowed. "Bite the bullet?"

"Sí, that's what I said."

"Great. Now that it's settled, let's eat. I will fill you in on the details after dinner."

Chapter 14

Henry couldn't remember the last time he had eaten a meal so delicious.

"Sophia, where did you learn to cook like this?"

Sophia smiled. "I've always loved to cook. My mother was a great cook. I remember spending hours watching her. I thought you might like an American dish. You've been a good sport with all the Colombian meals."

"I've enjoyed all your cooking. And I spoke with the minister today," Henry said quietly.

Sophia looked up from her plate in surprise.

"He can perform the ceremony tomorrow evening at the church here in town. Is that okay with you?"

Sophia nodded and blushed.

Henry reached across the table and covered her hand with his. "Hey, I'm going to keep you safe."

Sophia pushed her plate away. "Henry, I have to tell you something before we go through with this."

Henry pushed his plate aside and had a sinking feeling that he wasn't going to like what she had to say. "What is it?"

Sophia looked down into her lap for a moment. "I'm engaged to be married."

Henry felt like he had been punched in the gut. He sat back in his chair and crossed his arms.

"And you're just now thinking you should tell me this?" he asked with a calm that he did not feel. The thought of her with another man had Henry feeling emotions he had never experienced before. He didn't like them and, as a result, he was harsher than he should have been with her.

"I wanted to tell you but . . ." She began.

"So where was this *fiancé* when you decided to become a drug mule to save your brother? He was okay with that? Did he just wave and say *okay, honey, I'll see you when you get home?*"

Henry watched as her face became a deep pink. Tears sprang to her eyes at his harsh tone. His guts twisted.

Sophia shook her head. "No, he doesn't know about any of it. His name is John Williams. He's a missionary from England. I met him through our church in La Victoria. He's been on a mission trip deep in the Amazon jungle. He's been gone a year. He is scheduled to come home soon, and we were to be married and spend our honeymoon on another mission trip."

Jealousy swirled in Henry. He hated this saintly man. It dawned on him that these were the very same emotions that he had avoided all his life. With good fucking reason. He needed to keep his perspective. He was helping to save Sophia's life. She didn't belong to him and never would.

"Do you think this godly man will still marry you when this is over?" Henry asked, not realizing he was holding his breath.

Sophia was silent for a moment.

"Probably not, but I am doing this for Santiago. John doesn't like my brother, and was anxious to take me away from my village and Santiago."

Henry's hatred for this man increased tenfold.

"Apparently, John Williams doesn't understand the sibling bond. I would say that he doesn't deserve you," Henry said, with a little more gentleness in his voice.

Sophia smiled wanly. "No, John shouldn't be burdened with my problems. He's a good man. It's me who doesn't deserve him."

"Well, we will have to agree to disagree on that point. But I want you to be sure about what we are about to do, Sophia. I think it is the only way we can keep you in this country and prepare for your trial. But getting married isn't going to be as easy as driving to the church. In order for this plan to work, we must be convincing. Nobody can know the reason for our marriage. That would make them accomplices."

Sophia blushed and nodded. "Sí. I understand."

"It would just be when we were in public, of course. And when this is over, and you and your brother are out of danger, I can file the divorce papers and you can go home," Henry stated.

Sophia began to clear the table. "Sí," she whispered.

Henry could feel the hurt rolling off Sophia. Hurt for all she was giving up. Even though he knew she was hurting for another man, Sophia's pain affected him. He wanted to take all her pain away and shield her from the cruel world.

"I have some work to do before bed. I'll see you tomorrow afternoon," he said and left the kitchen. He walked to the office and closed the door. Jesus, he felt like shit.

He sat down in his father's old office chair with a thud. He wished his dad were here to talk to. His father had been the only person who was able to take what was in Henry's brain and make some sort of sense to it. He desperately needed that now.

Henry took the jeweler's box from his work bag. He opened the box to a brilliant split-shank emerald-cut emerald ring with diamond accents. All two carats of it.

It may be a pretend marriage to them, but friends and family wouldn't know that and they would expect no less than the best from Henry. To the world, he would be a man in love who wanted to give his bride the world on a platter.

He sat for a long time trying to decipher how much of that was truth and how much was make-believe.

Henry knew that he wouldn't be solving any of life's great mysteries tonight. As a matter of fact, nothing was going to be resolved tonight and sleep would also prove fruitless.

The main question that he wrestled with seemed to be, was he marrying Sophia to save her or were his motives more selfish? Was marrying her a way to keep her with him because he wasn't ready to let her go?

Henry knew the answer was more the latter and he could actually imagine the angel on his shoulder scowling as he crossed his arms and turned away from him. Guilt engulfed him.

****

Sophia lay awake staring at the ceiling most of the night. Guilt washed over her in waves. How could she ever repay Henry for helping her? The guilt she felt over the lie she was about to tell weighed heavily on her, as well.

She would be lying to God. This realization got her out of bed and kneeling on the floor, asking for forgiveness. She poured out her heart and prayed for guidance. After her prayers, Sophia felt lighter and was able to fall into a sound sleep.

In the morning as Sophia made her way to the coffeepot, she spotted a note on the counter telling her to not bother with cooking dinner. They would be dining out after the ceremony.

The ceremony. The guilt and angst hit her afresh. This was loco. A lie. But, it was also saving her and her brother.

Sophia sipped her coffee and decided to stop feeling sorry for herself. This was a temporary fix to a temporary life-threatening problem. She would try her best to not make Henry regret helping her.

Chapter 15

Henry and Sophia walked into the small country church on the edge of town a little after six. There were candles burning, giving a soft glow.

The minister and his wife greeted them as they walked to the altar.

Henry was very handsome in his dark work suit and tie. Sophia had chosen one of the skirts and sweaters Henry had bought her. If someone had told her two months ago that she would be married in an empty church with a casual skirt and sweater, she would have laughed from the absolute absurdity of it.

Sophia had dreamed of her wedding from her earliest memories as a child. This was not it. But this also wasn't forever. Something about that made her sad.

"You must be Henry Johnson and Sophia Rodriguez. I'm Pastor Mike and this is my wife, Sherry. Sherry will be witnessing the ceremony."

"Pastor, nice to meet you and thank you for taking care of this on such short notice," Henry said, shaking the pastor's hand.

"The Bible says love is patient but most couples in love are not. So, shall we get started?" Pastor Mike asked.

Sophia smiled and took Sherry's hand in introduction.

"Hola, you have a lovely church. I would love to attend this Sunday if that would be all right?" Sophia asked.

"Oh, that would be wonderful, Miss Rodriguez. Do you attend church in your homeland?" Sherry asked.

Sophia smiled and nodded. "Sí, I'm from Colombia. Many years ago a missionary started a church in my small village. My family were dedicated members."

The pastor and his wife exchanged glances and smiled.

The pastor stood before them and just before the ceremony began, Sherry asked Sophia if she had any flowers.

Embarrassed, Sophia shook her head. "I'm sorry, I did not have time to properly prepare," she said, smiling wanly at Sherry.

Henry took Sophia's hands in his.

Sophia looked down at their clasped hands and smiled up at Henry. He was trying to make her feel better. Henry had truly become a good friend. She felt blessed to know him.

The pastor began the ceremony. "We are gathered together . . ."

When the part about rings was mentioned, Henry reached into his suit and produced a silver band and slipped it on her finger. He then handed her a platinum band for her to put on his finger.

The entire ceremony took about ten minutes before the pastor announced that Henry could kiss his bride.

Sophia had forgotten that part. She looked at Henry with uncertainty.

Henry slowly lowered his head, and his lips hovered over hers before his mouth covered hers in a sweet, gentle kiss.

Sophia's heart was racing. She had never been kissed so sweetly. She wanted to kiss him again, but instead she felt her face heat and she looked away with a smile. She never saw the look of utter shock that crossed Henry's face.

With shaky goodbyes, Henry and Sophia made their way to the truck. As usual, Henry helped Sophia in. When he was seated in the truck, he was quiet for a minute.

"Well, that's that. Well done, Mrs. Johnson."

Sophia smiled. "Sí, gracias."

"So," began Henry a little awkwardly, "remember when I said this must look real in order for it to be believed?"

Sophia nodded. "Sí."

"Well, if we were a real couple, there would be no way you would be sitting beside the door as if you were ready to bolt any minute. You would be sitting beside me. It's kind of a thing in my family to have bench seats in our trucks. My father started it. He wanted my mother as close to him as possible," Henry explained.

Sophia smiled shyly and slid over close to Henry.

Henry smiled and nodded as he started the truck. "Much better."

Sophia's heartbeat thudded in her chest and her breathing was rapid. She couldn't think when she was close to Henry. And that kiss; she was still trying to process her reaction to it.

It wasn't as if she hadn't been kissed before, but she had truly never felt the shock and awe that came with Henry's kiss. Could he sense the intensity of her reaction? She needed to get a handle on her emotions. Henry was doing her a great favor by helping her. She couldn't make him regret helping her by placing her growing emotions for him into the mix. No, she must guard her emotions carefully.

They drove in silence for about twenty miles before they pulled into the parking lot of a steakhouse.

"I tried to find a place that was neutral to our cultures. I didn't want to bring you to an Italian or Indian restaurant, and we don't exactly have any Colombian establishments here in our small corner of the world. But I thought steak would be neutral," Henry said as he helped her out of the truck.

"Like Switzerland, no?" Sophia teased.

Henry laughed. "Yes, exactly like Switzerland. This place won't compare to your cooking, but you can hardly be expected to make your wedding meal."

The hostess showed them to their seats and Sophia couldn't help but notice how the pretty hostess watched Henry. If she was honest, she would admit to a pang of jealousy.

Henry held her chair for her before he sat down. The waitress came over at once and he ordered some house red.

He reached across the table and gently picked up her hands in his.

"There's one more thing that I need to give you that makes this marriage believable," he said. He reached into his suit jacket and pulled out the most extraordinary emerald ring Sophia had ever seen.

She gasped. "Henry!"

Henry smiled and looked at the ring. "It is beautiful, isn't it?"

He slipped it on Sophia's ring finger beside her wedding band. She was speechless.

"Anybody that knows me, knows that *if* I were ever married, I would only settle for the very best for my wife. This will be a good start for those who know us and those who may investigate the authenticity of our marriage."

Sophia swallowed and stared at the ring. It couldn't be real, could it? It would be too rude to ask.

Henry continued to hold her hands and watch her. "So, you like it?"

Sophia's eyes darted to his in surprise. "Sí, it's the most exquisite thing I have ever seen."

Henry looked almost relieved. He smiled.

"I didn't have a chance to tell you earlier, but you look very beautiful. I know it's not what you probably thought you would wear for your wedding, but you look beautiful all the same. And, I'm sorry I didn't remember some flowers for you," he said, caressing the tops of her hands as he spoke.

Sophia was having a hard time concentrating on his words. His touch did strange things to her equilibrium.

Smiling wanly, she answered. "Sí, a skirt and sweater is not what I dreamed I would wear for my wedding day. But your gift of help is just as precious to me as the beautiful wedding dress I dreamed about as a child."

The wine was delivered to the table and Henry lifted his glass in a toast.

"To your safety and the hope that someday you have the wedding of your dreams," he said.

Tears sprang to Sophia's eyes. She nodded and held up her glass. "Gracias."

The waitress came over to take their order.

"Do you need to look at the menu?" Henry asked her.

Sophia shook her head. "I will have what you're having."

Henry ordered for them and when the waitress had left, he sat back in his chair.

"So, what flower would you have wanted for your wedding?"

Sophia smiled. "White calla lilies."

Henry laughed. "You answered that rather quickly. I can see you're one of the women who dreamed of their wedding day when they were little girls. Tell me about it."

Sophia could feel her face redden. "Don't make fun of me."

Henry sat up and reached for her hands. "I would never make fun of you, Sophia. Never. I am teasing you a little because it's so rare these days that women dream of their wedding day. They are much more apt to dream of winning the Nobel Peace Prize or going into space. Most women wouldn't admit to dreaming of their wedding day. I think it's sweet and old-fashioned. I like it."

Sophia took a sip of wine. "You are right, of course. Even in Colombia women feel that unless they are dreaming to become wealthy and successful, they are setting womankind back. I have always been old-fashioned. It is how I was raised. But, more than that, it's who I am. I enjoy the simple things in life. Since I was a very small girl, I dreamed of falling in love and having a grand wedding and becoming a mother. That's it, really."

Henry was thoughtful for a moment. "That's monumental, Sophia. My mother felt the same way you do. She came from wealth and privilege and turned away from all of it. All she wanted was to be a good wife to my father and a mother."

"Obviously, she was very successful at both. Would it be too intrusive if I asked you to tell me about her?"

Henry got a faraway look in his eyes. "She was amazing. She was sweet and kind. Everyone who met her fell in love with her. Her name was Elsie. She was gifted in music and studied to be a music teacher. She never actually taught music in a school, but each one of us kids play at least one instrument. We were her music class, her life. Now that I think about it, you and my mother have a lot in common. She was old-fashioned, wanted a simple life, and she was a teacher."

"She sounds like a wonderful person. I would have loved to meet her," Sophia said sincerely.

Henry stared at Sophia.

The food was delivered to their table.

"Well, you're not able to meet my mother, but you will meet the rest of my family this weekend," he said, digging into his meal.

Sophia instantly felt fear wash over her.

Henry must have sensed it because he waved his fork in the air. "Relax, they are going to love you."

Sophia smiled but the feeling of dread stayed lodged in her gut all evening. Her mind swirled with doubts and guilt well into the night as she stared up at the ceiling. Eventually, she did what her heart told her to do: pray.

Chapter 16

Earlier on the wedding day . . .

Kent, Henry's temporary secretary, was a godsend. If Henry had been really smart, he would have had Kent sit in on all his meetings instead of running around for him and picking up the rings and making reservations for dinner.

Henry had been completely useless at work. All he could think of was how crazy this was, but also the most sensible and pragmatic solution to their problem. He had called his brother Marcus to set up a family meeting for Sunday at his house in Portland. He had no friggin' idea how his family was going to react to the news that he was married.

His siblings prided themselves on knowing everything in one another's lives. Henry was no different. He was the go-to guy and therefore was privy to information that his other siblings didn't know about each other.

Henry's only saving grace would be that he was the kind of guy who didn't spill details about his personal life as a general rule. He was the brother who would marry a cocktail waitress in Vegas because he felt like it. Thankfully, that had never happened because it was well known that he didn't ever want to get married. But he *was* the brother who would do it if he wanted to, and his siblings would simply roll their eyes. His family loved him exactly as he was.

If it had been a cocktail waitress in Vegas, it would be easier to shrug and smile. But this was a very serious matter and if not carried out with precision, could end up costing him his career. His family and everyone he knew must be convinced that he and Sophia were madly in love. Quite the undertaking considering he had never been madly in love.

Finally after the last meeting, Henry dashed to his truck in the parking garage and raced back to Harmony.

As he walked through the door, he was immediately bowled over by Sophia's beauty. She had twisted her long, dark hair into a French knot with long tendrils framing her face. She had makeup on, which she normally didn't use, that made her eyes sultry and mysterious. And, those red lips, sweet Jesus, he could stare at them all night.

She wore a skirt and sweater that she had purchased in Freeport, paired with her tall leather boots. She was beyond gorgeous.

"You look beautiful," he stated.

Sophia smiled shyly. "Gracias. You look very handsome too."

"Are you ready?" he asked.

"Sí."

The little church glowed in the darkness as Henry parked the truck along the curb. She had gotten used to his manners and stayed in the truck until he was able to open her door and help her down.

The minister and his wife were waiting for them. Henry had spoken to Pastor Flannigan yesterday afternoon. Henry handed the pastor the marriage certificate that he and his new wife would have to sign after the ceremony.

Mrs. Flannigan asked Sophia if she had any flowers, to which she smiled and shook her head.

Fuck. He should have remembered flowers. He sighed. Well, at least he had the rings. Hopefully that would make up for the lack of flowers.

The ceremony took no longer than ten minutes. Henry's brain was still trying to wrap around what they had repeated after the minister as they slid the rings on each other's fingers and then he announced they were husband and wife and Henry could kiss his bride.

The nerves in his gut churned worse than they had all day. But the moment he lowered his head and his lips touched hers, he was completely lost. A jolt of energy and desire unlike any he had experienced before washed over him.

As if on autopilot, his instincts took over. His tongue delved gently into her mouth for just a taste. She tasted of vanilla and confection. It was intoxicating. He never wanted the kiss to end but his senses must have kicked in and he quickly realized that they were not alone.

As he lifted his head, Henry could see that she was as shocked as he was in regard to the kiss. Guilt punctured his heart when he realized that Sophia hadn't been shocked that the kiss had been as amazing as it was; she was shocked and probably disgusted because she had a fiancé she was going home to marry as soon as she could.

Well, where the fuck was this godly man? Not here to make sure she was safe. *He* was.

Henry couldn't help but feel challenged. Sophia was with him at the moment, and he was going to make sure she was safe. Everything else was unimportant. He was determined to enjoy her company. She fascinated him with her sultry sexiness—that she didn't have a clue about—and her sweet innocence. And smart; she was the brightest woman he had had the pleasure to be around, excluding his sister and sisters-in-law.

The steakhouse was crowded. He saw many men's heads turn to look at Sophia. Whether it was warranted or not, he was proud as a fucking peacock that she was with him, however temporarily.

Henry couldn't have been more pleased that she liked the engagement ring he gave her. He had spared no expense. The moment the thought of an engagement ring came to him, he knew that she needed an emerald on her finger. Not only because her beauty screamed *precious gemstone*, but also because the emerald was mined in her homeland of Colombia.

Conversations with Sophia always surprised him. She was brilliant. It wasn't that she was brilliant that surprised Henry; it was the fact that he had never enjoyed just sitting and listening to anyone talk. Ashamedly, in the past, he preferred that his dates not talk much.

It also wasn't that he didn't date smart women. He did. Many of his female companions were attorneys or in business of some kind. And work or business usually dictated the conversation. Not that enjoyable to Henry.

But Sophia could talk about how she changed the lightbulb that day and he was pretty certain he would be spellbound. He knew he was sinking down the "bunny hole," as Sophia called it. He knew it, but whether he could or wanted to do anything about it was still up in the air.

At the end of the evening, he watched as Sophia shyly said good night and disappeared into his childhood bedroom.

The free-floating feeling of dread that he couldn't name or control snaked through his veins. It was this feeling of dread that he would blame as he drifted off to sleep, that took him back to the worst day of his life.

It was hot. He couldn't wait to go swimming. It had taken all morning to get his little brothers fed and dressed. He didn't help his mother and Bebe, their nanny, with the boys as much as he should but for the love of all things holy (as his mother's best friend, Gracie, said), why did his mother and father have so many damn kids?

Nine boys and his mother was pregnant again. He had heard his mother and father talking one night and they had decided that ten was it. But he didn't think his mother was happy about that. From that night on, Elsie had been a little sad.

He and his brothers Teddy and Bear sat on the porch and played their guitars. The little ones ran all over camp as his mother hollered to them to get dressed. At one point, four-year-old Davey ran onto the porch with his Spider-Man underwear on his head like a French beret. He was also bare-assed.

He, Teddy, and Bear laughed. When Davey could hear his mother coming after him, he gave a little hula dance and ran off toward his room.

Finally, when everyone was ready, he tossed his towel around his neck and headed outside. Davey begged for him to give him a piggyback ride. He stooped and Davey hopped on his back.

His mother watched and walked to him and kissed his forehead. She whispered, "You're a good big brother, Henry."

He smiled. His mother always made him feel good. He was old enough to have been around his friends' families and he knew hands-down that his mother stood above them all. She was kind and patient. Her love for her children knew no bounds.

He sighed as he began to walk toward the pond. The gravel dirt drive that led to the pond was dusty from no rain. His mother and Bebe directed the children to the tall grass instead of the gravel as they walked.

He was glad of that because he would look for grass snakes. As he was looking down at the grass, Marcus and Bobby zoomed past on Marcus's new dirt bike. He was a little jealous that Marcus got one for his birthday. His dad said when he turned sixteen, he, too, could have one.

But Marcus wasn't supposed to have riders and Bobby was waving and taunting them as he rode by on the back of the bike. Marcus would have to answer to their father for that.

"Lil bastards," he whispered as he felt sweat roll down his butt crack.

He was still looking at the ground when he heard Bebe holler out. He looked up to see his mother lying in the tall grass and all of her children surrounding her. In French, Bebe was pleading with his mother to open her eyes.

His heart was seized in fear like he had never known. He was frozen to the spot. Davey jumped down from his back and ran to his mother. Davey was already crying, as were all the other boys.

From a haze, he could hear Bebe talking to him in rapid French. He knew what she was saying because all of the Johnson boys could speak French as well as they could English.

He could hear her tell him to go to his mother while she ran to the house and called the ambulance. Bebe shook him and he was finally able to do as she asked. He ran to his mother and picked up her head and cradled it in his lap. She looked like she was sleeping.

She had some grass stuck to her face. He gently picked it off. His brothers' crying was distant but when he made eye contact with Ty, the sound became normal and loud.

"Ty, run and get Bobby and Marcus. Hurry!"

Marcus would know what to do.

Wetness dripped onto his mother's face. He wiped it off and looked upward to see where it had come from. Finally, he realized that it was his own tears that were dripping onto her face.

He wiped his face across his old T-shirt. But the tears wouldn't stop. He touched his mother's face. Why wouldn't she wake up?

Everything was a blur once the ambulance arrived. His father must have called Gracie and asked her to bring all of them to the hospital. Once he and his brothers got to the waiting room, what he saw gutted him and always would.

His big father sat in a chair that looked too small for his hulking body. His head was bowed and tears streamed from his eyes. He had never seen his father cry. All nine boys stood before him scared out of their minds.

He knew.

And the worst feeling in the whole world invaded his mind and soul that day.

Helplessness and a loss that would never leave him. He would spend his entire life making sure that he never felt such a loss again.

Chapter 17

There was no need for an alarm to wake him up. Henry had slept only a few hours and not at all after the dream. Funny, he hadn't had that nightmare for years. He couldn't help but take it as a sign that he needed to put this situation back into perspective.

Sophia wasn't his and even if that wasn't the case, he had spent his entire life running away from any romantic attachments. And that wasn't going to change. He was merely helping a damsel in distress. Nothing more.

He would admit that he had never felt the instant, intense attraction he felt for Sophia before. But she was a beautiful, sexy woman. So there was that. He had always been a sucker for a gorgeous woman. But getting them into his bed had always been the objective and he was usually successful.

He would also grudgingly admit that Sophia was different. He couldn't quite place why she was so different apart from the obvious: that she was as pure as the driven snow. Every detailed fantasy in which she had starred in his mind had left him feeling like he had defiled her in some way. It didn't stop the fantasies; but he did feel guilty about them.

He looked at the bedside clock: 4:00 a.m. He might as well get up and go to work. He felt like shit and he was in no mood to play nice. It would be best if he stayed away from Sophia and camp for a few days.

****

As the family jet was about to take off, Henry dialed Gracie's number. Gracie had been his mother's best friend and after she passed, Gracie had helped out with the Johnson kids as best she could. She lived in one of the cabins on his family's property. She and her husband, Sam, took care of the property when the siblings weren't there.

"Hi, Gracie, I didn't wake, you did I?" he asked.

Gracie laughed. "No, sweetie, I've been up for hours. What can I do for you?"

"Well, it's kind of complicated. I have to be away for a few days and my new bride is alone at camp. I haven't told Jack or my brothers, so I'd appreciate it if you wouldn't mention it to any of them. What I called for was to ask you if you would take Sophia into town and introduce her around. I don't want her to think she is a prisoner at camp."

There was silence for a moment.

"Well, I'll be. You are a sneaky devil! Congratulations, Henry. Of course, I would be happy to show her around."

Henry sighed. "Thanks. I'm getting together with the fam this weekend. Thanks, again, Gracie. I owe you."

"You don't owe me a thing. I'm happy to do it. I'll see you in a few days, then."

Henry tossed the phone on the table disgusted with himself. He was a fucking coward. He should be showing her around instead of running away. The angel on his shoulder nodded vigorously.

Henry scowled. "She's already engaged," he said to the empty jet.

****

Sophia stretched as she woke up slowly. Married. She was a married woman. Even though it was not a real marriage, she felt a connection with Henry.

She smiled and grabbed the old pink cotton robe belonging to Henry's sister, Jack, and padded down the hall. The camp was quiet. Henry must still be sleeping.

She made the coffee, and as she waited for it to brew, she noticed a note on the counter. She squinted to try and make out the chicken scratch. He had gone to work and wouldn't be home for a few days.

Sophia's stomach dipped to her toes. She knew the disappointment wasn't logical, but she couldn't help it. He hadn't even said goodbye.

Knowing she was alone, Sophia let out a string of cuss words, not the Lord's name, never that, but talking to herself in rapid Spanish about how he could have told her last night that he would be gone for a few days and that he was inconsiderate.

Her anger carried her through getting ready for the day. As she finished brushing her teeth, she looked at herself in the mirror and felt ashamed. How could she be angry with Henry when all he had done was help her.

She knew her anger was just covering her deep disappointment. She missed him. She was in deep trouble. She had fallen in love with her make-believe husband.

Dressed in her skinny jeans and fisherman's sweater, she made her way to the kitchen for another cup of coffee. There was a knock at the front door. Sophia's hand stilled halfway to the coffee pot. Should she answer the door?

Walking tentatively to the door, she opened it to find a beautiful older woman with salt-and-pepper hair, tanned skin with laugh lines around her eyes, and a big smile.

"Well, look at you! Henry didn't tell me that you were such a looker."

"You've seen Henry this morning?" Sophia asked.

The woman laughed and shook her head. "Nah, he called me a while ago and asked if I would show you around town. I'm Gracie."

Sophia held out her hand. "It's very nice to meet you, señora. I'm Sophia."

Gracie took her hand as she walked onto the porch before she pulled Sophia in for a big hug.

"None of this señora. Please call me Gracie."

Sophia blushed and nodded. "I was just about to have a second cup of coffee. Would you like to join me?"

"I have a better idea: how about you grab your coat and we can start with breakfast at the diner."

Sophia smiled and walked into the kitchen to shut off the coffee pot and grab her coat and boots.

The bell rang as she and Gracie entered the cozy diner on Main Street. There was a full table in the middle of the room. Gracie walked over and pushed another table beside the full one.

Everyone greeted Gracie and stared at Sophia. She could feel the heat rise to her cheeks.

Gracie looked around the diner. "Good morning, folks. I was just checking to make sure there weren't any Johnsons here. This," she said, pointing to Sophia, "is Henry Johnson's new bride."

There were gasps heard all around the table. Gracie held up her hand. "But the Johnson clan doesn't know yet, so let's keep it on the down low until after this weekend."

Each person got up and introduced themselves and smiled at her. Sophia would never remember everyone's name, but she felt their kindness.

"Gracias," she said, knowing her face was pink. The last two gentlemen that she was introduced to were the town's sheriffs.

Sophia was a little afraid, but they also smiled and made her feel welcome.

The waitress looked uncomfortable as she wobbled over to take her and Gracie's orders.

"And this beautiful pregnant lady is Dana. She and her husband own the diner," Gracie explained.

Sophia smiled at Dana. She looked tired, but that didn't take away from her beauty. With dirty-blonde hair pulled back in a loose braid and a smattering of freckles on her cheeks and nose, Dana was the closest thing to the American girl next door that she had ever seen.

"This is Sophia, Henry Johnson's new bride," Gracie said to a surprised Dana.

"Oh, my goodness! Congratulations! I hope you visit me and tell me how you managed to get Henry to the altar. Well, it's not hard to see why Henry fell for you—you're breathtaking. What can I get for you two for breakfast?"

Sophia instantly liked Dana. There was a gentleness about her.

As they ate their breakfast, Sophia answered the rapid-fire questions the folks at the table asked her.

"No, we haven't known each other long."

"I'm from Colombia, but was visiting a friend when I met Henry."

"Sí, it was love at first sight."

"I was a kindergarten teacher back home but am not sure what my and Henry's plan is for the future."

As she and Gracie were leaving the diner, a man with the most interesting looks Sophia had ever seen came in to pick up a takeout order.

The man smiled broadly at Gracie and Gracie smiled right back.

"Sophia, this is Blue. He owns the tattoo parlor across the street. Blue, sweetheart, this is Sophia, Henry Johnson's new bride."

Blue's big expressive eyes got big. He had blond dreadlocks down his back that had been gathered loosely with a leather tie. There wasn't a bare patch of skin anywhere to be seen that wasn't covered in tattoos. He even had tattoos on his face, along with several piercings. One would think that he would look intimidating, even though he was quite thin. But Sophia was drawn by his soulful eyes and a peacefulness that he exuded.

He held out his hand. "It is a pleasure to meet you, Sophia. I hope you learn to love this town as much as I have."

Sophia smiled. "Hola, Blue. I'm sure I will be very happy here."

After breakfast, Gracie walked Sophia across the street to meet Harvey, the grocer.

It was early afternoon before Gracie dropped Sophia back at the camp with the instruction that if she needed anything to just call. She said she would be back to check in on her in a day or so.

Sophia walked into the quiet camp, not knowing what to do with herself. She felt a sudden homesickness. She picked up one of the phones that Henry had given her to call her brother and dialed his number. She desperately needed to hear his voice and make sure he was okay.

****

Henry stared at the phone for the hundredth time that evening. He felt like shit.

He had paperwork scattered everywhere. In order to stop thinking about Sophia, he had thrown himself into his work. There was nothing like a good purchase and acquisitions case gone bad to get his head on straight.

Who am I fucking kidding, he thought, as he flung the papers he was holding into the air. He wondered what she was doing. He missed her smell. He wanted to put her against the wall and kiss her until she was breathless. He wanted to lift her shirt over her head and bury his face in her ample breasts. He wanted to pick her up and grind himself against her panty-covered core.

Fuck me. This wasn't helping his resolve to put distance between them. He would not call her tonight. He walked to the kitchen of the condo where he and his brother Caleb stayed when they were in New York.

Pulling out the top-shelf whiskey, he poured himself a generous glass. This was the only thing that would even come close to calming him the fuck down. Two months ago, when he needed to calm down, he would have gone to a club or called one of the hundreds of women's numbers on his phone. But he was a married man and he would honor his wife no matter how pretend it was.

Putting honor aside, he knew deep down that marriage or no marriage, the only woman he wanted in his bed and in his life was Sophia. And that, right there, scared the ever-lovin' shit out of him.

Chapter 18

Sophia woke early. If Henry had been home, she would have baked something for breakfast, but since she was alone, there wasn't really a need. She didn't even make coffee.

She took her time getting ready before she decided to walk to the diner for breakfast. It was so beautiful as she stepped outside the camp. The sun had just come up and the vibrant red and orange of the leaves was breathtaking.

Her breath danced in front of her face with every step. It was cold and crisp. Sophia was falling in love with the little town of Harmony. She only wished she wasn't falling in love with Henry.

Squaring her shoulders, she admonished herself. Whatever her feelings were, it wasn't fair for Henry to have to carry the burden of her emotions. He had sacrificed quite enough. She was sure that the sooner she straightened her legal troubles out and went back to Colombia, the better it would be for Henry.

It was so quiet along the gravel road. It was about a mile to town from camp. She heard some rustling in the woods ahead of her. Sophia stopped dead in her tracks as a big doe walked into the road and stopped, looking directly at her. A moment later, two fawns walked with wobbly legs to stand beside their mother.

Sophia didn't breathe. The mother, deciding there was no danger, began to walk across the road into the woods. Her fawns followed closely behind.

Swallowing hard, she didn't realize that tears had wet her face. She had never seen anything so beautiful in all her life. She wished Henry were here to see it with her.

Sniffing and wiping her tears away, she proceeded to the diner as loneliness settled in her heart.

When she arrived at the diner, there weren't too many people there at the early hour. Dana smiled as Sophia sat at the bar.

"Good morning. You're out early," Dana said.

"*Buenos dais*. I woke up early and decided to take a walk."

Dana laughed. "It's cold out there! Doug, come out here for a second."

A large gruff-looking man came to the counter from the kitchen.

"Doug, this is Sophia. She is Henry Johnson's wife. Sophia, this is my husband, Doug."

Doug raised his eyebrows at "Henry's wife," but smiled warmly and held out his hand.

"It's a pleasure to finally meet you. You're all the town has talked about since yesterday morning."

Sophia could feel herself redden. "I'm sorry."

Dana laughed. "Good lord, don't be sorry. Half the town is already in love with you and most of them haven't even met you yet. Word travels fast in small towns."

Sophia smiled. "When is the baby due?"

Doug looked at Dana with so much love that Sophia had to look away.

"Any day in the next two weeks," Doug answered. "We're trying to find someone to take over the waitressing, but nobody wants to work that hard," he said, furrowing his brow.

Dana rubbed his arm. "We'll find someone," she said to her husband. "We have a couple of high school girls who work weekends, but nobody to take my place for a few weeks."

"Like, eight weeks," Doug clarified.

"I can help you," Sophia offered.

Doug stopped as he began to walk back to the kitchen and turned around.

Dana shook her head. "You're a newlywed. You don't want to spend all day here. It's hard work."

Sophia laughed. "*Sí*, it is hard work. I have waitressed since I was a young teenager. I still waitress in the summers when school is not in session. Really, I would be happy to help. Besides, Henry is busy with work during the day. It would give me something to fill my time and help you out in the process."

Dana looked unsure but Doug stuck his hand out. "Deal. Can you start today?"

"Doug?" Dana admonished.

"Sí, after I have breakfast, you can give me a tour and leave me to it. I think your husband wants you home resting, *mamacita*."

A big smile broke out on Doug's gruff features. "Yes, that's exactly what I want my beautiful, very pregnant wife to do. Sophia has waitressed before. We'll be fine."

Dana sighed and smiled. "Fine, you win. Go fix Sophia a big breakfast. She's going to need it."

At three o'clock when Doug put the Closed sign on the door, Sophia wilted on the stool at the bar.

Doug smiled. "How ya holdin' up?"

Sophia smiled back. "I'm tired, but it's a good tired, you know?" she said in a thick Spanish accent. The more tired she was, the thicker her accent. And she was very tired.

"I know exactly what you mean. I can't thank you enough, Sophia. This means the world to us. Dana can rest easy now knowing you can easily handle the workload. It will only be for about six to eight weeks," Doug said.

"I'm happy to help," she said, putting her coat on.

"Hang on. Let me grab my coat and I'll give you a ride home."

****

Henry heard the crunch of the tires and a door slam. He was leaning on the counter bracing himself as the relief washed over him. He had been losing his shit.

He heard the key in the door and her footsteps into the kitchen.

"Hola, Henry," Sophia said cheerfully.

He whipped around and glared at her.

"Where the fuck have you been?"

Sophia took a step back in surprise.

"I have a job," she announced.

Henry tilted his head to the side. "You have a what?"

"I have a *trabajo*, a job."

"Where?"

His anger was scaring her. Had something happened?

"I'm filling in at the diner for Dana. Has something happened, Henry?" Sophia asked, not realizing she had slipped into full Spanish.

"Happened? Other than going out of my fucking mind worrying about you?" he shouted at her.

Sophia's eyes narrowed. Clearly she was angry now, and as she took her jacket off and hung it up, she began a tirade in rapid Spanish. He could only catch certain phrases such as, she was a big girl, he didn't have to shout at her, and he didn't have to bite her head.

She was the most glorious creature Henry had ever seen. He stepped closer to her and cupped her face just before he captured her lips in a scorching kiss.

He moaned as his tongue slipped inside her mouth. *Motherfucker.* Her taste was intoxicating. He could get addicted to her sweet mouth.

He was trying to hold on to a nugget of self-control when Sophia's hands circled his neck and she gave a little moan. *Fuck me.* He didn't think his dick could get any harder, but he was wrong. He deepened the kiss and backed her against the coat rack as he pressed against her.

Some inconsiderate fucking asshole chose that exact moment to call him as his cell phone began to play "(I Can't Get No) Satisfaction." Fucking apropos.

Henry made no move to reach for the phone in his back pocket, but he did break the kiss and rested his forehead against hers as they tried to regulate their breathing.

"It's bite my head off," he said breathlessly.

"Perdón?"

"You said I didn't have to bite your head. The correct phrase is *You didn't need to bite my head off,*" he said, smiling.

Sophia smiled back. "Sí, that's what I said."

"I'm sorry I was a jerk. I was worried sick. I've been calling all day and I couldn't get ahold of Gracie, so I flew home as fast as I could."

"I'm sorry to make you worry. I should have called you this morning, but I didn't know I was going to work until I got to the diner."

Henry stepped away and went to stand on the other side of the counter so she wouldn't see the effect her kiss had on him.

"Is everything okay with Dana and the baby?"

"Oh, sí, Doug just wanted her to be able to rest for the next few weeks. She is due any day."

"That is very generous of you, Sophia. That's hard work. Are you sure you want to commit to working every day?" he asked for purely selfish reasons. He wanted her with him when he was home. Whether or not that made him an asshole, he didn't care nor did his hard-on.

"It's not every day. I will work Monday through Friday and the high school girls will work the weekends. And, it's just for six to eight weeks. Besides, I am used to working hard. I'm not one to sit around reading all day."

Henry leaned on the counter and nodded. "I'll talk to Doug and see about getting a work permit. You know that will be about the time the trial is supposed to start."

There was an awkward silence. It would seem that neither of them wanted to speak about the kiss or the upcoming trial and the end of their temporary marriage.

Sophia smiled wanly. "I've brought dinner for us from the diner. I wasn't sure when you were coming home, so I got hamburgers and fries for two."

Henry clapped his hands together as Sophia went to the porch to retrieve the bag of food.

"That sounds great. I'm starving and Doug makes the best burgers."

Henry asked her about her day, and she began with the deer in the road and went on to expound on her eventful day as Harmony's most popular waitress. She didn't have to tell him that. He knew how men thought and right about now, Sophia, his wife, was the fantasy of every man who had the pleasure to be served by her today. *Jesus.*

He could listen to her talk all night. She was so animated and full of life. However, as he listened to her, two things he needed to do, pronto, came to his mind. Sophia needed a cell phone and a dependable car.

Chapter 19

"Will we be going back to camp tonight after we leave your family's house?" Sophia asked as they drove in her new Volvo sedan to Henry's brother Marcus's house in Portland.

The day after the "kiss," Henry gave Sophia a new cell phone and a new car. She told him repeatedly that she didn't need either, but he wouldn't listen. He was the most stubborn man she had ever met. *Dios.*

"No, we'll stay at my condo. It's not far from Marcus's house, the house I grew up in. And my condo is in a much cooler part of town—the Old Port.

"Do you like your car?" Henry asked.

"Sí, sí. I like it very much, but it wasn't necessary, Henry. I can easily walk to the diner. Besides, when I leave, what will you do with another car? It's not really your type of vehicle."

Sophia looked over at Henry as he drove. He was so handsome even as he glowered at her.

"This is the safest car on the planet," he said, stroking the dash like a lover. "I don't want you walking anywhere. That's not safe. You're not nervous to meet my family, are you?"

Sophia wrung her hands and looked out the window. "No, why would I be nervous meeting thirty members of your family?" she said sarcastically.

Henry smiled as he appeared to be doing the math in his head.

"I'm impressed. That is exactly how many that are going to be there. Right down to the babies.

"Listen, they're going to love you. But . . ." Henry began.

Sophia let out a string of Spanish. "But what?"

"But in order to be really convincing, we are going to have to really sell it," Henry said, glancing over at her.

Another string of Spanish. "What does that mean?"

"It means that we are going to have to act like newlyweds," he said, glancing over at her again.

Sophia smiled. "Sí, I understand."

Henry looked at her, confused for a moment. "Okay, good."

If Henry needed her to help him sell their marriage to his family, she would do all she could. But, for her, it wouldn't be an act. The only act would be not behaving like a lovesick fool once they were alone.

She hadn't dared to wonder why Henry kissed her the other night. She had convinced herself that he had been afraid for her safety. She knew firsthand that fear made a person do things that were not reasonable.

But, that kiss. Dios.

She was already feeling flustered when Henry turned off the main road and followed a pine tree-lined drive. It was magical.

The pine trees were mingled with vibrant autumn colors from the oak and elm trees. When the car finally stopped, the thick trees opened up to a majestic sage-green-and-white mansion with brickwork and several fieldstone fireplaces.

Sophia was stunned and then terrified when her eyes took in all the vehicles in the circular driveway.

"Breathe, Sophia. They're going to love you," Henry whispered as he picked up her hand and kissed her fingers.

That sweet gesture warmed her heart.

She smiled and nodded.

Henry held her hand as he guided her to the open garage door and then to the door leading to the kitchen.

"As you can see, this is the garage where there was and still is too much testosterone."

Sophia smiled. The garage alone was bigger than all the houses squished together in her small village.

The kitchen was large and empty. There were remnants of snacks and drinks that had been fixed to bring into another room along with coffee and creamer on the counter.

The granite counter was the biggest she had ever seen. There were twelve stools lined up with a step stool at the end for a small child.

"This of course is the kitchen. Copious fluffernutter sandwiches were made here and devoured."

"What is fluffernutter?" Sofia asked in a thick Spanish accent. She wondered if Henry was able to tell that her accent was more pronounced when she was tired and nervous. And when she was very angry, she lost the accent altogether because her brain just reverted back to complete Spanish.

Henry reared back and gave her a look. "You have never had a fluffernutter? Oh, the things I'm going to teach you."

Sophia could feel herself turn red.

Henry still had her hand and continued past the kitchen and pointed out Marcus's office, a large banquet room with colossal chandeliers. And finally, they entered another great room, but this one was warm and cozy and well lived-in. It was also full of people.

Henry had hung up their coats in the kitchen, so Sophia stood with her red plaid wool skirt, black tights, a black cashmere sweater, and tall leather boots. And she had never been so scared. She didn't think she was this scared when she was facing the drug lord Mateo.

The moment they stepped into the room, everyone fell silent and stared at them.

Sophia looked up to see Henry's huge grin on his face.

"Hello, my family, I would like to introduce you to my wife, Sophia Johnson."

Silence.

Sophia really felt like she was going to pass out. She waved her hand slightly. "Hola."

"Oh. My. God," said a tall, beautiful woman as she walked toward them. She was *really* beautiful and really tall.

She took Sophia's hands in hers. She had tears in her eyes.

"Hola, it is so wonderful to meet you, Sophia. Welcome to the family," she said in perfect Spanish. "I'm Henry's sister, Jack."

Henry laughed. "You know that you all look like a firing squad, right?"

As if a dam had broken, everyone swarmed in and greeted her with hugs and kisses. They each introduced themselves but there was no way she was going to remember all their names.

It was the children who enthralled her. And it seemed to be mutual because the children surrounded her and wanted to sit in her lap and hold her hand. They wanted to show her the nursery and their toys and books.

The family asked questions and Henry and Sophia had decided to just keep it simple and say she had been visiting a friend when they met and fell madly in love. That they were still figuring out the details, such as where they would live and if she would be finding a job as a kindergarten teacher in Harmony or Portland.

****

Henry found Sophia in the kitchen with the wives: Jack, MacKenzie, Zena, Riley, Ava, Emma, and Kate.

"Hey, what nonsense are you filling my wife with?" he asked as he pulled her into an embrace and kissed her softly.

The same electric current as from the kiss the previous night went straight through Sophia. She was lost every time he kissed her.

Henry continued to kiss her until a small voice said, "Oh, gross!"

Henry smiled as he broke the kiss and rested his forehead on hers.

"I guarantee you, John-John, that one day you will not find this gross in any way, shape, or form," Henry said as he turned toward his nephew.

"Will too," he said and took off running as Henry started after him.

The entire day was spent with the family getting to know her and, on more than one occasion, Sophia had spied Henry sitting on the couch so she came up behind him and wrapped her arms around his neck, nuzzling him.

It felt so good and right to touch Henry. She felt loved and cherished by his attention. Wherever she was, he would find and kiss her or even just make eye contact and hold her gaze.

Sophia was a ball of sexual energy. She felt like a dry piece of paper and Henry was the match. She was wound so tight that when Henry came to stand behind her and pulled her so close to could kiss her neck that she felt his arousal on her lower back, she thought her legs would buckle.

They had a dinner of delivered pizza, and when the kitchen was cleaned up, Henry brought Sophia her coat and helped her put it on.

"You leaving so soon?" Jack complained.

Henry kissed his sister's hair. "What part of *newlyweds* don't you understand? I thought you were some sort of genius?"

Jack laughed and hugged him tight.

Everyone again hugged and kissed goodbye. Henry's brother Ty was holding his two-year-old daughter, Eva, when she practically jumped from Ty's arms to Sophia's. Everyone laughed and said that it was a first because she was incredibly shy. Eva snuggled into Sophia and when she looked up at Henry, smiling, there was a look on Henry's face that was unreadable.

Henry hurried Sophia to the car and started the engine. He looked over at her and smiled. "I think that went well."

Sophia smiled back and wondered how he could be such a good actor. Touching Henry had come easily to Sophia. As a matter of fact, she had been in no hurry to leave because she knew that as soon as they left, they would revert back to whatever they were. She didn't want the magic to end.

Chapter 20

Henry was going to combust. He had struggled with an erection all damn day. It was painful. And now that they were driving back to his apartment, he had no friggin' clue how to move forward.

All day when Sophia had touched him or randomly sought him out and wrapped her arms around him, he had loved it. It felt so right. But, what the fuck did he know about these foreign emotions? Not that long ago it had felt *right* to pick up a woman in a club, go home with her and fuck her senseless, then leave with a smile and a thank you. That had also felt *right*.

They drove in silence as the angel and the devil on his shoulders did battle. He would set Sophia up in his bedroom, pour himself a drink, and try to get some work done. The angel sighed in relief.

Henry parked Sophia's new car in the private garage in the basement and took the elevator to the penthouse. Ten years ago, Henry had loved the building at first sight and bought it. It was a brick fifteen-story building that had seen better centuries. He gutted the building and made exclusive condos. He claimed the top floor for his own and he had been very happy living the ultimate bachelor life there.

As they rode the elevator in silence, Henry mused over the look Garrett had given him when he introduced Sophia to his family. Garrett, being the owner of the local newspaper in Harmony and up on the story that he and Henry had discussed about the "Colombian drug trafficker," had instantly known something was *off*. Henry had given him a slight shake of his head to tell him that he would talk to him later.

Henry looked down at Sophia. She looked as conflicted as he felt. The doors dinged open and the cold steel and gray of his condo opened up to them. He watched Sophia as she took in the professionally decorated masculine space. He had always been proud of this place. It made him feel successful and powerful. But, looking at Sophia's unimpressed face, he could see what she saw. A cold, lifeless space that was devoid of all emotion. Kind of like his heart.

"It's very big," she whispered and looked at Henry.

Mirth filled his eyes as he thought of the age-old response of "That's what she said." Their eyes met and the mirth in his eyes was instantly replaced with white-hot lust. Sophia's gaze mirrored his own.

Henry dropped the bags, cupped her face and found her mouth with his like a heat-seeking missile. The slight moan he heard from her sent him over the edge and he deepened the kiss. His tongue tasted her mouth and danced with her shy tongue.

Sophia wrapped her arms around his neck and pressed her body against his. He was dying. He unzipped her coat and pushed it off her shoulders. She finished ripping the coat off and reached for his coat and helped him off with it.

Henry reached for the hem of her wool skirt and pulled it up as he gripped her bottom and leaned her back against the wall. Her hands gripped his shoulders. Their mouths never parted.

Not able to stand it a moment longer, he pushed his erection to her core covered with warm black tights.

He moaned from the pure bliss of finally giving his dick what it wanted. "Fuck."

Sophia gasped. "Henry . . ."

He began to grind against her. He couldn't have stopped if he tried.

Sophia grasped his face in her hands and began to kiss him as she made little mewling sounds that were making him fucking crazy.

She broke the kiss and leaned her head against the wall and closed her eyes. He ground harder against her core. Crying out, she opened her eyes and the look of pure euphoria on her face and her cries of release sent him over the edge as well as he came.

Fuck me. He hadn't come in his pants since he was fifteen years old. *What is she doing to me?*

With ragged breathing, Sophia kissed his cheek so softly that his heart ached.

He kissed her forehead and gently set her on her feet.

"I'll show you to my room," he whispered, taking her hand and wondering why he was whispering.

They walked up the industrial steel stairs to his equally industrial but functional bedroom. He set her bag on the bed and excused himself to the bathroom to clean himself up. There was no need for her to know that he had completely disgraced himself.

He took a quick shower and threw on his old worn flannel bathrobe that he'd had since he was in college.

In the shower he had resolved to apologize for his aggressiveness. But, when he opened the en suite door, he nearly fell to his knees.

Sophia stood in front of his bed, facing him in nothing but a black lace bra and matching panties.

Holy Shit.

He had never in all his life seen anything so fucking sexy. He was instantly hard as steel. He slowly took his time, taking in every inch of her. His breathing was shallow and his heart was beating out of his chest. He walked over to stand in front of her and gently cupped her face.

"Sweetheart, I'm not strong enough to walk away from what you're offering," he said hoarsely.

Looking like a scared rabbit, she slowly took his hand and pressed it to her heart.

"I don't want you to walk away, Henry. I want you to make love to me," she said in her thick Spanish accent.

Henry swallowed hard. "Are you sure?"

Sophia smiled and released his hand. She reached for the belt of his robe, and untied it, and, with shaking hands, pulled it off his shoulders, leaving him standing before her, naked.

Henry watched her face as she looked at his body. He had no idea that he could get so aroused by watching her look at his body.

She slid her soft hands slowly down his chest. Her eyes fell to his almost painful erection. Her eyes widened and she quickly looked back into his eyes. What was she thinking? It was killing him to know.

She began to walk around him until she stood behind him and her hands softly stroked his back.

He gasped as she kissed the center of his back, sliding her hands down to his hips. This was the most erotic thing he had ever experienced. And he had done some kinky shit in his time.

He closed his eyes and let her explore his body. Thankfully, if he hadn't just come in his pants, he would not have been able to withstand her scrutiny and touch without throwing her down on the bed and burying himself inside her.

Sophia slowly walked around him to stand in front of him again, moved her hands to his chest, and, with a featherlight touch, she slid her fingers to his erection. He moaned loudly.

She pulled her fingers away instantly and looked at him inquiringly. "Did I hurt you?" she asked with concern.

Henry wasn't breathing. He shook his head. "No, it feels too good," he croaked.

With a small smile, her fingers touched him again. "You're so soft and hard at the same time," she said in awe.

His dick twitched and he moaned.

"Will you show me how to touch you?" she asked, still touching him softly.

That's it, he was going to die right here, right now.

He swallowed again as he took her hand in his, firmly gripped his dick and slid her hand up his length and back down. He could feel his eyes roll back into his head. He let go of her hand and she continued her ministrations, making him see stars.

He was getting close. He stopped her hand and she looked up at him questioningly.

"Sweetheart, it feels too good. I need to taste you and touch you. Are you okay with that?"

She nodded.

Henry cupped her breasts and ran his thumbs over the silk covering her hard nipples. She was fucking glorious.

She gasped at the sensation. He reached around her back, unhooked her bra, then pulled the scrap of silk away from her and tossed it to the floor.

Again, his knees threatened to buckle. He had never seen more perfect tits anywhere in his life. Not on supermodels or in magazines. He could worship them for the rest of his life. They were full and heavy with small areolas with the most perfect hard peaks.

He reached out and with reverence gently scraped his thumb nail across each nipple.

Her sharp intake of breath and the whispered sound of his name from her lips sent him in a frenzy. He pushed her back on the bed and pulled her up to the pillows before he lowered his head and began to worship her.

He drew her breast into his mouth and sucked hard. She cried out and he moved to the other and did the same. He alternated back and forth until he was again rocking his dick against her panty-covered core. She was writhing and once again close.

No, he had something else in mind for her next orgasm. He raised himself up and took her mouth again in a deep kiss. The moment her shy tongue slipped into his mouth, he moaned, knowing he was riding dangerously close to the edge once again.

He broke the kiss and began to trail kisses down her belly. She gasped as he nipped and sucked on her soft skin. He reached her dark curls and he gently spread her legs apart. He looked at her and then up her body to her shocked, desire-filled eyes. He knew in a heartbeat that no man had ever tasted her and that made him feel humble and ten feet tall all at once.

Still looking at her, he traced his tongue along her seam. Her breathing was coming in pants. He spread her lips and gently blew on her sex. Her head leaned back and she spoke in rapid Spanish. That was all it took for him to begin to devour her. He had never tasted anything so sweet. He was an instant addict.

Within minutes, she was hollering his name and coming apart. He never let up until she collapsed back onto the pillow. But he didn't stop. He began to lick her gently as he slowly inserted a finger into her tight wet heat. This time they both moaned loudly.

Fuck me, she was tight!

He continued to lick her and move his finger in and out of her. When he knew she was close again, he began to suckle her clit, the center of her bundle of nerves, and he inserted another finger and began to fuck her in earnest.

She screamed and came up off the bed. Henry held her bucking body tight with his hands on her thighs until her spasms subsided.

He kissed her thigh and crawled up her body. He was out of his mind with wanting her. He had never felt so out of control. He lined himself up with her entrance and kissed her mouth deeply.

"Are you sure, Sophia?" he whispered as if in pain.

Sophia kissed him softly and cupped his cheeks. "Sí, Henry, I'm sure."

With a groan, he pushed into her tight heat. He had never felt anything so good. He pushed harder and she gasped in pain. He immediately stopped. *Fuck me.* She was a virgin and he was hurting her. The pain in his heart at the knowledge that he was hurting her made him lose his breath.

Sophia opened her eyes to see what was the matter. "Don't stop, Henry, please don't stop."

"I don't want to hurt you, sweetheart."

Sophia kissed him gently. "Please don't stop," she said as she raised her hips to take more of him.

Henry groaned loudly and with their eyes locked on each other, he pushed until he felt her barrier break. He stopped to let the pain subside. It was she who, again, lifted her hips to cause a slight friction and she gasped as he saw the awareness of pleasure in her eyes. It was the single most amazing thing he had ever witnessed.

****

It hurt. She had been soaring on a cloud of bliss until he had started to push into her. She had a moment of panic as she was convinced that he was too big and wouldn't fit inside her. At that moment, he had stopped and the look of horror on his face—thinking that he was hurting her—seized her heart and she wanted nothing more than to bring him pleasure.

But it was Sophia who was surprised. When he had broken through her barrier and stopped, she had lifted her hips, determined to make him feel good, but it was she who felt the zing of pleasure begin at her core and resonate throughout her entire body.

She would never be able to put into words the feeling, but she did have a passing thought that this was the reason the world was populated. The good Lord had assured procreation with the promise of pleasure beyond comprehension.

That was her last thought because she began to climb higher and become wound tighter than she would have thought humanly possible before she exploded spectacularly.

She could hardly breathe as she repeated Henry's name over and over like a prayer.

Sophia opened her eyes just in time to watch Henry as he closed his eyes tight and hollered as if he was in pain for what seemed like minutes but was probably only seconds. She felt joy to know that she was the one that had made him feel such pleasure.

Henry collapsed beside her and pulled her in close to his side, hugging her with both arms. They both tried to get their breathing under control.

After a few moments, he pulled apart a little bit and looked at her and smiled. "Hello."

Sophia smiled. "Hola."

"How are you?" he asked quietly.

"Increíble," she whispered, looking into his eyes.

Henry chuckled. "You *are* amazing."

"How are *you?*" she asked shyly.

"I think I'm dead and I must be in heaven. I'll be kicked out soon enough, so I intend to enjoy my stay," he said, kissing her deeply.

Breaking the kiss, it dawned on him that he hadn't used protection. *Fuck me.* He wouldn't mention it right now. He didn't want to spoil the moment. How could he have been so stupid? She made him lose his mind.

Sophia let her hand stroke the dark hair on his chest. "You have a wonderful family, Henry."

Henry kissed her hair. "Yeah, they're okay," he said and yelped as she pinched his side. "They're the best. They fell completely in love with you."

The last thought Sophia had before being claimed by sleep was wishing it was Henry who had fallen in love with her. She never heard Henry whisper, "You know we can't get our marriage annulled now, sweetheart," nor did she see the small smile on Henry's face after he said it.

Chapter 21

The dream was unlike Henry had ever had. Usually he dreamed about his mother, but tonight his father had something to say to him.

It was hot and the air was heavy and humid. The sun beat down with a merciless hum. He was barefoot and walking on the beach at Moose Pond. He had his old worn Levi's on and the bottom was wet from the waves that covered his feet. He had his favorite Rolling Stones T-shirt on.

He'd been in this exact spot thousands of times. He looked around for his brothers, but no one was around. As he looked at the old wooden dock with the boats bobbing to and fro from the waves, he saw a large figure sitting at the end of the dock with his feet dangling in the water.

Dad? It couldn't be. He'd been gone for seven years. Henry walked slowly to the plank leading to the dock. He walked slowly toward the end of the dock. He could feel his heart thudding loudly. He swallowed.

As he reached the end, his father turned ever-so-slightly and raised his dark head. He had a wan smile. "Hello, son."

Henry's legs almost buckled. "Dad?"

David Johnson was larger than life and raised his sons with love, but he wasn't above kickin' their asses if they did something stupid or disrespected an elder.

His father patted the dock beside him. "Sit a spell with me."

Tears sprang to Henry's eyes. He had missed his dad so much. He sat down and stared at his father. He seemed as real as the solid wooden dock they were sitting on.

"You know you stole something very precious, Henry," his father said quietly.

Henry looked confused. He had never stolen anything in his life. Well, that's not true—he stole some mail from their neighbor's mailbox when he was eight. He was curious and had overheard his brother Marcus tell a friend that his neighbor got Playboy magazine delivered to his house. Henry wanted to see what the big deal was.

He didn't know his father was talking about that. He'd had to mow his neighbor's lawn free of charge for the entire summer. He would never steal anybody's mail again.

"What did I steal, Dad?" Henry asked hoarsely.

His dad looked at him for a long moment before looking out over the water.

"That young lady saved herself for a husband who loved her. You took what wasn't yours, son. You can never make restitution for what you took."

Henry felt like he couldn't breathe. "Dad, it was consensual. I would never have touched her if I thought she didn't want it as badly as I did."

A storm gathered at his father's brow. Henry knew that look. His father was pissed.

"Don't use your fancy lawyer-speak on me, boy. I don't give a flying fuck if it was consensual. What you took wasn't meant for you. It was meant for the man who would love and cherish her and build a family with her. Are you that man, Henry?"

Henry felt the anger rise in him. "Life isn't a fairy tale, Dad, and technically we are married, so there is that."

The anger left his father as he sat looking out over the black water. "You're right, son. Life isn't a fairy tale. You watched your mother and I love each other deeply, and then you saw what losing that love looked like. I was a broken man. I don't blame you for not wanting anything to do with love. But Henry, you had no right to take Sophia's innocence, knowing full well that when the danger

was over she would leave and you would just continue on with your
selfish ways. I'm disappointed in you, son."

Henry was speechless as he watched his father stand up and
walk toward the beach and then disappear.

Henry barely made it to the bathroom before he lost everything in his
stomach. A cold sweat had broken out on his brow.

Fuck me.

He picked up his watch from the bathroom counter, 4:00 a.m. Shit,
he needed to get out of here. He brushed his teeth and dressed quickly. It
was Sunday, so he grabbed jeans and a sweatshirt. He looked over at the
sleeping woman in his bed. His wife. Sophia.

She looked so sweet and peaceful lying there. Out of all the women
he had fucked in that bed, none had ever looked as sweet and innocent as
Sophia. It made him sick. His father was right. He had no right whatsoever
to take what wasn't meant for him. It had been meant for another man she
had promised to marry. A fucking missionary. A saint. A man who could
give Sophia all her heart desired because where he could give her money,
cars, expensive jewelry and fancy homes, this saintly man could give Sophia
what she really desired: love and a family.

Even knowing all that, Henry still wanted to punch the bastard in
the face.

****

Sophia stretched like a lazy cat. Muscles she didn't know she had were sore.
A big smile broke out on her face as she remembered the two times she and
Henry had made love.

She didn't think she would find so much pleasure in sex. Sure, she had
read books and watched a few movies, but she thought it was exaggerated
and over the top. But, no, now she knew the movies and books didn't do
the intimate act of sexual intercourse justice. It was better than she could
ever have hoped.

She glanced over at the empty space that Henry had occupied. Well,
to be fair, they both had occupied it because he had held her to him all

night. She had never felt closer to another human being, not even her brother.

She got out of bed slowly, put on Henry's worn plaid bathrobe, and made her way to the kitchen where she found a note propped up against a fancy coffeemaker. She frowned.

Sophia,

Something has come up at work that needs my attention. Your keys are here on the counter. If you punch in the camp's address in your GPS, it will direct you back. I will see you in a couple of days.

H.

Sophia just stared at the note. What did this mean? As far as she was concerned, they had shared the most amazing act of love that two people could share. So, why didn't he at least wake her up to say goodbye?

Her heart sank. Maybe it was only her world that had tilted off its axis. Maybe it had not been special to Henry. She knew he had been with many women. She must not have measured up. He must have been disappointed with her. Or, worse, maybe he didn't think anything at all about it.

Sophia swallowed, carefully set the note back on the counter, and made her way upstairs to dress. As she climbed the industrial stairs, she angrily wiped the tears away that refused to obey her direct command to not flow from her eyes.

****

She cried the whole way north to Harmony. As she entered town, she passed the little church where she and Henry had gotten married and saw that people were walking in for morning services.

Sophia slowed the car and parked. This was what she needed. She smoothed down the wool skirt that she had worn yesterday and walked into the small chapel.

Ironically, the sermon was about love. She loved Henry but she loved her God more. She needed to trust that this situation was in her Creator's hands and it would all work out. With a sigh of peace, she was once again centered.

She would be a wife to Henry and if all she had with him was a couple of months, then she would cherish them and count them as the blessing they were.

As she left the chapel, the minister, Pastor Mike, shook her hand and held it as she looked at him and said good morning.

"For a newlywed, Mrs. Johnson, you look a little sad. It's none of my business, my dear, but if you ever need to talk, my door is always open," Pastor Mike said.

Tears sprang to Sophia's eyes as she looked into the kind eyes of the pastor.

"It's Sophia, please, and I would like that very much. Thank you."

He nodded and let her walk away as he shook the hand of the next person in line.

Feeling much better, Sophia let herself into the camp and made a pot of coffee, pulling out the ingredients for a recipe for a New England favorite, corn chowder.

As the chowder simmered on the stove, she pulled out one of the burner phones and dialed Santiago. She desperately needed to talk to her brother. She wouldn't tell him she had fallen in love, at least not yet. She needed to make sure he was well and ask if Mateo had found out she was not going to be deported. She prayed Mateo didn't know about her marriage.

Chapter 22

Henry threw his pen across his desk in frustration. He had tried unsuccessfully all day to work. His brain refused to concentrate on contract breaches or trusts and wouldn't shut down the now constant movie reel of the events of last night.

Everything about Sophia was perfect and sexy. When he had her naked on the bed, it was as if a heavenly light shined down on her. She was spectacular. And not just the sight of her sexy-as-fuck-body; it was the way she completely gave herself to him.

His dream about his father had been spot-on. He knew from the moment she gave in to their lust that he was taking something precious. Something not meant for him. Not to mention the pregnancy issue.

Henry sighed and looked at his watch. His eye caught the shiny new platinum wedding band on his finger. *Fuck.* He was a fucking coward.

He pulled out his phone and dialed Will. He could use a friendly violent hockey scrimmage.

As he left his office, he called his contact in the state police that was investigating the two border patrol agents who had stopped Sophia. Henry's only true defense for Sophia was to get the charges dropped and not go to trial. How he was going to pull that off was a mystery, but getting Will's insight would help. Will was a brilliant attorney. Almost as brilliant as himself, he thought, grinning at the running joke between them since law school.

****

The scrimmage was intense. More intense than usual. It felt good. Will met him in the locker room after their shower.

"The pub?" Will asked.

"Yeah, I'm starved," Henry said, realizing that he hadn't eaten all day.

The meal of shepherd's pie was amazing. After they ate, Will sat back and narrowed his eyes.

Henry finished his Guinness. "Say what's on your mind, William."

Will motioned to the waitress. "Can we have a couple of fingers of your best Irish whiskey, please?" he asked the pretty waitress who smiled and nodded at Will.

"Well, where do I fucking begin? I'm going to start with the friggin' obvious elephant in the room. What the fuck is the wedding band about?"

Henry sat back and smirked. His friend missed nothing. He held up his left hand, displaying his wedding band. "This?"

Will chuckled. "Yeah, that."

"Remember Sophia? I married her."

Will started to say something but remained silent as the waitress brought the whiskey. As soon as she walked away, he leaned in. "You married your client so she wouldn't get deported? That is illegal as well as fucking beyond stupid, Henry."

Henry nodded. "Well, unless you're planning to announce it, you're the only one who knows. Well, I think Garrett thinks something is fishy, but I'll talk to him this week. It was the only way, Will. She is in a lot of danger."

Henry proceeded to tell Will the whole story, and when he was done, Will motioned to the waitress to bring the bottle of whiskey.

"Fuck me, bro, this is serious."

Henry nodded. "Very."

"So you've been in contact with the state police about the border patrol agents. Have you heard how their investigation is going? How can you be sure they can be trusted?" Will asked.

"I checked in with my contact at the state police before I met up with you. He said they were certain the border agents were dirty and that they were in the process of getting warrants for their cell phones and bank accounts. I trust my contact. I have to get these charges dropped against Sophia. I won't let her go to prison for protecting her brother against a psycho drug lord."

Will took another sip and chuckled. "For a guy who had his own life law of keeping things simple and never getting attached, you have broken it spectacularly. But I have another question. You've told me all about why you married Sophia, but now I want you to tell me when you fell for her? Was it when she was in jail or since she's been living with you?"

Henry finished his whiskey and narrowed his eyes. "Nothing gets by you, Perry Mason. What makes you so sure I've fallen for her?"

Will looked disgusted. "Please. I know you almost as well as your siblings. I know you would not have *married* Sophia just to keep her in the country. Shit, maybe you don't even realize you've fallen for her. But I'm telling you, you're up shit creek without a paddle, brother."

Henry stared at Will for a few long seconds before blowing out a breath. "I am in deep shit, aren't I?"

Will laughed. "Very deep. Speaking of, where is the gorgeous Sophia?"

Henry scowled. "She went back to Harmony," he said, without mentioning it was after he took her virginity and, like a dick coward, left her before she woke up.

Henry held up his hand to whatever Will was going to admonish him about and poured them another drink.

Will shook his head. "I have depositions in the morning."

Henry lifted his glass. "Since when did you enter middle age, Grandpa? We need to toast my marriage and the fact that Henry's Law has been repealed."

Will picked up his glass and clinked it with Henry's. "It's a day I never thought I'd see, and I wish you much luck, my friend. You're going to need it."

Henry and Will closed down the pub, but not before Henry sat at the piano and Will borrowed a band member's saxophone and they belted out "Only the Good Die Young."

****

"You look like shit," Henry's youngest brother, Caleb, said, grinning.

"Bite me," Henry growled. He was definitely not in the mood for his brother's smart-ass mouth. He had called Sophia's cell phone three times

112

that morning, but it went straight to voice mail. He had been reduced to calling the diner to make sure she had made it to work.

Not only did he have a massive hangover, he felt like the biggest shit that ever walked the earth. He would call her tonight and try to apologize. He wasn't sure how one went about apologizing for being the biggest dick ever. These emotions were all new to him and he didn't like them one bit.

The only good thing about drinking himself into oblivion last night was that he actually slept. He hadn't had a good night's sleep since he had met Sophia.

He and Caleb were on the family jet going to New York. There were several business meetings that they needed to attend on behalf of the company.

The day dragged on like no other day in his life. He and Caleb drove to the apartment on the Upper West Side that used to belong to his brothers Bobby and Ty. Now just Caleb and he used it when they were in New York on business.

Henry had just stepped out of the shower when Caleb hollered to ask him if he wanted to go to dinner and to the club they frequented when they were in the city.

"No, I'm going to order takeout and call Sophia," Henry said.

Caleb laughed. "Okay, be careful you don't hook that ring through your nose on anything. Peace out."

Henry grumbled about putting something through the little bastard's nose when his cell phone rang. It was Sophia. Fear washed over him. He picked up the phone and answered tentatively.

"Hello, how are you?"

"Hola, Henry. I'm sorry I didn't get your messages until I got out of work. It was crazy at the diner. The mountain crew have hired lots of new people and they were very hungry. How did your meetings go?"

She sounded as sweet as always. There was no anger. Any other woman that he knew would have let him have it if he had left without saying goodbye. Rightly so, but not Sophia. His heart constricted.

"Oh, the meetings were productive, if not boring as hell. Listen, I want to apologize for leaving without saying goodbye. Do you want to talk about what happened?" he said softly.

There was silence on the other end of the phone.

"Sophia?"

"I'm here, Henry. There's no need to apologize. I know you're a very busy and important man. And, as far as what we did, we did what most married people do, right?" she asked shyly.

Henry took a deep breath. He didn't think he could feel worse about what he did, but it seemed he was wrong.

"But we're not a real married couple, Sophia. I took something very precious from you. Something that wasn't mine to take."

Again silence.

"Henry, I'm not ashamed that we made love. I have done nothing wrong or immoral. You are my husband. We may not be together forever, but we *are* married in the eyes of God."

Henry was now speechless for a moment.

He cleared his throat. "So, are you saying that while we are married, we should act as husband and wife in *every* way?"

"I would like that if you would," she whispered.

Henry swallowed. He was painfully hard. He wished he were there to pick her up and tell her that yes, he wanted that more than he wanted to fucking breathe.

"Um, I would like that very much, Sophia. Are you sure?"

Sophia giggled. "Sí, I'm sure. When will you be home?" she asked in an almost whisper.

Fuck me. Not soon enough, that's for sure.

"I'll be home in two days. Now tell me all about your day," he said. And she did. She told him about the local people she had met and about Gracie and Sam visiting her. Henry settled down on the bed and just listened to her. Her enthusiasm and love of life was infectious. He could listen to her all night.

Chapter 23

Sophia lay in bed after talking with Henry and listened to the quiet. Occasionally an owl hooted in the woods or the logs shifted in the woodstove, but apart from that, it was silent.

As far as Santiago knew, Mateo didn't know she wasn't being deported just yet. But her brother did say that Mateo was getting very antsy about his drug shipment and that he was searching for her.

Sophia shivered, thinking about Mateo finding her, and then her terror increased as she thought about her brother having to be subject to Mateo's insanity.

Her fear pinged to the incident at the diner today. The mountain crew had increased, bringing with it men from out of town. Not that Sophia really knew the regulars yet, but they seemed to be good-natured in their teasing.

But there was one man who gave her the creeps. He was huge and huddled over his plate like a prison inmate and watched her. He had done nothing wrong, really, but she had a gut instinct telling her to be wary of that man.

She probably should have told Henry about him when she called, but she didn't want to be any more of a burden. She could handle this on her own. *Dios mío*, how did she get herself in so much trouble? She had lived her life quietly and tried to be a good Christian.

She shook her head in the darkness. No, she had prayed about it. It was out of her hands. After all, even with all the evil that she had recently endured with Mateo and the border agents, where did she find herself tonight, safe and warm? Not to mention she was married to a man she loved. No, her God had her in his hand . . . of that she was certain.

Smiling as the familiar peace enveloped her, Sophia fell fast asleep.

****

Henry pinched the bridge of his nose to stop the burgeoning headache. He had been trying to stuff as many meetings together as possible so he could get home to Sophia.

It was starting to feel like an addiction, and he needed his fix of sexy Sophia. He told himself that just seeing her was what he craved, but if he was in any way honest with himself, he knew that he wanted to bury himself inside her tight warmth and stay there until he got his fill. And that would not be anytime soon. Maybe never.

He walked out of the local deli—a short distance from the office building his family owned in downtown Manhattan—with a large coffee and a pastrami sandwich. He stood at the crosswalk waiting for the walk signal and took his first sip of coffee.

A white unmarked van squealed to a stop before him, and four large men with ski masks slid the door open and jumped out. They grabbed Henry and thrust him in the van, slid the door shut, and took off. All within a span of seconds.

Those at the crosswalk stared and stepped back, but none made a move to help him, and soon after, the walk signal began to blink and everyone proceeded to where they were headed.

There was one scraggly homeless man sitting on the street who watched the scene unfold. He stood and sauntered to where Henry had stood and looked down the street in the direction the van sped. Seeing nothing, he stooped to pick up the unopened sandwich that Henry had dropped, then slowly walked back to his perch against the dirty brick building and proceeded to eat it.

Henry glared at the masked men huddled around him in the van. He sat on the floor of the van waiting for someone to say something.

"You're buying me another sandwich, assholes," he said sarcastically.

The goons never said a word.

Henry sighed.

They drove about fifteen minutes out of the city to an abandoned warehouse. Why did these things always take place in abandoned warehouses?

The goons pulled him from the van and pushed him into the building.

"I'm capable of walking," he said flippantly as they continued to push him forward until they came to an empty open space that was probably the production room of something once upon a time.

In the room were two men and three wooden chairs. The goons gave him one last push into the space and turned and walked out of the warehouse.

"You should be proud of your workers—they've got personality for days. Now, who the fuck are you and why am I here?"

One of the suits motioned to the chair. "Why don't you have a seat, Attorney Johnson, and we will explain everything."

Henry rolled his eyes but walked to the nearest chair, sat down, and crossed his legs as if bored.

The two men sat as well. The tall, thin man with blond slicked-back hair spoke first. "I'm Jeb Sullivan from the FBI and this is Roy Smith from the CIA."

Roy Smith was short and stout with thinning dark hair also slicked back. He just sat there staring at Henry.

Henry looked to the ceiling. "Okay, FBI and CIA. Got it. Is there a particular reason you didn't just call me and ask me to meet with you? Why all the palace intrigue? The ski masks and white unmarked van were a little over the top. Just a little FYI for your next kidnapping."

Agent Sullivan smirked and nodded. "Duly noted. We have brought you here today to speak to you about Mateo Sanchez."

Henry narrowed his eyes. "Go on."

CIA Agent Smith sat forward and rested his arms on his knees. "We have been surveilling Mateo Sanchez for years. We have watched him climb his way to the top of the drug trade. He's methodical and psychopathic."

Henry nodded. "I'm listening," he said quietly.

"Sanchez has a large army, which has made it very difficult to get close to him. For the last few years, we have had very good intel via electronic means, but recently he must have garnered a super computer hacker who has all but wiped out our only connection to the Sanchez organization," Agent Sullivan informed him.

Henry had to play his cards very close to the vest. It didn't sound like they knew that Santiago Rodriguez, the computer genius, was Sophia's brother.

"So, this sounds like a problem for you. What does it have to do with me?" Henry asked coyly.

Agent Sullivan sighed. "Your client, Sophia Rodriguez, is right now our only and best link to Mateo Sanchez."

Henry began to drum his fingers on his leg. "So, do I hear complete immunity somewhere in this soliloquy?"

Agent Smith stood up angrily. "Your client was arrested with the biggest shipment of drugs ever confiscated in the State of Maine. Do you really think she will be able to just walk away free and clear?"

Henry stood up angrily as well to tower over the CIA agent. "Yes, as a matter of fact, that is exactly what I expect, but . . . that's not all on my list of *demands*."

Pulling out a business card and a pen from his inside jacket pocket, Henry scribbled his cell number on the back.

"When the pertinent branches of government are ready to really talk, give me a call. If you think you can just manhandle me in the back of a van to try and scare me and have me hand over my client on a silver platter, well, you clearly haven't done your homework. I have contacts so high that if I called them, you two may be meter maids starting tomorrow. They probably don't call them meter maids any longer, though. But you get my meaning. Do not waste my time again," he said, walking toward the warehouse door.

"We will be in touch, Attorney Johnson," Agent Sullivan hollered after him.

Henry never turned around but held up his middle finger as he continued to walk out the door to have the goon squad take him back to the city and buy him some fucking lunch.

Chapter 24

He watched her sleep. She was the most beautiful woman he had ever seen. He'd worked like a dog to be able to get home early. The pilot hadn't been happy to bring him home in the middle of the night instead of waiting for morning. He couldn't wait.

He'd been sitting there for about ten minutes just watching her breathe. It was the calmest thing about his last three days. Just being in her presence calmed him.

Sophia stirred and opened her eyes slowly and then started.

"Shhh, it's just me. I just got home," he soothed.

Sophia smiled sleepily, making his gut flip and his groin twitch. *Jesus, she is beautiful.*

"I'm glad you're home. Will you come to bed?" she said shyly, pulling the covers back slightly.

Henry silently moaned in rapture at the thought of crawling in that bed with her. He cupped her cheek.

"I'd like that very much. Are you sure?" he asked quietly.

"Sí," she whispered.

Standing he discarded his work clothes, down to his briefs, and slowly slid into bed. He cupped Sophia's cheek and lowered his head to kiss her. Something he had wanted to do from the moment he left her sleeping in bed three days ago.

He heard her little intake of breath before she opened her mouth to him. *Jesus.* He was going to self-combust.

Moaning softly, he deepened the kiss until neither of them could breathe. Breathing was highly overrated.

Henry kissed his way to the little crook in her neck that made him lose his mind with her scent. He was addicted to her scent. He couldn't quite place any specific smell, but it was a combination of vanilla, confection, strawberries, and lilacs, all making him lose his control and feel something else that terrified him.

He gathered her close and held her tightly. He could just stay like this forever. She had on her grandmotherly flannel nightgown. He felt her warmth straight to his bones.

"I want you," he whispered into her neck.

Sophia ran her fingers through his dark, mussed-up hair. The zings from her fingertips went straight to his painfully hard dick. He moaned as he pushed her onto her back and reclaimed her mouth in a deeply possessive kiss.

Henry began to pull her nightgown up. She lifted her bottom to help him. He peeled the heavy flannel material over her head. He looked down and moaned. Through the moonlight, he saw her glorious nakedness. She wasn't wearing any panties.

"You're so beautiful, Sophia."

"You make me feel beautiful, Henry," she said in a thick Spanish accent.

Sophia reached her hands out and shyly caressed his chest as she continued to stare into his eyes. The moment her hands were on him, his breathing became labored, his eyes dilated with desire, and his dick twitched.

She lifted herself and kissed his chest. Gently pushing, she turned him over onto his back and began to kiss her way down his chest and lower.

He wasn't breathing.

She continued lower until she was kneeling between his legs. She slid his boxer briefs off and began to stroke him with a look of wonder on her face. The distillation of love, or pre-cum, at his tip appeared to fascinate her. She ran her thumb over it and coated his throbbing dick with it.

Henry moaned and his hips lifted as if they had a mind of their own. He was powerless to stop his body's reactions. He watched her as she gazed up at him and lowered her mouth.

Fucking Christ, he was going pass out.

He watched as her little pink tongue darted out of her mouth and swirled around the crown.

He had never in his life been as turned on as he was at this very moment.

He moaned loudly.

She licked his entire length with that amazing tongue before she lifted her head questioningly.

"I do not know what I'm doing," she whispered. "Can you help me?"

Henry took a giant gulp of air.

"Um . . . your tongue is amazing. But . . . when you're ready, you can take me into your mouth and suck and use your tongue at the same time. The more that goes into your mouth, the greater the pleasure, but you might trigger a gag reflex," he explained. He was more embarrassed explaining this to Sophia than he would have ever imagined.

Sophia smiled and lowered her head again taking him into her warm, wet mouth.

"Fuckkkkkk," he moaned as she began to suck and swirl her tongue around his length.

She began slowly to take more of him every time she bobbed up and down. He wasn't going to last long if she continued. She was a very fast learner and soon she was taking him completely in and never once gagged. How was that possible?

With his head back and his teeth bared, Henry tried to hold back the explosive orgasm that was right there riding the edge. She stopped and lifted her head.

With a sharp intake of air, his head shot up and looked to see why she had stopped. His dick twitched in disappointment.

"What else?" Sophia inquired.

Henry swallowed hard. She was glorious.

"Um . . . that was amazing. Sometimes it feels good to use one hand to stroke while you suck," he said hoarsely.

Sophia nodded as she made a mental note.

"What else?" she asked.

He could feel his eyes widen. *I may just come from this conversation,* he thought.

"Ah, sometimes it feels good if you gently caress my balls as you suck," he said, embarrassed.

Again, Sophia nodded and was obviously thinking about what he had said before lowering her head again and completely ruining him for any other woman on the planet. He had a sneaking suspicion that he had already been ruined for any other woman, but her lips on his dick was giving him a come-to-Jesus moment he would never forget.

The firm suction along with her sensual tongue swirling around with every lift of her sexy mouth brought him right back to the edge. But, when she accompanied the taking in every inch of him with one hand working him and her other hand reaching beneath and gently caressing his balls, he couldn't help but reach for her soft raven hair to quicken the pleasure.

"Jesus, Soph, I can't hold back. You need to stop. I'm going to come . . ." he yelled as if in extreme pain.

Sophia never let up but just raised her warm brown eyes to his and that's all it took. He raised his ass off the bed, held on to her hair and let go.

Time stood still as he came to the realization of what he had just done. He gently cupped her face and she smiled. She looked like she had won a prize at the county fair.

Holy fucking Jesus! He was speechless. Not something that ever happened to him. Especially the lawyer in him.

"Sophia . . ."

"Did that bring you pleasure?" she asked with a shy smile.

Henry couldn't speak. He just hauled her up his body and held her tight.

"*Muy bueno,* sweetheart. So good. How are you?" he asked against her soft hair.

"*Muy bien,*" she whispered.

It seemed like only minutes passed when he felt her even breathing. He was right behind her in sleep. He had never felt so relaxed in his life. If he could have seen himself, he would have seen the most serene look upon his face as well as a smile on his lips.

****

Sophia slowly woke to the coziest feeling ever. Her back was facing Henry, but his strong arms were around her and held her to him tightly. She felt warm and safe.

She smiled as she remembered how she had pleasured Henry. It made her feel powerful and strong to bring such pleasure to the man she loved.

Shifting slightly, Henry pulled her closer still and Sophia felt his arousal against her bottom.

"Morning, beautiful," he said, kissing her hair.

"Buenos dais," she said, smiling.

Henry's hands began to caress her belly and slowly climbed to her breast. He gently tugged on her hard nipple.

She gasped as a rush of heat pooled in her nether regions. A strong rush. "Henry . . ."

"Shhh, I've got you, sweetheart. I want you to let go and just feel. Can you do that for me?" he asked as he worried her nipple between his fingers.

Her breath was coming in short pants. "Sí, I would like that very much."

As one of his hands pulled at her nipple, his other hand slid down to her soft curls and ran his finger along her seam.

Sophia instantly bowed her back in need and moaned.

He inserted one finger and then it was his turn to gasp.

"Oh fuck, Soph, you're so wet."

She smiled. She liked how he shortened her name. If felt intimate.

He inserted another finger and began to slowly pump them in and out of her. Her climax hit her hard as she bowed farther and cried out Henry's name.

He waited until her spasms stopped before pulling his fingers from her and reaching to the nightstand drawer, pulling out a condom.

He rolled her over onto her back and ripped the silver wrapper with his teeth. He pushed the covers back and rolled the condom onto his impressive length. He looked up at Sophia when he had finished. Their eyes met and pure heat once again pooled in her privates. Was it normal to want to make love so much?

Sophia cupped Henry's face and spread her legs.

He kissed her deeply as he settled between her legs and slowly entered her.

They both moaned at the bliss.

"I'll never get enough of you, sweetheart. You feel so good," Henry said between clenched teeth.

As the steady rhythm began to increase, every time he plunged into her, he touched a sensitive spot that made her see stars. She began to speak rapid Spanish, telling him to go faster and harder. She told him how much she needed him and how good he made her feel.

She wasn't sure if he was understanding her or it was his own urgency that made him drive harder into her. The orgasm built in her until she thought she would pass out. She cried out at the same moment Henry did in his own release.

They stilled, trying to regulate their breathing.

Henry lifted his head and looked at her.

"Buenos dais," he said, smiling.

"Good morning," she said, smiling back.

"I'm going to make breakfast this morning while you shower or do whatever you need to do. How does that sound?" Henry asked, kissing the tip of her nose.

She liked this Henry. He could be so loving. He could also be so distant. So, she was going to thoroughly enjoy loving Henry for as long as she had him.

"Sí, I won't be long," she whispered.

"Take as long as you need. We have the whole day. I'm scheduled for a couple of meetings today, but I'm going to cancel them."

Sophia smiled and watched Henry stand and grab a pair of sweatpants as well as a sweatshirt that read Maine Law School and tug it on. It was a little cold in the camp until the woodstove got going.

Tossing back the quilts, she padded naked and instantly chilled as she made her way to the bathroom and turned on the hot shower.

She looked at her reflection in the mirror. She looked well loved, her red lips swollen from biting them and letting the pleasure wash over her as Henry had asked.

Sophia shook her head at her flushed reflection. "Just enjoy the day."

Doug had managed to get Gracie to cover for Sophia today. He thought she had been working too hard. Dana was getting closer to delivering their baby but was still on strict bed rest as ordered by her husband.

Dressing in her skinny jeans, tall leather boots, and a thick dark-green tunic, she wandered to the kitchen where the smell of cinnamon and coffee emanated.

Silently walking to stand behind him at the counter where the griddle was set up, Sophia shyly hugged him from behind.

Henry jolted and turned around in her arms.

He stared down at her and smiled. He touched her long, shiny raven hair.

"That didn't take long. You look beautiful," he said, lowering his mouth and kissing her softly.

"Breakfast is ready, nothing fancy—just French toast and coffee. If you'd like fancy, I can add some rainbow sprinkles. That's about as fancy as camp gets," he said, grinning.

Sophia laughed. "No sprinkles, please. I'll save them for your nieces and nephews. What can I do to help?"

Henry took a sip of his black coffee and shook his head. "Not a thing, I have everything set up here at the kitchen counter. I only eat at the table when everybody is here."

Sophia looked over at the long table. It was beautiful. Henry had told her that his dad made that table from a felled tree out back. It was as long as two picnic tables set end to end. The edges of the table still had the original bark from the tree. The table had been shellacked and had developed a golden sheen over time. She could picture their large and boisterous family gathered around the old table.

Sophia took a sip of her black coffee and moaned. It was good. It had taken Henry a few times making the coffee for him to get it as strong as she liked. After all, she was Colombian, and they were known for their coffee.

"Okay, so, after breakfast I will shower and then we'll take off," Henry instructed.

Sophia nodded. "Where are we going?"

Shaking his head, he smiled. "It's a secret, but I will tell you that it is an event here in Maine in the fall. That's all you're going to get."

Smiling, she nodded and finished her breakfast.

Henry stood to take care of his plate, but Sophia touched his arm.

"I will clean up while you shower. You cooked breakfast so I will do the dishes."

Henry picked up her hand from his arm and kissed her fingers. "Deal."

Chapter 25

The road was so bumpy Sophia had to brace herself on the dashboard as Henry maneuvered his big four-wheel-drive pickup through the woods. Well, it looked like woods to her.

They were both laughing as the GPS finally said they had arrived at their destination. An apple farm where you pick your own apples.

Sophia gasped. "Oh, Henry, this is wonderful! I can make an all-American apple pie."

The air was crisp and cool as fall often is in Maine. It sometimes snows in Maine in the fall, Henry had told her.

They were bundled up warmly, and the morning sun also took much of the bite out of the cold.

Henry paid the man at the barn and brought back a large bushel basket to put the apples into. The trees were somewhat low, so Sophia was able to pick some for herself. But eventually Henry had resorted to picking her up to help her get the apples she thought were the best.

At one point, Henry was holding her when he tripped on an apple on the ground. They both hit the ground but Henry made sure that she landed on top of him so he could absorb the brunt of the fall.

"*Estás bien?*" she asked urgently without realizing she had switched to Spanish.

Henry laughed. "Yes, I'm okay. But I do have several apples poking into my back."

Sophia laughed and stood up fast so he could get off the ground. They continued to pick until the basket was full. As they were heading back to the barn, Henry spotted an apple above Sophia's head.

"I think that is the most perfect apple from the bunch. Like Eve-tempting-Adam perfect."

She was facing him as he hoisted her up and held her by her thighs against his chest.

"I've got it. It is quite an apple, I think," she said as Henry slowly let her body slide down the front of him until her face was level with his.

"Yeah, I think it's perfect," Henry whispered, not looking at the apple in her hand.

Sophia held his gaze as desire whipped deep in her belly. Dios mío, how could she possibly want to make love again? It had only been hours since they last made love. It's times like this that she wished she had her mother or a sister to talk to. It was clear that her parents hadn't prepared her for becoming a woman.

"Henry . . ."

He didn't let her finish that thought before his mouth was on hers. A hungry, searching kiss. Sophia would never get enough of his kisses. He tasted of toothpaste and just of Henry.

When they finally broke for air, Henry gently set her back on her feet and cupped her face.

"What kind of witch are you, Soph? You've put some sort of spell on me and I can't think straight when I'm in your presence."

Tears sprang to Sophia's eyes. "You say that like it's a bad thing," she said in a thick accent.

Henry smiled and caressed her cheek. "Not bad but definitely disconcerting. Come on, let's pay for the apples. I have another surprise for you."

They rode in comfortable silence as they both seemed to be lost in thought. Sophia watched the gorgeous display of vibrant-colored leaves on the trees that lined the roadway as well as the distant hills and mountains. She had never seen anything so beautiful. Not only had she fallen in love with Henry but with his home state of Maine, as well.

When they reached the camp, Henry picked up the bushel of apples.

"I'll take these to the kitchen. You should use the bathroom and see if you can find a hat and mittens," he said.

Sophia looked at him suspiciously but did as he suggested and made use of the bathroom. Then she found a hat and some mittens in the coat closet.

When she emerged onto the porch, Henry was waiting for her with a bright orange knit cap on and leather gloves.

He looked at her and a big smile broke out on his handsome face.

"I like the hat," he said.

Sophia giggled. She had chosen a pink hat that looked like a bunny with ears and whiskers.

Henry took her hand and led her out back to the barn. He slid the big barn door open and walked toward the back where several large four-wheelers sat. He pushed one out and fired it up. He smiled and held out his hand for her to hop on back.

She felt a little nervous as she got on and wrapped her arms around Henry's waist. He must have sensed it and took off slow and easy. They headed into the woods behind the barn to a well broken-in trail. They traveled through the woods for a long time.

It was magical. The sun was filtered on the tree-covered trail but where the it did break through, it shone on babbling brooks and rocks covered with soft, green moss. At one point, Henry stopped and turned off the engine and pointed a little ahead of him. There were four baby foxes, or kits, frolicking like kittens beside a fallen dead tree.

They watched them for a while until Henry wondered aloud if the mother was watching and waiting for them to leave so she could be with her kits. Eventually, the trail broke out to an open space and Henry killed the engine.

The view was breathtaking. They sat atop a small mountain that overlooked what seemed like hundreds of miles of trees and mountains. The colors were so vibrant that even if Sophia had wanted to, she would never be able to describe the many variations of reds and oranges that demanded her attention.

"Henry," she whispered in awe.

They had gotten off the four-wheeler and Henry was standing behind her. He suddenly enveloped her in his arms and kissed her hair. It was so intimate and loving that it broke her heart a little.

"Yeah, it never gets old. Are you warm enough?" he asked, hugging her tighter.

"Sí. Thank you for sharing this with me. I will remember it always."

That seemed to put paint to it. Henry stiffened and walked back to the four-wheeler. What had she said? Did he not want her to think of him when she was back in Colombia? Because that simply wasn't going to happen. She loved him with her whole heart.

"We should get home, it's going to be dark soon," Henry said, climbing on the four-wheeler and holding out his hand to help her on.

As she took his hand, her heart sank when he refused to make eye contact with her. She wrapped her arms around his waist, rested her head between his shoulders, and inhaled his unique scent.

****

What the fuck. He needed to get a fucking grip. He was angry with himself for spoiling the special moment he and Sophia had been sharing. The moment she mentioned that she would always remember their foliage ride, he was reminded that this was all temporary. Eventually she would be back in Colombia, getting ready to wed the man she was supposed to marry.

In his defense, he had never experienced jealousy before and it was a son-of-a-bitch. He had never experienced any of the feelings he felt with Sophia. Was this love? This all-consuming need to protect as well as an unreasonable rage at the thought of another man touching her? He wasn't sure he was built for these emotions. But that was the stick in his eye; love didn't seem to give two shits if you wanted it or not. It just blew the fucking doors off your heart.

He needed to make this right. As they pulled into the dark barn and he killed the engine, she climbed off the four-wheeler, but he caught her wrist.

"Hey, wait a sec. Can you come back?" he asked quietly.

She turned and looked confused but walked the few steps back to him. He surprised her and picked her up and sat her on his lap on the four-wheeler. She was straddling him with her hands on his shoulders to support herself.

The little yelp that escaped her went straight to his dick.

"I'm sorry I got weird back there. Sometimes I get stuck in my head. Or, as my brothers would say, my head gets stuck in my ass. Either way, I'm sorry. I had a great time today. I haven't been this relaxed in a long time and it's all because of you."

Sophia smiled and nodded. "Sí, I had a wonderful day."

He pulled her tighter against him. There was no way she could not feel his arousal. He saw the moment she felt his hard-on and he watched as desire washed over her and she shivered. At that moment a surge of lust so strong washed over him that he couldn't stop the growl that erupted from his chest.

"Fuck, Soph, I can't get enough of you. I want to be buried inside you so deep right now that I can hardly breathe."

Sophia shifted so her core was even tighter against his jeans-covered dick and she moaned from the friction and cupped his face. She kissed him deeply and the moment her tongue darted into his mouth, he thought he was going to fucking pass out.

He moaned and grabbed her hips and began to grind her up and down his painfully hard dick.

"Henry," she moaned, panting. "I need to feel you inside me, *por favor . . .*"

Her plea sent him over the edge of any rational thought. He picked her up and set her on her feet. He reached for her jeans button and zipper.

She was on the same page because she unzipped her boots and shucked them off with her jeans and panties next.

Henry sat back on the four-wheeler and unbuckled his belt, his top button and zipper and lowered his jeans and briefs, giving him relief from his cramped dick.

She was looking at him with hunger and he wanted to hold that picture in his brain to refer back to when she was gone.

With that thought urging him on, he picked her up none too gently and set her back on his lap. He was in a fervor and had only one thought in his head: bury himself in her tight warmth and claim her. She was fucking his.

She must have been feeling the same fervor because she clasped her hands around his thick arousal and guided him until he was entering her. Then she slowly sat on him until he was totally seated inside her. It was the single greatest feeling he had ever felt.

"Fuckkkkk, Soph," he groaned.

She kissed him and began to rise and fall. He was going to die from the sheer bliss. She broke the kiss and let her head fall back. He leaned back so he could watch her and let her take her pleasure at her own pace. He let her use him and it was fucking glorious.

He pushed his hands up her sweater and caressed her breasts. He grazed over her sensitive hard peaks.

Sophia cried out loudly and repeated his name over and over as she came apart. The urgency of her cries and his name on her lips sent him straight into a frenzy. He grabbed her hips tightly and began to drive into her as he, too, fell over the edge.

Henry's head lay wedged in her neck as he tried to recover his breath and inhale her scent at the same time. That's when it hit him. He hadn't used protection. Again. Jesus, he couldn't think when he was around her and especially when he was about to bury himself in her. Which he wanted to do all the damn time.

Sophia hugged his head and gently stroked his hair. He felt like a shit, but he needed to tell her.

"Um . . . sweetheart, I didn't use any protection. I'm sorry, baby. I was out of mind with wanting you."

She was silent for a beat and then two before she spoke and, swear to Christ, he didn't breathe.

"I guess we'll drive off that bridge when we come to it," she said in the thick Spanish accent that she had when she was aroused or upset.

Henry couldn't help the smile and brought her face in front of his.

"It's *cross that bridge when we come to it*," he corrected.

Sophia smiled, letting him breathe again. "Sí, that's what I said," she said, without missing a beat.

Chapter 26

The diner was busy, but Sophia couldn't wipe the stupid smile off her face. She and Henry had had a wonderful weekend.

The lunch crowd included the ski mountain trailblazing crew. Sophia whipped around the tables effortlessly. She had grown up helping to serve meals in her village and waited tables to help pay for college to become a teacher.

She missed her students back in Colombia. She was thinking about them when she missed Gracie asking her about Henry. Gracie was helping her and making the drinks for the tables and filling customers' coffee cups.

Gracie used to own the diner but retired with Sam to an island not far from the beach on Moose Pond. She had been a huge help to Dana and Doug.

". . . did Henry go to New York this morning?" Gracie asked.

Sophia was delivering lunch to a table of sweaty workers when she realized Gracie was talking to her.

"Perdón?"

"Is Henry away this week?" Gracie asked again.

Sophia smiled. She loved to talk about Henry. She was so proud of him.

"He is in Maine this week, but he had meetings in Portland today so he is staying in his condo for the night. He will be home tomorrow night. He is a very important man," Sophia boasted.

Gracie chuckled. "Gawd love ya. Henry struck pure gold with you, sweetheart."

Sophia smiled. Gracie had become a good friend to her. She was small and the entire town loved her but feared her. She looked like an older, wise

Indian princess. Her salt-and-pepper hair was plaited into a single braid down her back and her skin was the shade of soft leather.

Sophia heard several of the men utter distasteful things as she walked by, which fueled her temper. As she went about slicing a pie, she let loose in rapid Spanish how the younger generation had no civility or manners. She glanced behind her to find Doug smirking. *Dios.*

The diner crowd thinned out considerably before she was forced to bring the check to the same creepy man who watched her every day. He made her skin crawl.

She set the check on the table, but before she could walk away, the man grabbed her wrist and leered at her.

"Sounds to me like your husband is nothing but a pussy. What you need is a real man, chica."

Sophia tried to wrench her wrist free, but the man let go when Doug grabbed him and had him pinned against the wall.

"Get the fuck out of here and I don't want to see your sorry ass in here again. Do you hear that, you fucking loser?" Doug ground out.

The man's face turned beet-red because he couldn't breathe. Gracie gently laid a hand on Doug's arm, which seemed to bring him out of the trace he was in. He released the man and told him to leave in a disjointed voice.

The man scurried from the diner without paying his bill. Doug turned to Sophia.

"Are you okay?" he whispered, not looking at her.

"Sí, sí, I'm fine, Doug. Thank you."

Doug nodded and walked silently back to the kitchen. Dana had confided in Sophia that Doug suffered from PTSD as a result of several tours in Iraq. Sophia wondered if she should tell Dana about the incident. No, she was about to deliver their baby. They had enough on their plates.

Sophia didn't mention it again, and as they closed up the diner, Doug was still quiet. She said her goodbyes, got in her car, and drove home. She had multiple apple pies to make.

****

Stifling a yawn, she pulled the last apple pie from the oven. She was exhausted. Henry had called to say good night a while ago, which warmed her right down to her toes.

She shut the oven off and covered the hot apple pie with a clean dish towel. She shut the lights in the kitchen off and made her way to the bathroom to get ready for bed. She was exhausted.

She was asleep before her head hit the pillow. But not for long. Sophia woke to a massive hand over her mouth. Her eyes flew open and held pure terror. The room was dark so she couldn't see her attacker. But it didn't take long to recognize that gravelly, hate-filled voice.

"Now I'm going to show you how a real man pleases a woman, chica," the creepy man said and licked her forehead.

"Your husband is a fucking idiot to leave you alone. By the time I'm finished with you, you won't even remember his name."

Sophia began to struggle but he held her down with iron arms. Tears began to fall down the sides of her head. Her eyes were pleading with him not to hurt her.

It was dark, but as Sophia's eyes adjusted to the darkness, she could see his evil smile as he peered down into her terrified face.

The man was breathing heavy and his breath was rancid. He flung the quilt off her and sneered at her flannel nightgown.

That's when she saw the knife he held close to her throat. He lifted it and began to rip the nightgown down the center with the blade. It was sharp and the material gave no resistance as the knife made its way to her waist.

Sophia began to plead under his hand which sounded muffled.

Her attacker was transfixed by her plump breasts. He set the knife on the pillow to free his hand to grasp her breast tightly, making Sophia moan in pain.

But, somewhere in Sophia's brain, a voice spoke to her. Maybe it was God. Maybe it was an angel. Maybe it was her own badass self that had taken care of herself for too many years. But whoever it was, it told her to fight. It told her to not be a victim.

Taking advantage of her attacker's current obsession with her breasts, Sophia bucked him off her with all her might. He dove back on her, they tussled a bit, and Sophia caught his elbow in her eye socket just before she used her feet to push him off the bed.

She launched herself out her bedroom door and ran down the hall to try and make it to the porch door. If she could make it outside, maybe she could make it to Henry's brother Garrett's house by the pond.

She had almost made it to the door when a massive hand grabbed her nightgown and pulled her backward.

They both landed in a heap, but Sophia refused to give up. She knew there was an electric guitar on a stand by the front door. She lunged where she thought it might be and fell into it. She stood up and swung the instrument into the face of her attacker with all her might.

Crying out, she didn't stop to see if he was going to stay down, throwing open the door and running down the driveway, right into the headlights of a large SUV.

Sophia screamed and tripped on the gravel driveway as the SUV came to a screeching halt inches from her body. The dust and pebbles scattered everywhere.

The next moment she was being held by Garrett.

"Sophia! What happened? Are you hurt?"

She couldn't quite focus but she managed to tell Garrett that her attacker was still in the house.

Sophia heard Lilly's voice next.

"Garrett, I've got her. I'll call the police."

The screen door slammed, which alerted Garrett that there was still danger. With his pregnant wife cradling Sophia and calling the police, Garrett took off on a dead run to immobilize the fucker who dared to fuck with a Johnson.

Everything happened in slow motion after that. Sophia found herself being held by Garrett and transported to the bed where she had been sleeping in so soundly.

"Sophia, look at me," Garrett implored.

She looked at him even though she wasn't really comprehending much.

"The police are here. You're safe. I've called Henry. He's on his way home. Are you hurt?" Garrett asked as he wrapped a blanket around her.

Tears began to stream down her face. Her mind knew it was an adrenaline release, but her body was a little in shock.

She shook her head. "I'm not hurt. But please don't call Henry. He has had a busy day. I don't want to worry him," she sniffed.

Garrett smiled wanly and gently caressed her hair. "Sophia, Henry won't be able to get here fast enough, sweetheart. You're safe now. I'm going to go talk to Officer Lancaster for a minute. Lilly will stay here with you, okay?"

Sophia nodded as Lilly grasped her hands.

"Oh no, hold on just a second, Soph, I'm going to get a bag of frozen peas for that shiner," Lilly said, striding toward the kitchen.

****

As Lilly gently settled the bag of frozen peas on Sophia's throbbing eye, Henry's brother Bobby, the surgeon, entered the room along with his wife, Ava.

Sophia was surrounded by Johnsons and any danger that was skulking around was gone. Evil would have to pass through them to get to her and that was never going to happen. Sophia felt very safe indeed. But she just really needed Henry.

****

Henry paced back and forth on the roof of their company's headquarters in Portland. He was going out of his fucking mind. He was over two hours away from Sophia and that was fucking unacceptable.

He continued to pace as he waited for the helicopter to arrive. He absolutely couldn't wait two hours to make sure Sophia was all right. Hence the helicopter. He wasn't one to flaunt his money but what the frig was the point of having any if he couldn't make the world shift on its axis to get to the woman he . . . loved. Holy fuck, he was in love with Sophia. The crater in his chest was growing larger by the second with absolute terror for her. Not to mention the fucking rage that was almost blinding him toward the motherfucker who tried to hurt her.

137

He had gotten the call thirty minutes ago from his brother Garrett. He was still at the office trying to get shit done so he could get home at a reasonable time the next night. He hated being apart from Sophia. Every time he left her presence, he felt like he literally left part of himself with her. The only good part of himself.

"Where the fuck is that helicopter?" Henry growled.

"Bro, you called them like three minutes ago. Relax, Bobby and Garrett are with Sophia. They will keep her safe," Caleb said, standing with his arms crossed and a concerned expression on his too-handsome face.

Henry stopped and faced Caleb. "I should have been there. This is my fault." Jesus, he felt like he was going to be sick.

Just then the whir of a helicopter came into focus. The brothers watched as the bird landed securely on the Johnson building.

Henry and Caleb piled into the helicopter and put on their headgear. "You got the coordinates I sent you, right?" Henry asked the pilot.

The pilot nodded. "Affirmative. We will touch down in Harmony in less than thirty minutes."

And, with that, the helicopter rose and flew like the wind.

"Did you call Marcus?" Caleb asked.

Henry nodded. "Yeah, but I told him to stay home. There's nothing he can do, and I didn't want to wait around for him to drive back to the office."

Caleb smirked. "Bet that went well."

Henry scowled. His brother Marcus was the oldest and thought the fifteen months that separated them made him king of the fucking world. It did, kinda, but Henry knew that Marcus loved them all fiercely and only wanted to protect them. He would call Marcus as soon as he'd seen with his own fucking eyes that Sophia was unharmed. Jesus, his heart felt like it was being constricted in a vise.

It was the longest twenty-five minutes of Henry's miserable life. When they finally touched down, he shot out of the helicopter like a bullet. His feet couldn't carry him fast enough. The camp was lit up like a Christmas tree, was his last thought before he burst through his childhood bedroom door to find Sophia wrapped in a blanket on the bed with her knees drawn up to her chest. Lilly was sitting on the bed with her.

The moment Sophia saw him, she vaulted off the bed and into his arms. She was speaking rapid Spanish. Her body was shaking.

"Henry, *estaba tan asustado. Por favor, no me dejes!*" she cried into his neck.

He visibly swallowed and nodded as Lilly pointed to the door and left them alone.

"I'm not going to leave you, sweetheart. I'm so sorry. So sorry," he whispered into her hair. He stroked her soft raven hair and her back until her shaking eased.

He walked them to the bed and sat down, bringing her on his lap. He needed her as close as he could get her. And that's when he saw it.

He cupped her chin and turned her so he could see better. Her eye had swollen shut and the bruising had already begun. Rage like he had never felt before began to swirl inside him.

She must have sensed him losing control because she cupped his face.

"I'm okay now, Henry. He tried to hurt me, but I wouldn't let him. And Garrett came along at the perfect time. I'm unharmed," she whispered as her eyes implored him to calm down.

He swallowed again. "Tell me what happened," he asked with a voice that sounded like crushed glass.

Just then, a knock at the door sounded.

"What?" Henry growled.

The door opened to Chief Ben Keister. "Sorry, Henry, but I need a brief statement tonight to process the perp. You know the drill. You both can come down tomorrow for a formal statement."

Henry nodded. For the first time Henry looked at her flannel nightgown and saw that it had been cut open to her waist. He grabbed the blanket and wrapped it around her and set her beside him on the bed. He grasped her small hands in his. The rage began to roil.

"Mrs. Johnson, can you tell me what happened tonight?" the chief asked quietly.

Sophia nodded. She liked the chief of police. He and his crew came to the diner every day.

"Sí," she said and slowly began to recount how she went to bed early and from the hand over her mouth to the man slicing her nightgown. She was still in shock because she wove back and forth from English to Spanish without knowing it.

The moment she recounted the knife by her throat and him slicing her nightgown, Henry's rage boiled over and he had no control over his legs. He jumped up, ran to the kitchen and grabbed Sophia's keys off the counter, and bolted out the door.

All three of his brothers were standing outside in the driveway when they spotted him.

"No way, brother," Garrett said, holding out his arms to hold him back.

"Get the fuck out of my way, Garrett," Henry growled.

"No, stop. You are not going to the jail. That will only make it worse," Caleb growled.

Henry never lost a step. He just intended to plow right through them to get to Sophia's car and then, as Caleb had deduced, to the jail and rip that motherfucker a new asshole.

What he didn't expect was all three of his brothers using every bit of force they had to overpower him. All four of them landed on the ground and wrestled with every ounce of their hearts, until they had Henry in an irreversible chokehold.

Chief Keister knelt down before him. "Don't do it, Henry. You know better than most that that will only fuck up the case. Stay home tonight. That's an order."

"Sophia needs you, Henry," Bobby said quietly.

Henry's face was turning purple from lack of air. He tried to nod so his brothers released him. He rolled onto his back with a thud and began to cough, trying to suck in air.

After getting his breath back, he stood and so did his brothers, slowly. He swallowed and looked at Garrett and cupped his cheek. "Thanks for saving her," Henry said hoarsely.

Not trusting himself to say more, he just turned and walked into the house and went straight to the one room where his heart was.

Chapter 27

Bobby gave Sophia a sedative to help her sleep. She made Henry promise her that he wouldn't leave her. A promise he freely gave. He wouldn't be so careless with the most important person in the world to him again.

He didn't know a lot about this love shit, but he was pretty goddamn sure that protecting said love interest was way up there on the list of things not to fuck up.

But he had. He had already fucked things up and she had almost gotten raped or worse. He was so freaked out by his emotions concerning Sophia that he continued to push her away.

Had he—in some sort of unconscious way—tried to get her pregnant so she would be forever tied to him? Jesus, that was fucked up. But was it true? And, deep down, he knew it was. Shame washed over him. But only for a moment because the angel and lil' devil were back on his shoulders. And this time, he wasn't looking to the angel but to the devil because his message was clear: *take what you want no matter the consequences.*

Henry held Sophia close and smoothed the dark hair away from her brow. So, this was love. And, by Christ he *would* do what was necessary to keep this woman safe.

He eased out of bed, grabbed his phone, and scrolled through his contacts until he landed on the one person equipped to help him.

"Attorney Fucking Johnson, how the hell are ya?"

Henry smiled into the darkness. "Hey, Snake. It's been a minute. I need your help, buddy."

****

Sophia's eyes popped open. Had she dreamed her attack last night? She knew she had not because Henry was wrapped around her like an anaconda. She smiled, and then faltered. Last night had been awful. She had never been so scared in her life. But Henry was here now and she felt safe.

She wiggled her behind as she snuggled closer to his front. She knew she was shameless, but almost instantly she could feel his growing erection.

"Are you trying to kill me?" he muttered sleepily.

"No, of course not. I was just making sure you were my husband," she said over her shoulder.

Henry's sharp intake of breath told her that she should not have made light of last night's situation.

"I'm sorry I said that. I didn't mean to joke about it. I'm fine, Henry. Believe it or not, last night's horror is a reminder of the threat I've had to live with most of my life with the drug cartel in our village. It had never happened to me, but the threat was always there. Last night I fought and won. I can move on," she said quietly.

Henry was silent for a moment before he squeezed her tighter to him.

"You're fucking amazing. Do you know that?"

She giggled until his hand drifted to the junction between her thighs and stopped.

"Why did you stop?" she whispered, wanting him to touch her.

"Jesus, Soph, I'm no better than that fucker last night. I can't be within six feet of you without wanting to fuck you on any available surface. I'm sorry," he whispered into her hair.

Sophia took his hand and slid it inside her panties. "Dios mío, Henry, do not ever say you're sorry for what happens in our marriage bed. There is nothing shameful that takes place between us. That man had evil intentions and I refuse to let him rob me of my happiness for one second. And it makes me happy when you touch me and . . . do other things to me," she said shyly.

"Jesus, fuck, where in the hell did you come from?" he moaned and continued his path to her most sensitive treasure.

Henry had magical hands. Within seconds he had her panting and crying out in orgasm as his fingers slipped in and out of her and his thumb massaged her most sensitive spot.

He reached into the nightstand and retrieved a condom and pushed her onto her back. She pulled her nightdress over her head and discarded her panties.

She grabbed the condom from his fingers and tore the silver package with her teeth just as she'd seen him do. All the while never losing eye contact with him. He took his briefs off and threw them somewhere in the bedroom.

Sophia took the condom out and slowly slid it down Henry's impressive hardness and length.

Henry closed his eyes as if she were hurting him.

As soon as her mission was accomplished, he flipped her back on her side and lifted her leg wide as he lined himself up with her entrance.

"Tell me you want this, Soph. I want to hear it," he said urgently.

"Sí, Henry, I need you inside me, por favor," she cried.

And he obliged. He gave a swift hard stroke and he was completely seated inside her. She gasped at the wave of pleasure that rippled through her. Dios mío, would she ever get enough of him? Was this normal?

"Jesus, Soph, you feel so fucking good," he growled into her hair as he grasped her hips and began to drive into her.

It was seconds before she was crying out his name as she fell over the edge. It wasn't long before he, too, chased her over that same edge.

As they captured their breath, Sophia rolled over to face Henry.

Henry gasped and cupped her face. "Jesus, sweetheart, that's quite a shiner. Does it throb?"

To be truthful, she had forgotten about her black eye. Last night it had throbbed and her eye had threatened to button up. But this morning there was only slight swelling and bruising.

"No, I had forgotten about it, actually," she said, laying her hand over his that cupped her cheek.

"I'm so sorry I wasn't here," he whispered.

"Stop. You're here now. The man is in custody and can't hurt me. I'm not a damsel in distress. It will bother me if you start treating me as such."

Henry grinned. "Yeah, you're a badass, all right. But you know we have to go to the sheriff's department and make a statement, right?"

Sophia nodded. "Sí," she said as she stroked his beard. "How long have you worn your goatee?"

Henry smirked. "That's very random but a nice subject change. It's actually not a goatee, it's called a Balbo. In college and law school I was clean-shaven. but once I became an attorney, I felt like I needed to look older for my peers to take me seriously. One day I watched an old black-and-white cowboy movie. The bad guy wore a Balbo beard and he was a friggin' badass. I decided that day to grow one. Eventually, they became popular when the Marvel movie *Iron Man* came out and that actor sported one. But I had it first."

Sophia stopped stroking his beard and looked incredulous. "You do look like a bad guy in an old western! You look like you should be wearing all black and a black cowboy hat."

Henry laughed and then looked serious. "Well, little lady, I can assure you that my intentions with you are very far from pure," he said in an exaggerated southern drawl.

He rolled on top of her and kissed her thoroughly.

Breaking the kiss, he sighed. "Okay, I'll go start the coffee and see what I can rustle up for breakfast. You take your time and get ready, okay?"

Sophia nodded and watched him get out of bed, scoop up his briefs, and walk naked out of the bedroom. Dios, he was a sight to behold. He was so big. Broad shoulders, that V waist, perfect muscular bum, and to top it all off, that swagger. She had it bad for her husband. That should send her over the moon, right? Then, why did she feel like they were living on borrowed time?

After breakfast they loaded the car with two of the apple pies she had made for the diner. When they were finished at the sheriff's department, she would drop the pies off and tell Doug that she would be in to work tomorrow morning.

Henry had been very pleased with the pies and wasn't sure he was satisfied with only leaving one pie at camp. She assured him that she could make more. As a matter of fact, warm apple pie and coffee was what they had for breakfast. It seemed like they were breaking the breakfast rules, and if she had learned one thing from her husband, it was that he liked to break the rules.

The trip to the sheriff's department wasn't as bad as she thought it would be. Chief Keister was kind and considerate. It was Henry who made her uncomfortable. She'd had to relate everything, including what the man had said to her. When she relayed that the man indicated that her husband was an idiot to leave her home alone, Sophia felt Henry stiffen.

Chief Keister thanked her for coming in and told her he would be in touch.

"What is he being charged with?" Henry asked menacingly.

"Aggravated assault, attempted gross sexual assault, breaking and entering, and, the best one, violating conditions of probation. He's on probation in Massachusetts for rape. He served four years of a ten-year sentence. He's now going to serve the remaining six years of that sentence as well as what the judge gives him for what he did last night," Chief Keister said.

"And bail?" Henry asked.

Chief Keister shook his head. "Held without bail pending a bail hearing. But since he skipped out on his probation and has no ties to Maine, there's no way in hell a judge is going to grant the fucker bail. Um . . . sorry, Mrs. Johnson."

Sophia smiled. "Please call me Sophia, Chief."

The chief nodded and Henry shook his hand. With Henry's hand at the small of her back, he led her out the door. His hand on her felt good. It felt right.

They walked down the street to where the car was parked in front of the diner. Henry gathered the pies and followed Sophia inside.

There were gasps heard throughout the diner. Her customers had heard what happened and righteous anger that filled the diner made Sophia feel loved. She assured them that she was fine. Gracie hugged her tightly. But it was Doug stomping out of the kitchen like a storm cloud that concerned her.

The big, quiet man stood before her shaking with anger. His hands fisted at his sides.

"Did he hurt you?" he whispered, his face a deep red.

Sophia shook her head. "No, Doug, he only scared me."

Doug's brows furrowed together as he looked at her black eye.

Sophia touched his arm lightly. With her other hand she pointed to her eye. "This was just a result of a struggle. I fought with him. I didn't let him hurt me."

Doug's eyes got big and a big smile burst out on his face. Something not many had ever seen before. Sophia knew he was proud of her. It showed in his eyes.

"I should have taken the sonofabitch down yesterday when I had the chance," he mumbled.

Now, it was Henry's turn to scowl. "What do you mean?" he asked quietly.

Sophia's stomach sunk. She should have told Henry about the creepy man, Clint Striker, and his rudeness toward her and especially about yesterday morning's incident, last night when they talked before she went to bed.

"That asshole has been talking shit to Sophia since she started waitressing. But yesterday he put his hands on her and I lost my shit. I guess I should have been more convincing to get him the fuck out of town."

Sophia took a giant gulp of breath. "That's all in the past. I will be in to work tomorrow morning," she said in a rush.

Doug shook his head but before he could speak, Sophia held up her hand. "No arguments, por favor. I will be here in the morning," she said with finality.

Doug stared at her for a moment before nodding and turning back to the kitchen. Sophia could feel the anger rolling off Henry. She refused to look at him and took the pies to the rack on the counter. Several regular customers hugged her before she turned to see Henry standing by the door with his arms crossed and a stern scowl on his handsome face.

She squared her shoulders and marched out the door. As soon as they were on the sidewalk, Henry grabbed her arm and spun her around to face him.

"Why the fuck am I just hearing about Striker verbally abusing you and why in the Christ am I just hearing that he actually laid hands on you? Yesterday, no less!"

Sophia yanked her arm away from his grip and looked around, embarrassed.

"Baja la voz," she hissed.

"No, I will not keep my goddamn voice down! If you had told me last night what happened, I could have come home and I would have been there when that fucker attacked you!"

Tears sprang to Sophia's eyes. "Por favor, Henry," she whispered.

Henry looked like he had been kicked in the gut. He groaned and pulled her to him and wrapped his arms around her.

"I'm sorry, Soph. When I think of him hurting you, well, I can't fucking think straight. Why didn't you tell me?" he whispered into her hair.

"I didn't want to worry you. You have done so much for me already, Henry. I didn't want to add to your worries. I'm sorry. I promise I won't hold back again."

Henry pulled apart slightly and cupped her face gently. "I'm sorry I hollered at you," he said and lowered his mouth to hers in a deeply possessive kiss.

"Get a room, Johnson," a voice said from someone walking into the diner. It was Officer Josh Lancaster. Henry spirited Sophia to the car and silently held up his middle finger as he walked behind her.

They left the diner and went grocery shopping. It warmed her heart at how the simplicity of doing something so mundane as grocery shopping with Henry made her happy. Henry loaded up the cart to overflowing.

"Who do you think is going to eat all this food?" she asked.

"We're going to have company. He'll be here tonight."

"You're not going to tell me who this guest is?"

Henry shook his head. "You'll see soon enough."

"Well, it must be a giant," she groused in Spanish, by the looks of all the steaks they bought.

By the time the groceries were taken care of and they made a lunch of toasted ham-and-cheese sandwiches and tomato soup, it was late afternoon.

Something had been on Henry's mind, but Sophia couldn't tell if he was still processing what took place last night or if he was still a little angry that she hadn't told him about Striker. She decided to just leave it alone.

She got up to do the dishes, but Henry stopped her before her hands landed in the soapy water and hoisted her up on the counter beside the sink.

"I'll do the dishes. There's something I want to talk to you about," he said, taking the dish towel and throwing it over his shoulder.

How could having a dish towel on his shoulder make him twice as gorgeous? Sophia could feel her pulse increase and her thoughts turn in the direction of the bedroom. Or, maybe in the kitchen with him still wearing the dish towel. She rolled her eyes at herself and snorted.

"You okay?" Henry asked as he rinsed the frying pan.

She could feel the heat rise to her hairline. She nodded.

"So, I've been contacted by the FBI and the CIA about your case," he began tentatively.

Sophia could feel her eyes grow big.

"I think I can get you full immunity if you are willing to tell them what you know about Mateo Sanchez."

Sophia clapped her hands together. "Henry, that is wonderful!"

Henry didn't smile, which slowly wiped the smile from her face, as well.

"The FBI and the CIA do want to know what you know about Sanchez, but what they are really after is the computer genius who works for Sanchez. They don't know he's your brother."

Sophia hopped off the counter like it was on fire. She wasn't aware that she wasn't speaking English any longer. She told him there was no way she was going to put her brother in any more danger than he already was in.

Henry braced himself against the sink and closed his eyes as if she was trying his patience.

"Sophia, be reasonable. You are in this situation because your brother couldn't stay out of trouble. When are you going to stop sacrificing your life for his? He needs to grow up and take responsibility for himself."

The anger threatened to rob her of her voice as she glared at Henry. Who did he think he was, asking her to serve her brother up on a platter so she could take a deal? He didn't know the first thing about what she and Santiago had endured since her parents died. He didn't know what it was like growing up in poverty and always living with the threat of physical violence. He grew up like a prince, surrounded by people who loved him. She and Santiago were all each other had in this world and she would certainly not be putting him in any more danger.

"How dare you pass judgment on my brother! You have no idea what my brother has been through. Yes, I've tried to protect Santiago and as a result probably enabled him to lean on me to fix his messes, but it's my job to take care of him."

"Even go to prison for twenty years?" Henry shot back.

Tears welled up in her eyes and she nodded. "Yes, even go to prison. Tell me, Henry, would you give up one of your siblings to save yourself?" she asked and walked away so he wouldn't see the tears that wouldn't stop falling.

The next thing she heard was a frying pan hitting the wall with a thud and him hollering, "Goddamn it."

Chapter 28

Henry sat at the piano on the porch, letting his fingers choose the notes they wanted to play from muscle memory. His thoughts were fully engaged in wondering when exactly he had turned into a selfish asshole.

Sophia asking him if he would save himself at the expense of one of his siblings had gutted him. Of course he couldn't. Not in a million years. But, yet, that is what he was asking her to do. He wouldn't deny that he was a selfish bastard. If there was any way he could save Sophia from going to prison, he wanted to grab it. For himself. He didn't want to lose Sophia. Not to prison or to Colombia. She was fucking his.

But she wasn't his. That was never so glaringly obvious as it was now after he stood outside his bedroom and listened shamelessly as she spoke with her brother on the phone.

He had come to find her after waiting an hour to let them cool their tempers. And what he could understand chilled him to the bone.

"Hola, Santiago."

"Santiago I can hardly hear you. I'm going to put you on speaker so I can hear you better."

"Has something happened, Sophia?"

"No, I'm fine. I just wanted to hear your voice. Is Mateo still treating you well?"

"Sí, as long as I continue to outsmart his enemies and make him money, I'll be okay. Although, I am getting tired of sleeping on a cot beside my computer. He hasn't let me go home since you were arrested. He thinks I'll run. I'm his insurance policy, he says."

"I think this will be over soon, and you can get on with your life. But I want you to promise me, Santiago, if I get sent to prison, that you will escape and disappear forever. Okay?"

"Sophia, you can't go to prison. You were only protecting me. I thought you said Henry was a smart and important man and that he would find a way to help us both."

"He is, Santiago, but sometimes things don't go the way we think they should. I had a choice and I broke the law. You let me worry about me going to prison. I want you to have an escape plan in place if that happens. If I go to prison, Mateo will know that he is not getting his drugs back and he will take it out on you. Promise me you will escape."

"Sí, sí, I promise. John Williams came to see me yesterday. He was looking for you."

Silence.

"Sophia?"

"What did you tell him?"

"I told him you were teaching as a missionary in America for a few months. And, that you didn't expect him back until the end of the year, which was why you took the mission job."

Silence.

"Sophia?"

"Oh . . . sí, that's good."

"He said he hated being away from you, so he came home to ask you to marry him now instead of at the end of the year like you planned. He said after you married he wanted to bring you with him back to the Amazon and finish the mission work until the end of the year."

"Oh . . . um, I've got to go, Santiago. I will call you when I can. Be safe. I love you."

Henry quietly walked back to the porch and stared at the keys of the piano. She had never been his and never would be. He had never felt so empty in his life.

As if on cue, the rumble of a revved-up exhaust barreled up the driveway and stopped suddenly, sending gravel and dust flying.

****

Sophia heard a loud engine drive up to the camp. She made her way to the porch and stopped dead in her tracks.

The biggest man she had ever seen stepped out of a black SUV with tinted windows and shiny silver wheels.

Henry was shaking his hand. Now, Henry was big, but this man must have been at least six foot six and solid muscle. She swallowed as she took him in. He wasn't handsome in the traditional sense. As a matter of fact, he looked more dangerous than the devil himself.

He had short blond hair, a little longer than a crew cut, hair that was mussed up maybe from a hat taken off. His whiskers had no rhyme or reason. It wasn't exactly a beard, but it was far from a clean shave. The whiskers on his chin jutted out longer than the rest of his patchy beard. And those eyes. She could see from inside the house that they were piercing. She couldn't tell what color but she could tell that she wouldn't want that stare trained on her when he was angry.

Henry and the giant stranger talked for a moment longer before they made their way inside. Sophia stood on the porch, waiting for them.

Henry entered first, met her gaze, and held it for a beat before stepping aside and waving toward the giant.

"Sophia, this Snake. Snake, this is my *wife*, Sophia. Snake is going to stay here for your protection. He will drive you wherever you need to go and accompany you everywhere."

Sophia bristled and felt anger shoot through her. He never thought to talk to her about this? But she would not give Henry the satisfaction of showing her anger.

She smiled and held out her hand. "Mr. Snake, it is a pleasure to meet you. But I'm sorry you had to travel here because I don't need a babysitter. No offense, I'm sure you're very good at what you do," she said in a very thick Spanish accent and glared at Henry.

Snake held her hand gently, not letting it go.

"What the fuck did you do in your past life, Henry, to get this kind of karma in this one?" he asked, never letting his eyes leave Sophia.

Sophia's smile widened.

Henry cleared his throat. "I'll show you to a room where you can bunk down."

Snake gently kissed the back of Sophia's hand and let it fall back to her side. "It was a pleasure to meet you, Miss Sophia."

Henry walked toward the bedrooms with Snake behind him. "By the way, it's Mrs.," he said over his shoulder.

Snake barked out a laugh and clamped his hands down on the back of Henry's shoulders. "Don't worry, brother, I don't poach what belongs to another man. I mean, come on, do I look like I can't get my own girl?"

Henry looked physically sick at the shot about poaching what belongs to another man.

"I think I would prefer to bunk down here in the living room on the couch. I want to be between any invader and Sophia. I'm used to sleeping on the ground, so this couch will feel like the Ritz, trust me."

Sophia stood watching the exchange, fascinated.

Henry nodded. "I've got to be out of town for the week, so I'll let you do whatever recon you do to prepare. Let me know if you have any questions."

Snake nodded. "I'll have a look around outside first," he said and walked toward the kitchen.

He had barely left the room before a string of Spanish curses flew from Sophia's mouth.

"You are not leaving me here with a stranger, Henry!" she hissed.

Henry sighed as if the weight of the world was on his shoulders. "He's not a stranger. I would trust Snake with my life. As a matter of fact, that's exactly what I'm doing. You have nothing to fear from Snake, Sophia."

Sophia was rattled as she tried to figure out if Henry had said what she thought he had and if so, why he was so distant, cold.

"I have to be out of town for business all week. I will call every day to check in," he said, and then just turned and walked out the door.

Sophia watched him speak with Snake for a minute and they shook hands again. Henry got in the old truck that usually stayed in the barn and roared down the driveway away from her.

What had just happened? Was he so angry with her over not helping the FBI and the CIA that he couldn't stand to be in the same house as her? Did he really have to leave Maine or was he just staying at his condo in Portland?

****

After an hour of Snake walking through every room and checking windows, he met her back in the kitchen where she was having a cup of tea.

"Mr. Snake, you must be hungry from traveling. Can I make you a toasted ham-and-cheese and soup?"

Snake eased on a bar stool and nodded. "I'd like that very much. I don't expect you to cook for me, though."

Sophia smiled as she got up to get the ingredients. "I don't mind. We both have to eat and besides, I like to cook."

"I see on the back of your leather vest, it says 'The Four Horsemen.' do you like Revelations?"

Snake grinned. "Actually, I do. It's my favorite part of the Bible. What's your favorite book of the Bible?"

Sophia looked over her shoulder and grinned. She was feeling more comfortable by the minute with this giant named Snake.

"The book of Ruth, of course."

Snake chuckled. "Yeah, everybody loves them some Boaz. But, if you ask me, he was a lucky shit to find such a strong and loyal woman like Ruth."

Sophia turned and studied Snake for a minute. "You're right. I've only ever thought of it as how lucky Ruth was to find a strong, handsome man to love and take care of her."

"Don't forget he was rich, that don't hurt either."

Sophia burst out laughing. No, she and Mr. Snake were going to get along just fine.

"Is protecting people what you do for work?" she asked, setting down his dinner before him. "Would you like a beer or milk or water?"

"Milk would be great, thanks. Um, yeah, me and my crew take protection jobs when we can find them. There are four of us, me, Jax,

Shorty, and Mac. We all served in the military but not together. I was a MARSOC, Marine Corps Special Operations Command. We were responsible for special reconnaissance and counterterrorism," he said and took a big bite out of the sandwich, eating half of it in one bite.

"Wow, why did you leave the military, if you don't mind me asking?"

Snake grinned. "Darlin', with your accent you could ask me anything and I would tell you just to keep you talkin'. Your voice is the sexiest thing I heard in a long time. I left the military on a stretcher and wasn't supposed to live," he said and knocked on the front of his skull. "Full metal plate right there. I like to refer to it as my bionic head. Forget I said that . . . it just sounds dirty when I say it to you. Anyway, each one of my crew was injured and tossed to the curb by Uncle Sam. We bought Harleys and live on the road most of the time. Going from job to job."

"You didn't ride your motorcycle here? How come?"

"Sweetheart, this is Maine; it could snow in friggin' July. I don't trust the weather. I left my hog back with my crew in Florida. How 'bout you, how are you finding the cold weather?"

Sophia laughed. "Sí, it's not Colombia, for sure, but I've fallen in love with Maine."

"And an asshat named Henry Johnson."

Sophia sighed deeply. "Sí, that is very true, Mr. Snake."

Chapter 29

Sophia grimaced as she walked into the diner and heard Gracie gasp at her black eye as well as the others sitting around the long table already enjoying their coffee. Also included in the bunch were the chief of police, Ben Keister and his deputy, Josh Lancaster.

Everyone thought that she should be home resting. It was her turn, however, to gasp as she spied Sam, Gracie's husband, doing the cooking instead of Doug.

Gracie beamed. "Their little girl was born early this morning. All are doing well."

Sophia clutched her chest. She was so happy for her friends. They had waited a long time for this miracle. She made a mental note to find out what room at the hospital Dana was in. She and Snake would be taking a little road trip this afternoon after work.

Hanging her coat up, Sophia walked to the long table, dragging Snake along with her.

"Everybody, I would like to introduce mine and Henry's friend, Mr. Snake. He has graciously agreed to keep me safe while Henry is working. At least for a little while."

Sophia introduced everyone to Snake who looked like he would rather peel a layer of his skin off than be standing there at that moment. He nodded and headed to the back of the diner by the window so he could see everyone who entered and surveil the room in a glance.

It was a busy morning and Sophia was glad Gracie was there to help her. She was a little tired from all the excitement. Sophia never let Snake's coffee get cold or empty and never asked him what he wanted for breakfast or lunch because she knew he would have said nothing. She set before him the lumberjack's breakfast platter for breakfast and the BLT with fries and milk at lunch. He just smirked and nodded.

After work, Sophia informed Snake that they would be going to the local department store in Skowhegan and then to the hospital to see her friends. He nodded and punched in directions on his SUV dashboard screen and they set off to shop for a newborn baby girl.

"Has Henry told you about my situation?" Sophia asked quietly.

Snake didn't answer right away.

"Henry told me only what I would need to know to do my job and keep you safe. He has given me the names of those who want to find you. I will tell you that I have my crew researching, as well. If there is anything you can tell me that I couldn't find on the dark web, I'd appreciate it. But if it's too personal, I understand."

Sophia shook her head. "No, I don't mind. I think it would make me feel better if you knew the whole story."

She told him about she and Mateo were childhood friends until he began to get involved in the cartel. How her father forbid her to see him and, as a result, Mateo left for the city of Bogotá to work and eventually climb to the top of the most dangerous drug cartel in Colombia.

She told him about her parents' deaths and her having to raise her brother, Santiago. She didn't leave anything out. She talked about how disappointed she had been in her brother for his drugs, gambling, and getting involved with Mateo.

And, last, she told Snake about the fight she and Henry had had before he left for New York.

"I won't put my brother in any more danger than he already is," she explained.

Snake had been quiet for the whole ride to Skowhegan. He let her tell her story at her own pace.

"You know Henry is just scared for you, right? He doesn't want to put your brother in any danger. But, with that said, it's *you* that he's focused on," Snake said quietly.

Sophia nodded. She didn't have the heart to tell Snake that their marriage wasn't real. Maybe she just wanted to pretend a little while longer.

She didn't want to admit to herself that Henry had a life before her and he probably wanted to get back to it. As a single man.

"I know. But, as close to his own siblings as he is, I would have thought it would go unsaid that I wouldn't give up my brother for my own safety."

Snake sighed. "Don't underestimate Henry, darlin'. I've seen him work up close and personal. There's no one better out there, trust me. I've known your husband for a long time. He helped me and my crew out more than once. That man can bend the law to whatever he wants it to say to meet his objective. Don't give up on him. He will find a way to save you *and* your brother. Mark my words."

Sophia smiled a little sadly as they pulled into the small department store. She didn't doubt her husband one bit. What she feared most was him doing his job so well that he would have no reason to stay married to her and she would be sent home to Colombia by herself. Empty and sad. Yes, her biggest fear was having to go on with the business of life without Henry.

Sophia looked back at Snake as they left the store. She smiled. This giant biker dude was carrying the biggest pink teddy bear that she had ever seen. Even carrying the bear, he looked dangerous and people gave him a wide berth.

She had picked up some outfits and a few books as well as the giant pink teddy bear. She spent quite a lot of the money she had earned at the diner.

Peeking into the hospital room, Sophia almost cried. Dana was holding the baby. Doug was draped on the side of the bed with his arm around Dana. They both peered down at the miracle with so much love in their eyes, it almost made Sophia not want to disturb the intimate scene.

Sophia knocked and slowly walked into the room followed by Snake. Dana and Doug both smiled at Sophia and then looked questioningly at Snake and the giant pink bear.

"Dana, Doug, this is Mr. Snake. He will be staying with me when Henry is traveling. Snake, these are my friends, Dana and Doug. They own the diner where I work. And this beautiful, perfect girl is . . ."

"Snake, I'm so happy you will be staying with Sophia. I heard about what happened. Are you okay, Sophia?" Dana asked, holding out her hand for Sophia.

Sophia came forward and grasped Dana's hand. "Sí, I'm fine. Now please introduce me to the newest citizen of Harmony, Maine."

"This is Tessa Ann. Doug's late mother was named Tessa and my mom's name is Ann," Dana said, holding out the baby for Sophia to hold.

Sophia tried to swallow the lump in her throat as she cradled baby Tessa in her arms.

"Oh, she's perfect. I'm so happy for you both," she said with tears in her eyes.

"Yeah, she's a keeper. I thought I was pretty content at this point in my life, but when I look at Dana holding our baby girl, well . . . I can't even breathe, there's so much happiness," Doug said.

Doug got up and walked around the bed and held out his hand to Snake. "Nice to meet you. I feel better now that Sophia won't be alone."

Snake shook Doug's hand and turned his forearm over. "Special Forces?"

Doug nodded as they broke the handshake and pointed to Snake's forearm. "Marines? MARSOC?"

Snake nodded. "You bet, brother. Three tours before they kicked my ass to the curb."

Doug nodded. "Two for me, but the same outcome."

"Well, I'm not much for chitchat, but I'd sure like to sit a spell with you before I leave town. At the very least, find out what your secret is for surrounding yourself with beautiful ladies," Snake said, smirking.

Doug returned the smirk because he was the king of "no small talk," but Sophia could tell that Doug was comfortable around Snake, and that was saying something.

Sophia handed Doug the baby and leaned down to hug Dana.

"Get some rest, both of you. Between Gracie, Sam, and me, we will have the diner under control and Mr. Snake will keep the peace. All you have to concentrate on is taking care of your beautiful family," Sophia said with tears in her eyes again.

****

As Sophia and Snake rode back to camp in companionable silence, Snake was the first to break it.

"How many kids would you like to have?"

Sophia tried to hide her small gasp as her heart constricted. "Um, one or two, I think. I'm a kindergarten teacher, you know. I'm used to being surrounded by children. I miss my pupils."

Snake looked over at Sophia. "Of course you're a kindergarten teacher," he said, shaking his head and smiling as he turned back to the road.

"What's that look for?" Sophia teased.

Snake sighed. "I'm not quite sure if Henry knows what a lucky sonofabitch he is."

Now Sophia sighed. She wished with all her heart that Henry did feel blessed to have her love. Even though she hadn't actually told him she loved him. But, instead, she was certain that Henry felt the opposite of lucky to be saddled with the likes of her. And who could blame him. Not Sophia.

****

Henry's phone buzzed with a text. He had just gotten on the road to Portland for the night. The jet would take him to New York in the morning, but he'd had to get away from camp. No, if he was going to be honest with himself, he needed to get away from Sophia. He knew if he stayed with her tonight, he would fall to his knees and beg her not to leave him.

Oh, he wasn't afraid she would leave him and be sent to prison, no, that was never going to fucking happen. He knew deep in his gut that as soon as the danger was over, she would leave him and go back to Colombia and her fiancé, John Williams, the goddamn saint.

He didn't have any idea how to handle these unfamiliar emotions roiling around in his gut. But his flight-or-fight instinct was in perfect fucking order.

The text was from Officer Mary Ellen Landry at the jail. It just said, "Come now."

Suddenly, Henry knew exactly how to *handle* his emotions. He stepped on the gas and made his way to the Skowhegan jail.

****

The fist to the gut of one Clint Striker, attempted rapist of his wife, should have kept the guy down. Henry had spent the last ten minutes beating the shit out of him, but the sonofabitch was tough as nails. Probably why he was a member of the mountain crew.

But Henry had one thing on his side: rage. They beat each other against the bars of the holding cell until they were both bloody. The mental image of Sophia sitting on that bed, trying to make herself small because of fear and humiliation, spurred Henry to reach deep down and deliver the final blow that sent Striker's three front teeth skidding across the floor and him to the floor, unconscious.

"Jesus Christ, Johnson, I said five minutes and punch below the neck. He looks like he's been in a meat grinder!"

Henry took out his handkerchief and wiped some of the blood dripping from his split lip before scooping up the three teeth and then pocketing the bloody handkerchief.

"Mary Ellen, I'm sorry, but that asshole deserved what he got. Was it legal, no way. You shut the camera off and went to the restroom for five minutes. You have no idea who got into the cell and beat Striker. And, if they decide to pursue actions regarding your job, give me a call. I know a fucking amazing attorney who won't charge you a dime."

"Get the hell out of here before someone sees you. You're going to have some explaining to do yourself after people see your face."

Henry grunted and tossed his hoodie over his head to keep his face in the dark as he exited the jail.

****

The plane ride from Portland, Maine, to New York was less than an hour. Even for such a short distance, he still brooded over the deal he was going to have to broker for Sophia and her brother.

He had sat all the previous evening at his condo, nursing a half bottle of Johnnie Walker with an ice pack covering his face. His face felt a little better, but his head was throbbing.

He kept his sunglasses on as he made it to his office without seeing either Marcus or Caleb. Marcus didn't come to New York much now that he had a family, but occasionally he had to make an appearance like today. Which Henry had completely fucking forgotten about.

There was no way he was going to be able to fly under Marcus's radar until he went home, leaving Henry in New York to handle any loose ends. But he was going to try.

Henry called Kent, his secretary in Maine, to call Marcus's secretary and tell her that Henry had been delayed but if Marcus forwarded the information from the meeting, he would read it over and make any suggestions if needed.

Henry took his sunglasses off and leaned back in his cushy office chair. Marcus burst through the door and stood in front of his desk with his arms crossed.

"Oh, hey, Marcus, you need to fire your secretary. She is lousy at relaying messages," Henry said dryly.

"Oh, she relayed the message, but I could smell your bullshit all the way down the hall. What the fuck is going on? And, so help me, if you make some comment about how I should see the other guy, I'm going to clock you myself."

Henry furrowed his brow. "Well, all right, Grandpa. First off, no one says they're going to clock someone anymore, and second, you *should* see the other guy. The other guy happens to be Clint Striker, the man who tried to rape my wife. And, yes, I cleaned his fucking clock. Satisfied?"

That took the wind out of Marcus's sails completely. "Oh fuck, sorry, Henry. But you should have called and I would have helped you so maybe your face wouldn't be so Quasimoto-ish. That's what brothers are for, asshat."

"Thanks, but I handled it. I suppose you insist on me attending this meeting?"

Marcus nodded. He was back in full oldest-sibling, head-of-the-family shoe empire mode.

"Yes, and after, we're going to have a talk. I know there is shit you haven't told me. I've waited long enough for you to tell me and you haven't. That ends today," Marcus said, already striding out the door.

Henry sighed. He actually didn't mind Marcus pulling family rank on him. He needed to tell his brother the whole story. Maybe, just maybe, between the two of them, perhaps they could come up with a deal that would satisfy everyone. Well, everyone except the asshole who was threatening Sophia, Mateo Sanchez. That fucker was going down in flames.

Henry called Snake three times during the day to check on Sophia. He said she was fine and on the last call, Snake said they were baby-shopping. Henry really couldn't picture his giant friend shopping for a baby, but did know that Sophia could charm the socks off any man with a pulse.

Marcus called his wife, Zena, and told her that he was staying with Henry. She gave no argument, so Henry was certain Marcus and Zena had talked about what he wasn't telling them. Families—you couldn't get shit past his before they busted your balls. Out of love, of course, but it still had the ability to irritate him to no end.

Henry ordered a pizza and they drank beer while Henry told Marcus every detail. Especially about the government's involvement.

"How about if you tell the Feds that Sophia and her brother will make a deal to serve Sanchez on a platter to them if they both get immunity and Sophia's brother comes to live here in Maine? I'm sure we could find a place for him in the company."

Henry smirked at his brother. "I like the way you're thinking, bro, but I don't think we have a lot of need for hackers who work for the Colombian drug cartel. But you're on the right path. I want to make a deal for both of them and have her brother live here in the States. He's her only family and it would make Sophia happy to have her brother close to her. But there is a fly in the ointment, so to speak. What I didn't tell you is that Sophia was engaged before she agreed to do the drug-trafficking job. I would guess she still intends to go back to Colombia when this is over and marry the bastard. I'm selfish, but even I can't take her away from all she knows and loves."

"So the marriage was just to keep Sophia from being deported?"

Henry nodded. "Every bit of it was my brilliant idea."

Marcus blew out a breath. "You're fucked."

Almost choking on the beer he was draining, Henry sat the bottle on the counter. "I'm certain I am, but what part exactly am I fucked?"

Marcus pointed his beer bottle at him. "You're fucked because you're in love with Sophia. Like little heart-emojis-in-your-eyes fucked."

Henry swallowed hard. "You're right, as you often are, according to you, but what disturbs me most is how you know what little heart emojis in my eyes are."

Chapter 30

Sophia barely made it to the bathroom before she retched until there was nothing left. Dios, she had never felt so horrible. Luckily, she didn't have to work today.

Several weeks had passed and Dana was going crazy staying home, so she brought the baby into the diner and worked a couple of days a week. Henry was working all the time. He was distant toward her, but sometimes in the middle of the night he would caress her and they would make love and he would hold her after. She began to hope every evening Henry was home that he would touch her. She wasn't disappointed; it was magical.

She also knew within the passing weeks that her feeling awful and barely making it to the bathroom was not a flu bug. She was pregnant. But she still wanted to take a test before she completely had a meltdown.

One morning at breakfast on her day off, after Henry had gone to work, Snake sat at the counter, sipping his coffee.

"So, are you going to tell him?" he asked quietly.

Sophia's hand that held her dry toast stilled midway to her mouth. She tried to swallow but it seemed the dry bread particles had lodged in her throat.

"Tell who, what?" she croaked out.

Snake set his coffee down and looked at her. "Tell your husband you're pregnant."

Sophia set her toast back in her plate and couldn't have held back her tears if she tried.

"Shit," Snake mumbled as he held out his big arms for her.

She happily let herself be enveloped into his comforting warmth as she cried. When the tears stopped flowing, Sophia sat back on her stool and blew her nose.

"It's not that simple, Snake."

"It must be pretty friggin' complicated because that's the first time you have called me Snake instead of Mr. Snake. Come on, spill it."

Sophia confided that her and Henry's marriage wasn't real. That Henry only married her to keep her from being deported back to Colombia, where Mateo was waiting for her. She told him how she loved Henry, but he had made it clear that he didn't have relationships and that was how he liked his life.

"You're right about how Henry used to be—I can attest to that. As far as I know, he's never had a serious relationship. I think his mother dying when he was a teenager did a number on him and then he got a front row seat to watch his father suffer from missing her for twenty years. But also, let's not forget that he sees people at their worst in his job. Nasty divorces, custody battles, humanity at its worst. Who could blame him? But all that was before you, Sophia. You and Henry are married. And, whatever the reason for that marriage, it doesn't negate the fact that you *are* married and you have made a child together. That is a game changer."

The waterworks began again as Sophia nodded. "But I can't trap Henry with a child to make him stay married to me. I've been nothing but a burden for him since he laid eyes on me."

"The man deserves to know he is going to be a father."

"Sí, sí, of course I will tell him. But I don't know officially if I am pregnant. Would you go to the drugstore and get me a test?"

The color drained from Snake's face. She almost laughed at his expression of terror.

"I can't go into the pharmacy . . . people will know! But nobody will say a word to you if you go," she said with pleading, watery eyes.

Snake pointed his finger at her. "If any of what I've done since coming to Maine gets out to my crew, especially going to pick up a pregnancy test, I'm going to have to turn in my man card. I'll never live it down."

Sophia looked confused. "Man card?"

Snake looked confused as he tried to explain what a man card was. He just shrugged.

"It doesn't matter, you are a very large man and no one would dare ask you any questions. As a matter of fact, most of the people in town cross the street when you're walking down the sidewalk."

"Fine. Let's go before I change my mind," he said, grabbing his keys.

****

Sophia sat in Snake's SUV with tinted windows waiting for him while he went into the pharmacy.

When he returned, he had a bag with every brand of pregnancy test they had. She just looked at him.

"I didn't know which one to get and you were completely wrong about no one asking me any questions. The little old lady who cashed me out said she noticed I wasn't wearing a wedding ring and asked if the test was positive, was I planning to marry the lady. She said she sincerely hoped I was. You owe me big, Sophia," he said, grinning.

Sophia burst out laughing. It felt good to laugh.

****

Henry had taken the first bite from his sandwich as he stood at a tall table in his favorite deli which was located down the street from his office in New York when the goons who kidnapped him before stood around the table. To their credit, they weren't wearing ski masks.

"Do you people try and ruin my lunch? Is that a thing with the Feds?" Henry asked sarcastically.

Goon one shushed Henry. "Keep your voice down. You need to come with us. You can eat in the car."

Henry glared but took one more bite and tossed the rest as he let them flank him to the waiting double-parked black Suburban.

Henry called his secretary and told him he was going to be late getting back to the office, which pissed him off because he had wanted to be back to camp by dinnertime. That was not going to happen.

****

They arrived at the same rundown warehouse with three chairs.

"Well, if it isn't Agent Sullivan and Agent Smith. I've been waiting for you to contact me. You are aware that we can meet at a nicer establishment, right? I know the country is broke, but this is pathetic," he said, waving his hand around before turning a chair around, sitting down and leaning his arms on the chipped wooden back.

"Are there new developments since we last talked and you refused the deal we offered?" Agent Smith asked.

"Um, yeah, Sanchez is getting very antsy. He wants his drugs back or Sophia. Preferably both."

"I'm sure he is but we've told you your wife can have immunity if you give us the computer hacker. I need a name, today," Agent Smith demanded.

Agent Sullivan sighed. "This is getting us nowhere. Attorney Johnson, I'm sure you have something in mind. Tell us what you want."

Henry liked FBI Agent Sullivan. CIA Agent Smith was a dick.

"The computer hacker is my wife's brother, Santiago Rodriguez. I want complete immunity for both. I want Santiago to be brought to the States and given a permanent visa."

Agent Smith stood up. "Do you have access to Mr. Rodriguez? Is he in your custody? Because that is the only way any deal like that will go down. I'll tell you what I think is going to happen. We give your wife immunity and her brother disappears and we get squat. No, unless you can gift wrap Mr. Rodriguez for us, there's no deal. And, what makes you so sure, the US isn't planning on locking Mr. Rodriguez away for life? Hell, we could even get Homeland Security in on this. Santiago Rodriguez could very well end up in Guantanamo as a terrorist."

Henry stood up and started for the short squat Agent Smith.

Agent Sullivan held up his hands. "Calm down, everyone. Mr. Johnson, I understand your predicament, but Agent Smith is right; unless you deliver your wife's brother to us and he agrees to help us take down Sanchez's drug cartel, there can't be a deal. If you can make that happen, I will gladly give both your wife and her brother complete immunity. I will even go so far as to draw up the papers and have them delivered to you."

Agent Smith turned to Agent Sullivan. "You have no authority to authorize that deal."

"Shut the fuck up, Roy," Agent Sullivan said. "Attorney Johnson, that is the best we can do. I'll be in touch in one week to see if you've made progress," he said, holding out his hand.

Henry shook his hand and glared at Agent Smith.

On the trip back to his office, his head felt like it was going to explode. How the fuck was he going to infiltrate the biggest drug cartel in Colombia and spirit away their ace-in-the-hole computer hacker back to the States to wrap him in a fucking bow for the Feds?

****

Sophia and Snake stared at the white tube on the bathtub. They sat in the hall in front of the open door of the bathroom like it was some sort of portal they were terrified to jump through.

"Is it time?" Sophia whispered.

Snake shook his head. "It's one minute past the last time you asked. We have eight more minutes."

He took her shaking hand in his huge paw. "It will be fine, Sophia. Don't count Henry out just yet."

Sophia smiled and nodded. Maybe it would be okay.

They waited out the remaining time in anxious silence.

"It's time," Snake said. "Do you want me to go look?"

Sophia shook her head, got up and walked to the tub and picked up the test. In big, bold letters it read Pregnant. It didn't get much clearer than that. She touched her belly and looked at Snake.

"I'm going to have a baby," she whispered as the tears began to flow. It only took a fraction of a second to know deep in her soul that the tears she was crying were happy ones.

****

After an hour and a cup of tea, Sophia wanted to talk to her brother. No, she *needed* to talk to her brother.

Taking a burner phone from the top of the refrigerator, Sophia dialed her brother's number. Snake began to rise from his stool, but she put a hand on his arm.

"No, stay por favor."

Sophia put the phone on speaker and they listened as the loud dial tone filled the kitchen. The phone was answered but Santiago didn't speak.

"Santiago?" Sophia asked nervously.

"Hola, Sophia. I've been waiting for you to call. It seems that you haven't told your brother your whereabouts. That wasn't nice of you, *princesa*."

Her blood ran cold. "Do not hurt him, Mateo. I'm begging you, please don't hurt him," she said on a sob.

Snake put a hand on her back to steady her.

"Oh, it's too late for that, but rest assured, your brother is not dead . . . yet. I want my drugs, Sophia. I'm done waiting."

"Mateo, please! I can't get the drugs for you. Please just let Santiago go. If I ever meant anything to you, please don't hurt my brother. I'm begging you, Mateo."

"You're the only thing I've ever cared about, *mi amor*. You know our deal, Sophia. You either delivered the drug shipment or become my wife. Those are still the terms of our agreement. I expect you to deliver your end of the bargain or your brother is made an example. I've already given Santiago too many chances and that is only because of you. It makes me look weak. And, you know I'm not weak. Your father could attest to that."

Sophia gasped. "What could my father attest to?" she whispered.

There was silence for a beat. "Do you really think I would let anyone take you away from me, Sophia? Your father tried and died because of it. Don't think I won't kill Santiago, mi amor. Your time is up. I will kill your brother and I *will* find you."

"You killed my parents? You caused the car crash?" she sobbed.

"I'm not a weak man, Sophia. You have always been meant to be my queen. I will give you one week to get back to Colombia. I will keep your brother alive for that time. When you come home we can be a family, mi amor. The way it was always meant to be."

The line went dead and Sophia just stared at the phone with tears streaming down her face.

Snake cupped her face. "Sophia, look at me."

She slowly raised her eyes to his steely blue eyes.

"I'm not going to let anything happen to your brother or you. Do you understand me?"

Sophia nodded.

"Good. Now I need you to go lie down and rest. Try not to worry. It's really important for you not to worry. Too much stress isn't good for the baby."

Sophia could feel her eyes grow big at the mention of her baby.

"What are you going to do, Snake?"

"What I do best, little one. Just go rest. I need to make a few calls."

Sophia nodded and walked toward the bedrooms but stopped before leaving the kitchen and turned back around.

"Thank you, Snake. You're a good man and a better friend," she whispered.

As she left the room, she didn't see the sheen of tears in Snakes eyes or the pure rage that lurked right behind the tears.

Chapter 31

Snake pocketed the burner phone and whipped out his own phone. He walked outside to the cold midmorning air.

"Jax, how's that intel-gathering going, brother?"

"Snake, man, not good. Not good at all. That fucker Mateo Sanchez is one feared motherfucker. There's no way we're going to get close to him. He has an army surrounding him."

Snake chuckled. "That's what makes it fun. But don't worry about getting close to him. We're going to have help with that. What I need you and the boys to do is get as many schematics of the lay of the land you can find and then get the arsenal ready. We will be flying by private jet to the abandoned airfield you found not far from the compound. Just be ready for boots to the ground as soon as you get my call."

"Will do, brother. It will be good to be back in the saddle instead of babysitting these rich fucks."

"Amen, brother," Snake growled and disconnected the call.

With plans swirling around in his head, he couldn't ignore the dread in his gut. The same gut he trusted and had kept him alive more times than he cared to count. He thought about the difficult conversation he'd had just a few nights ago with his crew after Henry and Sophia had gone to bed. His crew knew the risks involved in this mission and hadn't hesitated a second when Snake had outlined his plan and told them this mission was personal. Jax had been right about feeling good about getting back in the saddle again. Men like them needed a purpose and for too many years they had just been drifting in the dark.

The US government had left them with broken bodies and broken spirits and if it hadn't been for them finding each other and Jesus, they would be sitting in an alley with a brown paper bag and piss-covered pants. No, he wasn't going to leave it to the government to save Sophia; he and his crew would be the avenging angels in this particular story. Their halos may be crooked but when you have the Almighty on your side, you can't lose. And, losing wasn't an option. No, sir, not a fucking option.

****

He had just tucked his phone back in his pocket when Sophia padded into the kitchen looking considerably better.

"I'm hungry," she stated.

Snake smiled. This woman was as tough as fucking nails. She may cry a little when she gets knocked back, but her tears meant that she loved deeply. And anyone who was worthy of her tears, well, they were lucky sonsabitches.

"How about we go to the diner and have a late lunch and you can check up on Dana and baby Tessa?"

The most gorgeous smile graced Sophia's face. It almost took his breath away.

The diner was pretty full, so they sat at the counter. Sophia held baby Tessa while they waited for their burgers.

The baby cooed and made funny faces that made Sophia giggle. The bell on the door chimed and as Sophia looked up, her smile left her face, as well as all her color.

Snake immediately looked at the new arrivals and stood up with hands fisted. Two border patrol agents stood in the doorway and stared at Sophia. The very same border patrol agents who were going to rape her.

Jax had sent him pictures of the agents several weeks ago after Sophia told him everything.

The agents swaggered to stand before Snake and then peered around him.

"Well, hello there, chica. We've been searching for you. I'm afraid you have violated your bail conditions. We're taking you in, and you, big guy, you need to step away or there's a bullet meant for your head. Obstructing justice and anything else we can come up with. Now move out of our fucking way and get someone to grab this kid from Miss Rodriguez."

Snake's blood was boiling and he was reaching inside his leather vest to grab his Glock when Harmony's finest stepped up beside him.

"What seems to be the problem, boys? You're a long way from the border," Chief Keister said.

The border patrol agents looked a bit surprised but recovered quickly.

"Miss Rodriguez here is a fugitive from justice. She is charged with drug trafficking and has violated her conditions of bail. We're taking her in, so I suggest you step aside, Sheriff," one of the agents growled.

Chief Keister and Officer Lancaster stood their ground beside Snake. These officers were hard ass. If there's one thing Snake learned since stepping foot in small town Harmony, Maine, it's that they take care of their own. And seeing it in action was a sight to behold.

Chief Keister shook his head. "No, sir. Miss Rodriguez has checked in with me every day. There's been no violation. I suggest you go and have a word with your superiors or better yet, why don't you come to my office and we'll both have a word with your superiors."

The other border patrol agent snarled. "There's also a little problem with immigration. Go check your computer; she is to be deported back to Colombia," he said, smiling menacingly.

Officer Lancaster chuckled. "Where do you boys get your intel? Miss Rodriguez is now Mrs. Henry Johnson. She's all legal, fellas."

Chief Keister nodded. "That's right, so I suggest you get the fuck out of my town or I'm going to go back to my lunch and let my friend, Snake here, have some fun with you both."

Snake smiled and fisted his giant hands.

"This isn't over," one of the border agents snarled and they stomped out the door.

Chief Keister turned to Snake. "Get her somewhere safe. I'll have a patrol car set up in front of the camp."

Dana gathered baby Tessa. "Are you okay, Sophia?"

Sophia nodded but looked shell-shocked.

"We'll take our lunch to go, please, Dana," Snake instructed.

Sophia turned to Chief Keister. "How did you know?"

The chief smiled. "How do I know about your charges? It's my job to keep this town safe. Do I think you're a drug trafficker and a threat to my town? Not a chance. I don't know what this was about today, but I know those two agents are bad news. You're one of us now and we protect our own. You just go with Snake and let him keep you safe." Then the chief turned to Snake. "And, yes, I know who you are too, Sergeant Jake "the Snake" Whitehall. You're one of us too. Now get your asses out of here and think about going dark for a few days."

There was a lump in Snake's throat that burned as he hustled Sophia out of the diner and beat feet back to camp where he called Henry and told him to get his ass home, stat.

****

Henry sat back in the leather seat of the jet and pulled out the tattered, worn paper from his pocket. Tears blurred his eyes as he reread the last words his father ever said to him.

Hello Son,

Henry, I cannot put into words how proud I am of you. I know your mother is proud, as well.

You, along with Marcus, carry the weight of the world on your shoulders. That's my fault. I know that you think that there was something you could have done to save your mother. There wasn't. Your mother was given to us for a short time before she was called home. She just burned too bright for this world. You take after your mother and shine too brightly too.

I remember your mother looking at you as a little boy and marveling at your wit and intelligence. She would say, "My Henry, he's going to be a star." And she was right—you are the shining star of this family. I know that when your mother passed and then I sent Jack away, you blamed yourself, thinking that you should have been able to save them both.

I know this because I stood outside your room and listened to your heated and probably your last discussion you had on your knees to the almighty God. It broke my heart how you railed against him for taking your loved ones away from you. I heard the vow that left your lips with tears running from your eyes that you would never let anyone other than your family get close to you and if he ever decided to fuck with your family again, you would stop him. It would be you and not the Almighty that took care of them.

And you have taken that vow to the extreme and made sure your family was safe. Above your own wants and needs.

You need to stop, Henry. You must accept that life gets messy sometimes.

Someday, God is going to send a special lady into your life. Probably when you least expect it. And all your white-knuckled control is going to fly right out the window. Don't be so stubborn and angry at God that you miss your chance at happiness, Henry.

Take a knee, son. God is waiting to hear from you. As your father, I know how painful it is to see your children in pain. Your father in heaven is waiting to ease your pain, Henry. All you have to do is ask.

I love you more than you will ever know.

Dad

Henry could barely see his father's signature for the tears. His father was right, he was angry at God. When he had let God have any semblance of control in his life, the people he loved had been taken away. No, he wasn't going to let that happen again. He had managed to keep his loved ones safe by his own ingenuity and he would continue to do so. But, judging by the hole in his heart, he wished his father was here to talk to. But God had taken him too.

Henry folded the letter and slid it back into his pocket. He wiped his tears away and sat forward with his elbows on his knees and tried to lessen the knot of terror that had been there since Snake had called and told him to get his ass home ASAP. He said Sophia was all right, but some decisions had to be made tonight.

When Henry finally drove down the camp driveway, he was shocked by what he saw. Officer Josh Lancaster was sitting in his cruiser at the end of the driveway. Henry waved as he went by and then saw a civilian helicopter sitting in the middle of the gravel road that led to the pond.

Snake was talking to the helicopter pilot when he spied Henry. He jogged to Henry's truck.

"What the fuck is going on, Snake?"

Snake held up his hands and told Henry about the border patrol officers finding Sophia.

"Is there a safe place you can go to for a few days?" Snake asked.

Henry thought for a minute and pulled out his phone.

"The helicopter pilot is a friend of mine. He owes me a favor. Wherever you're going, get the coordinates," Snake demanded.

Henry nodded and dialed a number.

Arrangements made, Henry wrote down the coordinates for Snake and handed them to him.

"Good, now I need you to pack a bag and be out here in under fifteen minutes. Sophia is already packed. I want you both somewhere safe. And Henry, leave all electronics here. I will pick you up at these coordinates when it's safe. Hopefully, it will be within three or four days. But, no matter how long it takes, you need to stay put and keep Sophia safe. Got it?"

Henry nodded. "Where are you going to be?"

Snake shook his head. "I've got some business to take care of. The less you know the better, my friend. Now go—clock's ticking."

Henry started toward the house and turned back to Snake.

"I wasn't able to make a deal with the Feds. They will only grant immunity to both Sophia and her brother if her brother can be handed over to the Feds willingly with a fucking bow. I'm going to try and work on a plan B in which Sophia simply disappears off the face of the planet. I won't let her go to prison."

Snake grabbed Henry's shoulders tightly. "Now is not the time to worry about that, bro. All you need to do is get your wife to safety and love the shit out of her. Do you hear me, Henry? Make her forget about all the bad shit. Just love her for a few days. We'll hash out a plan later."

Henry nodded and ran toward the camp where he could see the love of his life staring out at him from the porch door. His heart constricted. He loved her so much.

Smiling, he opened the door and Sophia jumped into his arms. The whole world ceased to exist when he had her in his arms. Her scent, her curves nestled against him perfectly, it was as if she was made for him.

His lips found hers and he couldn't stop his moan. He had missed her so much. He had been trying to distance himself from her so he wouldn't be destroyed when she left him. But that ship had sailed probably from the first moment he laid eyes on her in an orange prison jumpsuit and her big brown eyes that he got lost in.

Yeah, he was a goner for sure. There was no way he would survive without her. But, as he broke the kiss, he decided that for however much time they had left, he would make the most of it. He would spend every moment making her smile. And the orgasms he planned to give her, well, just the thought had him getting uncomfortable in his jeans. It also spurred him into warp speed to get her where they were going.

"I need to pack," he murmured against her lips.

"I have already packed for both of us," she whispered against his mouth as she kissed him deeply.

Henry moaned and broke the kiss and cupped her cheeks. "Hey . . . hola, how are you?"

Tears appeared in her eyes, but she smiled. "Hola. I'm okay now that you're here with me."

Henry smiled. "Good answer! Now let's get out of here," he said as he took her hand and grabbed the suitcase.

Henry shook the pilot's hand and helped Sophia into the helicopter.

Snake walked Henry away from the bird.

"I need your jet," Snake said flatly.

Henry pulled his phone from his back pocket. He had planned to give his phone to Snake so he would have access to all his siblings' numbers if he needed them.

He dialed his pilot.

"Hi, Brownie, Henry here. Listen, I'm going to authorize a friend of mine to have access to the jet. Take him anywhere he needs to go. I trust him with my life. I'm giving him my phone. I'm going to disappear for a few days so just do whatever he asks, okay?"

"Of course, Henry. I'm happy to help."

"Great, I'm going to hand over the phone to him and he will let you know what he needs. Thanks, Brownie."

Henry handed over the phone to Snake. "My pilot is on the line waiting for instructions. His name is Brownie Jones, ex-military."

Snake grabbed the phone and held his big paw out. Henry grasped his hand and pulled him close. "Stay safe, my friend," Henry hollered in Snake's ear.

Snake nodded and mouthed "you too." Henry climbed into the waiting helicopter with the woman he loved.

As they flew off, Henry could see Snake talking and making hand gestures as he spoke with the Johnson family pilot. He didn't know what Snake was up to, but he was certain it was extremely dangerous. If he were a praying man, he would have offered one up. But, seeing that he wasn't, he just picked up Sophia's hand, kissed her palm, and held it to his cheek.

Chapter 32

Snake threw his duffel in the SUV and tore out of Harmony, en route to the Portland International Jetport, where the Johnson family jet was on standby.

Pulling out the burner phone Sophia had used, he dialed the only number she called. Santiago Rodriguez and he were going to have a little tête-à-tête.

"Sophia?" Santiago asked urgently.

"No, my name is Snake and I've been protecting your sister. She's in a great deal of danger right now. How are you? I heard the conversation Mateo had with Sophia while you were getting beat."

"I'll be okay. Is my sister safe?"

The love and fear in Santiago's voice made Snake feel a little better about the little fucker who was responsible for his sister's shitstorm of a life right now. Just a *little* better. He couldn't be sure what he would do when he had the guy in front of him. But right now he needed to focus.

"Yeah, she's safe for the time being. But you, not so much. You're going to help me and my crew get into the compound and take Mateo out. You'll be coming back to the States with us when this is over."

There was silence on the other end of the phone.

"I'll do anything to save my sister. Just tell me what you want me to do."

Well, Snake liked him a little more.

"Okay, I need you to text me the exact coordinates of the closest airfield where we can land a jet. Then, I need you to have a vehicle there to transport a crew of four men."

"Only four? Mateo has lots of men on the compound!"

Snake chuckled. "Trust me, amigo, the four of us are all that's needed. I need you to listen carefully. I need you to send the schematics of the compound to the email address I'm going to text you. You need to do that as soon as you get off the phone with me."

"Sí, sí. Anything else, Mr. Snake?"

Snake smiled. Just as polite as his big sister. "Um . . . yeah, I need you to find me and my crew a way into the compound."

Silence.

"Sí, I'll do my best, Mr. Snake."

"You do that, amigo. And one more thing . . . a few prayers wouldn't hurt."

Santiago chuckled. "Ah, it's been a long time, but I'll do anything for my sister. And I happen to know for a fact that she and Dios are very tight."

"Amen, brother. That's what I'm counting on," Snake said and disconnected the call to text Santiago the email address.

Snake then called Jax to tell him the tentative plan and to expect an email with the schematics of the compound. He told Jax to have the crew ready to roll out with every available ammunition and weapon, including the rocket launcher and explosives.

He made record time getting to the Portland Jetport. As he made his way to the jet, the pilot, Brownie Jones, stood at the bottom of the stairs and held out his hand.

Snake returned the handshake. "Good to meet you, Brownie, I'm Snake, formerly of MARSOC. If I was a betting man, I would guess Air Force Special Tactics?"

Brownie grinned and nodded.

"Please tell me Vietnam is part of your story," Snake inquired.

Brownie furrowed his brow. "It was indeed."

"Thank Christ, because we are going to need someone with serious combat flying. We may be going in hot and we definitely are coming out hot."

Brownie looked at ease again. "That, my friend, is my specialty," he said, patting Snake on the back as they climbed the stairs to the jet.

"First stop, the private airstrip in Florida that I told you about, and then, Colombia," Snake said as Brownie made his way to the cockpit.

Snake lay on the couch to try and get an hour of shut-eye. Every soldier knew that the more well rested you were, the increased chances of you staying alive. Besides, he had no idea when he would get a chance to sleep over the next four days.

He woke up as the wheels touched down in Florida. He looked out the window to see if his crew were there. Of course they were, along with all the fucking bells and whistles he had asked them to bring.

Brownie opened the jet door to hooting and hollering from his crew. Obviously, they had never flown in a private jet before, nor had he. It would be good to see his guys again.

Snake jumped down and gave them all the official man hug. Jax, his righthand man, as he liked to call himself because he only had a right hand. His left arm to the elbow had been blown off during his last tour. None of his crew were as big as Snake was, but Jax came close. He was as dark as Snake was blond. Dark hair with a full, black beard. Not many men would choose to fuck with Jax. The most dangerous thing about Jax was his combat skills, but these days that included a bayonet as his prosthesis when he was working. Badass didn't even begin to cover it.

Shorty was anything but short, but, as a bomb specialist, he was known for setting his fuses short, which meant you had to haul ass or get blown up. Ironically, he was blown up in a roadside IED. His convoy was on their way to bring humanitarian relief to impoverished villages in Iraq. He was left with facial scars, burns, and no right leg. His prosthesis was identical to the runners in the Special Olympics, a lightweight steel that looked as though it could bounce, making running possible. So, as long as Shorty could still run when he set a fuse, then he wasn't fucking disabled by any stretch of the imagination. He was bald and with his scars, burns, and tattoos, well, he was a gnarly fuck with the tenderest heart of any of the crew. He would cry over commercials.

Lastly, was Mac. The Romeo of the crew. And with his baby face and dark curls, he could charm the panties off any female. A member of the exclusive Navy SEALS, Mac was a weapons specialist like no other, as well as a sharpshooter. The fucker could shoot a tick off a dog's ass from a mile away. Mac lost his left leg on his second tour. A suicide bomber took out a bar in Kabul while he and his mates were having a cold one.

With the arsenal loaded, the guys threw their duffels up and hoisted themselves into the plush jet.

"Sweet ride, buddy!" Mac gushed as he plunked down in the leather seat.

"Yeah, I could get used to this," Shorty said, sitting at the table.

"For fucking sure," Jax said, sitting down at the table and laying out the schematics of the compound.

Brownie fired up the jet and began immediately to taxi down the short runway. As the jet reached the end of the runway, it rose seemingly effortlessly into the sky. That was some fucking skill.

Snake sat down at the table and they began to study and brainstorm. Once they had a tentative plan, Snake dialed Santiago again. Hoping he was alone.

"Mr. Snake, I've been waiting for your call."

"Are you alone, can you talk?"

"Sí, Mateo is gone until tomorrow, which is how I'm going to get you into the compound. I have transport scheduled to be at the airfield to pick you up and bring you to the compound. You will be able to come right through the front gates."

"No shit?" Snake said, surprised.

Snake went over the possible plan with Santiago. He was able to fine-tune it as they mapped it out on the schematics. Santiago told Snake to call him once they had passed the front gates.

Dread settled in his gut. Snake knew the risks Santiago was taking. If anyone found out about him helping Snake's crew, Santiago was a dead man. Telling Sophia that her brother was dead was not a conversation he wanted to have. No fucking way.

With the plans in place, Snake told his crew to get some sleep. He continued to study the compound and to try to go over every possible outcome. It's how his mind worked. It was kind of his superpower. Well, that and his metal head.

****

The helicopter touched down in the middle of the dirt driveway. The little log cabin looked like a magazine cover with smoke coming out of the fieldstone chimney and the tall pine trees standing sentry.

It was late afternoon and the sun was setting earlier and earlier so it looked more like twilight as Henry and Sophia entered the cabin.

It was toasty warm from the woodstove in the kitchen and the fireplace in the living room. It was beautiful and perfect.

Sophia clutched her hands to her chest. "Oh, Henry, it's beautiful. So rustic and cozy. How did you know about this place?"

Henry slid her coat off her shoulders and tossed it on the bench by the door along with his own. He walked to her and embraced her.

"I found this cabin a couple of years ago when my brother Bear's wife, Kate, needed a place to recuperate. I think if you threw a rock it would land in Canada. This area doesn't even go by town names. I think they call it Township 12."

"I love it. Thank you for bringing me here. Do you know what Snake is going to do?"

Henry shook his head. "I don't know but how about we not talk about any danger or what ifs. Let's just give ourselves a few days to just breathe."

"I would like that very much," she whispered.

"You know what I would like very much?" Henry asked with a wicked grin.

"I can probably guess," she giggled.

"Well, if you were guessing a kiss, then you would be right," he said with his lips barely touching hers. Their breath was intermingled as they gazed into each other's eyes.

"Kiss me, Sophia. Please put me out of my misery," Henry whispered.

Sophia tilted her chin up just a little more and let her lips slide over Henry's. He moaned and pulled her close to him as he deepened the kiss.

The kiss spoke of love, misunderstandings, fear, and a passion so great it threatened to turn them both to ashes.

When Sophia let her tongue slip into Henry's mouth, he physically grunted like he had been punched in the gut. He turned his body slightly and picked her up without breaking the kiss.

"Need you, Soph," he groaned as he began to open doors until he found a bedroom.

He set her down beside the bed and they both began to undress each other urgently, all the while not willing to break their kisses unless a shirt was heaved over one of their heads and unceremoniously tossed to the floor.

It was as if they had both been starving and were now sitting before a banquet fit for a king. They were gorging themselves on each other's scent and taste.

"Henry, I've missed you," Sophia whispered.

"Shhh, I'm here, baby, I'm not going anywhere," he said as he laid a naked Sophia on the bed.

He stood over her and looked at her longingly. "You're so fucking beautiful."

Sophia watched as he finished undressing. He was the most breathtakingly handsome man she had ever seen. His shoulders were broad, his biceps big and strong, his flat, muscled stomach narrowed in a V to his slender hips. She wasn't an expert on men, but she was quite certain that Michelangelo himself would have wanted to sculpt Henry if given the chance.

"If you keep looking at me like that, Soph, this is going to be the shortest lovemaking session in history."

Sophia smiled and opened her arms in invitation. Henry climbed on the bed and kissed her deeply before kissing and nuzzling her neck. He bit her earlobe and sucked it to soothe the bite, making her squirm under him.

"Henry, I need you."

Henry began to descend again. Kissing and licking.

"I know, sweetheart, I've got you."

He made his way to her breasts and once he began to suck and lick, she gasped and bowed her back, trying to capture his mouth and keep it in one place.

She moaned and writhed on the bed as he continued lower until he reached her apex. The center at which all her need was aching desperately for him. Only Henry could relieve her pent-up need.

That first lick brought her behind off the bed and she cried out. Henry grasped her thighs and held her down as he began to feast on her. He was like a madman. He moaned as he wielded his tongue like the finest swordsman.

The orgasm came suddenly and hard as Sophia cried out. She fisted Henry's soft dark hair and rode out the waves of desire.

But Henry didn't stop; he slowly, ever so slowly, began to lick her from top to bottom until she felt like she would explode if she didn't have more. More pressure, more friction, more of Henry.

Henry was like a maestro tuning a beloved violin; he knew exactly what she needed. He inserted one finger into her aching core and then another.

Sophia gripped the comforter and moaned. He worked her slowly in and out until she thought she would burst. He began to pump his fingers faster and added a little more pressure until she could stand it no longer and fell over the cliff once again.

As her spasms calmed, Henry kissed her thigh, tickling her tender skin with his beard and grabbed his jeans from the floor. He brought a condom to his teeth and ripped the package. Sophia didn't have the heart to tell him at his moment that a condom wasn't necessary.

She took the foil package from his mouth and pulled the condom out and waited for Henry to raise himself to his knees. She slid the condom on his hard length as she held his gaze. The desire in his eyes shot new heat to her core. Would she ever get her fill of him? Again, the passing question of "is it normal to want to make love with the man you love all the time," fluttered through her thoughts only to be completely disregarded as Henry lined himself up to thrust into her.

They both cried out from the utter bliss of that moment.

"Fuck, fuck, fuck. Don't move, baby. It feels too good. Just give me a minute," Henry begged.

Sophia began to caress his tight backside. He moaned.

She brought her hands to his face and kissed him with all the love she felt for him.

He began to move slowly in and out of her.

"Oh, baby, you feel so good. You're so warm and tight and so fucking wet for me," he crooned in her ear.

Sophia began to match his rhythm until she too was wanting more.

She gasped. She was so close. "Henry, more, harder, faster, please," she panted in Spanish.

Henry began to drive into her. He hollered her name at that precise moment she fell into the abyss with him. Nothing existed but Henry's body clinging to hers and their love.

Chapter 33

The jet touched down on a private runway not far from Bogotá. Snake shook Brownie's hand after he opened the jet door.

"Will you be available by phone for pickup?" Snake asked.

Brownie shook his head. "I'm not leaving. I have everything I need here," he said opening a cupboard and retrieving an assault rifle.

"Damn!" was heard from the crew.

"But, with that said, if you give me a heads-up that you're coming my way, I'll be ready. Especially if you're coming in hot," Brownie advised.

"Yeah, unfortunately, coming in hot is the only fucking setting we seem to have," Shorty grunted.

Snake patted Brownie on the back. "Stay safe, brother." He jumped to the ground and looked around for their transportation and just about fell to his knees.

In the dark, a covered truck was parked not far from the jet. In the headlights stood the most gorgeous woman Snake had ever seen. She was petite, tiny even, with black leather thigh-high boots with a stiletto so sharp it could be used as a weapon. She wore a leopard-print minidress that barely covered her ass. Her long hair was pulled to one shoulder. It appeared light brown but there were so many red highlights that it looked copper. Jesus, it was as if the good Lord himself had peered into his fantasies and created this woman for him.

He swallowed hard and glanced behind him, jealousy coating his gut. His crew would get one look at her and want her as badly as he did. Fuck 'em, she was *his*.

Snake stalked over to stand before the tiny woman. She never flinched. Her eyes never left his. And, those eyes, Jesus, they were as blue as the ocean, and those red lips . . .

"You Snake?" the goddess asked in a thick Spanish accent.

Snake nodded. "Yeah, and you?"

"I'm Mia. Santiago sent me to pick up you and your crew."

By this time, the rest of his crew were flanking him and ogling Mia. He could feel their eyes on her and knew that their dicks were already swelling in their goddamn pants.

Snake turned. "How about we get that gear loaded in the truck?" he growled.

"Ain't you gonna introduce us to the little lady?" Mac asked, smiling.

Fire shot out of Snake's eyes. "No, this ain't no fucking high school dance. We have a job to do. Now let's get loading," he barked.

As the guys brought the first load to the back of the truck, Mia and Snake walked before them. Mia threw back the cover to reveal ten scantily dressed women smiling at them. None as breathtaking as Mia but attractive, nonetheless.

The crew wore big smiles and they helped the ladies out of the truck so they could put their weapons and ammunition at the front of the truck bed.

Once the truck was loaded, the guys helped the ladies back in the truck and followed them in. The ladies were not shy as they draped themselves over Jax, Shorty and Mac.

Snake threw the cover back in place and followed Mia to the driver's-side door and opened it for her.

She looked surprised as he helped her into the big truck. Snake walked around to the passenger side and hefted himself into the truck.

"When we get closer to the compound, you can pull over and I'll get in the back. But for now, I will take care of any trouble that comes along," he said, leaning his assault rifle against his leg.

Mia started the massive truck and looked over at Snake. "I can take care of any trouble that comes along," she said as she hefted her own AR-15 onto her lap.

Snake grinned. She was fucking awesome. A woman straight from his fucking imagination.

"The Four Horsemen? Are you a motorcycle gang?" she asked in very broken English.

Snake chuckled. "I guess, in a way. We do pretty much live on our Harleys, but it's more about friendship and brotherhood.

"You speak pretty good English—better than my Spanish."

Mia glanced at him sideways. "When I still lived at home, my mother taught me. She was a teacher. But it's been a long time since I've been home. Sometimes I struggle to find the right words."

"Mateo and his army kidnapped you? How old were you?"

At this, Mia looked fully at Snake. He knew she was deciding if she could trust him.

Finally, she nodded. "I was ten years old."

"Jesus," he grunted angrily. "Do you and the women live at the compound?"

Mia shook her head. "No, we live a few miles away. We all live together in a small house. We live like dogs," she said disgustedly.

"Have you ever thought about running away?"

Mia shrugged her shoulders. "Some girls have run and they were caught and beaten as well as passed around to hundreds of men. Others have run and Mateo just let them go. Fear of which fate it will be keeps us here."

"What about you?" Snake asked quietly.

Mia sneered. "I could never run. I'm Mateo's personal *puta*. He would never let me go. He would kill me for running."

Rage raced through his veins. "Listen, if I ever hear you call yourself that again, we're going to have trouble," Snake growled.

Mia looked over at him sharply. "I didn't think you would be offended quite so easily," she spat.

"I'm not just offended by what Mateo has done to you, I'm fucking outraged. You are not Mateo's slut. What happened to you was in no way your fault. You were a goddamn child. No, you're so much more. You're a fucking survivor. And, if I have any say at all, when this shitshow is over, Mateo will be dead and you can do or be any fucking thing you want."

Snake watched her as she looked at him with tears in her eyes. She nodded.

"So, you and the girls are going to the compound under the pretense of a party to smuggle us in?"

Mia cleared her throat. "Sí, Mateo is away until late tonight or morning. The men will think Mateo is rewarding them. We will get them drunk and distract them so you boys can do what you need to get ready for your battle."

Snake nodded.

Mia pulled the truck over to the side of the road, which was Snake's cue to get into the back.

He opened the passenger door and turned to Mia. "If I think this is going south at the gate, me and my crew are going to take over. If I tell you to drive, you step on the gas no matter what. Are we clear?"

"Sí," she whispered.

****

The cupboards and the refrigerator and freezer had been well stocked before Sophia and Henry arrived at the log cabin lodge.

Sophia sat cross-legged on the bed, wearing Henry's long-sleeve Boston Bruins T-shirt, eating mint chocolate chip ice cream from Henry's spoon.

"Mmmmm, did you tell the owners to stock mint chocolate chip?" Sophia asked incredulously. Even with everything going on when they had to leave quickly, Henry had made sure that she had her favorite ice cream. If it was possible for her to love him any more, she would right now.

"Of course. I take my job to take care of you very seriously."

Sophia opened her mouth to speak but Henry served her a large spoonful of ice cream before she could.

Sophia giggled and held her hand to her mouth. "*Para!* I'm too full."

Henry set the bowl on the nightstand and gently pushed her to a lying position as he hovered over her.

"Are you tired?" he asked, tracing his finger along her lower lip.

"No, I should be. It's the middle of the night."

"Well, to be fair, we have been napping off and on," Henry said, cheekily.

Sophia raised her hand to run them through Henry's mussed-up hair. "Sí, that must be why I'm not tired," she whispered.

Heat blazed in Henry's eyes and he lowered his head to thoroughly kiss her. He broke the kiss, however, and rolled over, bringing her close to his body.

"Even if we don't sleep, I want you to rest. You're going to be sore tomorrow as it is. Tell me what you were like as a little girl? What was your favorite thing to do?" Henry asked softly into her hair.

Sophia's heart was so full. She knew she should tell Henry about the pregnancy, but she was loath to break this spell they seemed to be under. If she was to only have a short while left with Henry, then she wanted it to be spent loving each other.

Oh, she knew they would be connected forever by this child. She had decided that if she went back to Colombia when the danger had passed, as was the original plan, she would wait to tell Henry after the baby was born. It would be too painful to have contact with Henry while she was pregnant. The heartbreak and stress wouldn't be good for her or the baby. Once the baby was born, she would introduce Henry to his son or daughter and they could work out a plan for Henry to have visitation. There was no use fighting about it before the baby was born. She had no intention of fighting, period. She would never withhold their child from him. With the issue settled in her mind, she pushed any guilt over not telling him out of her mind. She was going to embrace her time with Henry. Lock every memory away so when she was at her lowest, she could call the memories up to sustain her.

She wasn't sure exactly when she fell asleep but she thought it was somewhere in the middle of describing her seven-year-old self climbing high into a tree so she could read in peace and no one would find her. Her village had a little library, more like a small shed, with used books piled up. In that shed, she found a series of Nancy Drew mysteries. She had been hooked. She would stay up in that tree for hours.

The last thing she remembers Henry saying was, "So, my Sophia was a little bookworm.

****

Fuck me. He was so fucked. When had he fallen so hopelessly in love with this woman? Who was he kidding, it had begun the moment he saw her at the jail. Now he knew what his father was talking about. Love. It was such a small word for such an enormous emotion.

More than ever he didn't want to be parted from Sophia. But was it fair to ask her to give up her whole life for him? When she had talked about her happy childhood in Colombia, he could hear the love she had for her family, her village, her country. Would she eventually hate him for manipulating her to stay here with him? He wouldn't be able to stand that. It would gut him if he saw bitterness and resentment in her gaze. No, he would respect her decision whatever it was when this shitshow was over. He knew without a doubt that if she chose to leave, he would never be the same. He wouldn't recover from losing her. Suddenly, he remembered the bastard who had asked her to marry him and then left her alone. Jealousy burned like fire in his belly. He would never leave her alone. That guy was an idiot.

Henry caressed her face lovingly before what felt like a bucket of ice water had been dumped on him. The little angel on his shoulder reminded him that he was no better than her fiancé in Colombia; he, too, had left her alone. He had been so terrified of his feelings for her that he had been avoiding her for weeks. He would hold her at night and take what she freely gave to him in the dark of the night. And then he would run away at first light like the coward he was.

Jesus, he felt sick. He looked down at her content face. She deserved so much better than him.

Chapter 34

The big truck jerked to a stop at the gate. Rapid Spanish was exchanged with Mia's voice getting sharper as she spoke. Fuck, she was a force to be reckoned with.

The girls must have heard what Mia was saying, so to reinforce what Mia told the militants, the girls hung out the side of the canvas and waved at the men. That seemed to do the trick. As usual, the men thought with the wrong heads, with the promise of what was to come.

Soon the truck surged forward and the gate was opened to let them through.

"Shorty, take a look at that gate and see what you will need to blow it if necessary," Snake whispered.

Shorty nodded and looked out the side of the canvas as the rest of the crew also looked to take in the layout and see where exactly the guards were. Santiago had already told them, but they felt more comfortable seeing things for themselves.

Mia drove the truck around to the back of the compound. As soon as the truck stopped, Mia got out and gave the compound door a bang as she pulled the canvas back.

"*Rápido!*" she hissed, looking around.

They all hauled ass out of the truck and to the open door. Snake and the crew quickly unloaded the weapons into the building. Snake waited until everyone was inside before he waved his hand for Mia to go ahead of him.

She gave him the side-eye again. She was fucking adorable. Especially with an assault weapon hanging off her shoulder.

"Are you Mr. Snake?" a tall man asked him. It was Santiago. He looked so much like Sophia, they could be twins.

Snake nodded and held out his hand. Santiago smiled and shook his hand enthusiastically.

"Come with me. You girls can go upstairs . . .you know what to do," Santiago said and started toward the stairs that would lead to the basement.

As the girls started for the stairs, Snake grabbed Mia's elbow. "Not you. You stay with me . . . por favor."

Mia hesitated and looked down at the big paw holding her arm. She smirked and nodded. She immediately bent down to help Snake with the weapons. She was fucking amazing. She could do everything his crew could do *and* all while wearing heels and lipstick.

He was glad she had agreed. He had never had a wave of possessiveness hit him like that, ever. He most certainly didn't want any of these men laying their hands on her. Which made no fucking sense. He had only set eyes on her an hour ago, and they had hardly spoken.

They crouched down in the far corner of the dank basement as Santiago pulled out the compound schematics.

"Okay, so, we have gotten very lucky. Mateo had to leave the compound last night because of trouble with a shipment. He took most of the soldiers with him. There is just a skeleton crew. There are two at the gate and about ten inside the compound. All ten should be upstairs with the girls."

"Fuck yeah," Mac mumbled.

"When is Mateo due back?" Snake asked.

"Either late tonight or in the morning, it depends. If he found some *puta*, he won't be back until morning."

At the word *puta*, slut, Snake's hands fisted. Mia must have been watching him because the next thing he knew, her tiny hand found its way into his. It calmed him instantly.

"Shorty, you set the fuses in the compound like we talked about. Once we have the militants in the compound secured, we will then take out the guards at the gate."

"Fuck yeah, it's been too long since I've been able to play this much," Shorty said as he immediately began to gather his equipment.

"Jax and Mac, grab what you need for weapons. We're going to secure the soldiers in the compound. Santiago, take Mia some place safe until I tell you to come out."

Santiago nodded but Mia shook her head and gripped her rifle. Snake and Mia had a stare down that he knew he wasn't going to win, so he nodded once. "Stay behind me," he growled.

The crew—minus Shorty—took the stairs and quietly made their way to the large denlike room where a literal orgy was taking place. And Santiago was right, all ten soldiers were in the room, engaging with the women.

It was like shooting fish in a barrel. Jax, Mac, Mia and Snake surrounded the men with their weapons drawn. The naked men simply held their hands up in surrender.

Mia said something to one of the women and she tossed a backpack to Mia. She unzipped the bag and produced a handful of zip ties. She was fucking brilliant.

Mia and the women proceeded to tie the men's hands and feet. The women grabbed the men's weapons as if they knew exactly how to handle them. Why the fuck wasn't it advertised that the women of Colombia were badasses? He would have been on the first plane here twenty years ago . . . but he was here now. Thank Christ.

The men hauled the bound, naked soldiers into a back room. Shorty crossed the room to set more fuses in other parts of the compound.

"Shorty, make sure there aren't any detonations near the back of this room. Those soldiers are just following orders—no reason to blow them up," Snake said, jerking his head in the direction of the back of the compound.

Shorty never faltered in his steps as he continued in concentration. "Already taken care of, bud."

"Jax and Mac, you take the truck to get to the gate and take the two guards down. Zip-tie them and put them in the truck and unload them in the same room."

Mia held up her hand and spoke in rapid Spanish. Snake looked to Santiago to translate.

"She says she needs to drive the truck or the guards will get suspicious. We can't take the chance that one of the guards calls Mateo to warn him."

Snake was silent for a moment before nodding. She had a point. But he was loath to put her in danger.

"Fine, Mia, you drive, Jax, come with me."

They headed to the truck. Snake opened the driver's side door but before Mia climbed up, he held her elbow.

"If things go sideways, you just drive through the gate and keep going," he said, using his hands like he was driving and then chopped one hand down the middle. "Do you understand?"

Mia grinned and nodded.

Snake and Jax hung on to the back of the truck.

What Snake didn't count on was Mia stopping at the gate and getting out of the truck to stand in front of the truck grill. She motioned to the two guards and pulled her minidress higher.

Fuck. What was she doing?

The two guards walked to her and began to touch her ass and breasts. She was a fucking genius. She had managed to completely distract the guards and pull them away from any phones or alarms. Also, making them easy prey as Snake and Jax came around the truck and held their guns to the back of their heads.

The guards surrendered immediately. Snake and Jax zip-tied them and put them in the truck. Mia jumped back in the truck and drove to the back of the compound once again. The compound was secure. All they had to do was wait for Mateo and the rest of the army to show up.

When they all met in the den, Mia clapped her hands together and spoke to the women who came with her. Two of them got up and began to strip.

Snake and his crew stared for a minute before Snake muttered for them to turn around to give the women privacy.

After about five minutes, the two women walked to stand in front of them, wearing uniforms from the naked soldiers. Their hair was tucked under their hats, which were drawn down low on their faces. All traces of makeup were gone. Unless you knew they were women, it would be impossible to tell.

Mia pointed to the two women. "Gate," she said.

Realization dawned on the crew. If these two women were at the gate and opened it when Mateo returned, Mateo and his soldiers would be taken completely off guard.

"That's fucking awesome," Jax said, smiling.

The two women smiled back and slung assault rifles over their shoulders and walked out the front door.

"You boys keep watch. I've got to go over some things with Santiago," Snake said, motioning for Santiago to take him somewhere private.

Santiago nodded and led Snake to his makeshift office. It was a bare room with a laptop and a cot.

"So, here's the deal. Henry has made a deal for you and Sophia with the Feds. But, to fulfill that deal, you must turn yourself over to them and give them everything you have on Mateo. Everything. They want training facilities, drug warehouses, bank accounts, everything. And just so we're clear, if you don't go willingly, I'm gonna kill you along with Mateo. You have caused your sister enough grief. It ends here. It's time you man up and take care of her."

Santiago swallowed hard and nodded. "I would do anything for Sophia. You didn't have to threaten to kill me."

"It wasn't a threat."

Santiago smiled. Snake smiled.

"My sister cares for you a great deal, Mr. Snake. I can see why. There are some things I would like to run by you."

Snake leaned up against the wall and crossed his arms. "Shoot."

****

Sophia tried to brush whatever was on her face away. She tried again before opening her eyes quickly, suddenly wide awake.

Henry sat on the edge of the bed smiling. It was still dark in the room, but the hall light filtered into the bedroom.

"Is something wrong?" she asked fearfully.

Henry cupped her cheek. "No, no, I'm sorry, I didn't mean to scare you. I wanted to gently wake you up. I want to take you somewhere."

Sophia looked confused but smiled all the same. "Where? And how can I be expected to go anywhere without coffee? Strong coffee."

Henry smiled as he took her hands and helped her out of the bed. "Come on, Sleeping Beauty, time's a wastin'. Your coffee is made, strong, just how I know you like it. Dress warm; it's cold outside."

Sophia stood in the middle of the room as Henry went back to the kitchen. She was in a fog and a little nauseous. Her morning sickness hadn't been too bad so far. Most mornings it was just a little nausea, which seemed to pass by midmorning.

She fumbled with the clothes in the open suitcase until she found a pair of jeans and a cream-colored fisherman's sweater. She washed her face and brushed her teeth before carrying her thick wool socks to the kitchen.

She had forgotten to comb her hair, so it stayed wild and rumpled around her shoulders.

Henry lifted her onto the counter and took the socks from her hand. He replaced the socks with a travel mug of hot coffee and then he proceeded to put her socks on for her.

Tears stung her eyes. He was so sweet. She loved him so much.

When he finished, he looked up and saw her tears.

"Hey, are you sad you had to get up so early?" he asked, kissing her gently.

She giggled and shook her head. "No, I just think you're sweet."

Henry smiled and rubbed his hands together. "My plan is working perfectly," he said and gave an evil laugh.

All bundled up, they made their way to the old battered Jeep in the garage. Henry had started it, but it was still cold.

"Are you going to tell me where we're going?" she asked.

"*We* are going heater hunting," he said very smugly.

"What is heater hunting? Henry, I would never kill an animal," she said, horrified.

Henry shifted the tall stick and smiled over at her. "That's the beauty of heater hunting. We stay in the confines of this not-very-warm Jeep while we look for animals. We drink our coffee and eat some donuts as we romp along the old tote roads."

"What's a tote road?"

"A tote road is a kinda cross between a road and a path. The logging companies up north here have to get the felled trees out of the woods, so they just drive their skidders into the woods and haul the trees out, which makes a rough sort of road. We can travel for days on old tote roads through the thickest part of the woods. Which is where the animals are. And, if we're very lucky, we'll get stuck in the mudholes. But don't worry—I've got four-wheel drive and cables and chains. We're golden."

Sophia smiled and sipped her coffee. His excitement was contagious. She couldn't think of a single place she would rather be than right here, heater hunting with Henry.

Henry pulled out a box of chocolate sugared donuts and waggled his eyebrows.

Sophia took one, nibbled on it, and drank her coffee. The sun was just starting to come up.

She was glad she finished her coffee and donut when she did because before too long, the Jeep began to bump and tip so much from the huge potholes in the road that Sophia had a hard time staying in her seat, even though she was buckled up.

At certain points, she was laughing so hard, tears rolled down her face.

As they rounded a corner, Henry slammed on the brakes. A huge female moose with her calf stood in the road.

Sophia gasped. They were so big and majestic. They watched the mother moose and her calf stare at them for a while before meandering into the woods.

"They are so beautiful," Sophia whispered.

"Yeah, and they're good eating too. Mainers eat a lot of moose and deer. Does shooting animals bother you?"

Sophia shook her head. "No, I used to kill our own chickens and pluck them. I just don't like unnecessary killing of animals. I would be sad if the mother or baby were shot."

"Yeah, I agree. Me and my brothers stick to bull moose and bucks. It's kind of a challenge who can bag the biggest buck in any given year."

Henry unbuckled his seat belt, leaned over, and kissed Sophia, softly at first, and then the passion zinged off every part of her. She slid her tongue into his mouth, and he groaned.

He unbuckled her seat belt and hauled her onto his lap so she was straddling him. Sophia dug her fingers into his soft hair and kissed him like she would never see him again.

Henry broke the kiss and cupped her face. "Hey, is everything all right?"

No! I'm not all right. I feel like you will be ripped away from me at any second, she wanted to scream.

"I want you," she said shyly.

Henry took a gulp of air and began to kiss her feverishly. His hands ghosted up her sweater until his thumbs were teasing her swollen buds.

Sophia could feel his hardness through her jeans. She began to move her core over his hardness. The friction was delicious. She was moaning and biting his lower lip.

Henry gripped her hips and ground her against him, making her see stars.

"Henry . . ." she gasped.

Henry unbuttoned her jeans and slid the zipper down. He found the tiny treasure that held all her nerve endings, and he began to stroke slowly.

Sophia gasped. "Henry . . . I need . . ."

"Shhh, I've got you, Soph, I didn't bring any condoms. Take what you need. Grind on me, baby. I want to watch you come apart."

That was all the permission she needed as she grasped his shoulders and began to slide and grind on his hard length. He continued to stroke and flick at her bundle of nerves.

Sophia cried out.

"Come for me, Sophia. I want to feel your wetness."

That was all it took for Sophia to bow her back and let the orgasm take over.

She rested her head on his shoulder as she tried to get her breath back.

Henry pulled his hands from her jeans and put his thumb in his mouth. He moaned as if in pain.

"Jesus, you taste good. I'm going to fuck you hard when we get back to the cabin, Soph."

Sophia lifted her head and gazed at him. She could see the desire all over his face.

"I could . . . I could suck on you?" she offered.

"Oh, my fucking word. I'm going to come in my pants just from you saying that sentence," he said and shook his head. "No, there's not enough room in this Jeep for you to be comfortable. But I like the way you think," he said with a wink. "Does it bother you when I'm crude and say things like *I'm going to fuck you hard?*"

She could feel her face heat up. "No, it shocks me, but I think that's why I like it. It makes me want you more."

Henry leaned his head back and looked at her for a long moment. "You couldn't be any more perfect."

He buttoned and zipped her jeans back up and set her back in the seat. He buckled her back up and nuzzled her ear.

"I *am* going to fuck you hard when we get back to the cabin."

And just like that, she was a molten mass of need again. The question that ran through her mind on repeat these days was front and center in her mind. But, instead of asking herself if it was normal to want Henry as much as she did, this time her subconscious asked if it was normal to *need* Henry as much as she did. It was becoming an all-consuming need and she had a terrible feeling that it was going to end with her heart shattered into a million pieces. Never able to be put back together.

Chapter 35

Santiago had some mad skills on the computer, for sure. He also had some interesting thoughts on how to wrap up Mateo's empire for the Feds.

Once they had wrapped up their business, Snake went back to the den with Santiago following behind.

"All right, we wait. The ladies at the gate have walkie-talkies and will notify us when they see them coming and just open the gate. Be ready when that call comes. You can rest, but stay ready."

The crew sank down into the couches and chairs followed by the girls curling up against the guys.

Mia took Snake's hand and pulled him toward a room off the den. It was a room with a bed. That was it. No blankets, just a red satin fitted sheet and no pillows. There were, however, handcuffs hanging from the bedposts.

Snake scowled.

Mia shut the door and set her assault rifle against the wall. She walked to Snake and began to kneel in front of him.

Oh hell no. There was no way he was going to let that happen. Not because he didn't want to fuck her more than he wanted to breathe. Literally. But because he wanted to be different than all the motherfuckers who'd come before him, he wasn't going to touch her until he was sure she wanted him and not because she felt like she owed him or some stupid shit like that.

Snake pulled her up to standing and cupped her face. "You don't get on your knees for anyone, Mia. You're a goddamn queen."

"You don't want me?" she asked in broken English.

"Sweetheart, I want you so bad my balls are blue. But I want our first time to be special. Not some shithole where you've been treated like shit your whole life. Do you understand that?"

Mia smiled and her whole face lit up. She nodded. "Special," she repeated.

Snake nodded. "And, my name isn't Snake; it's Jake Whitehall. You can call me Jake."

"Jake," she repeated.

Snake crawled onto the bed and held out his hand for her. She took it and snuggled into him like she was fucking made for him.

He gently caressed her arm. "Would you like to come back to the States with me when this is over?" he asked, not knowing if she understood him.

"How can you take me with you?" she asked with a thick accent.

Snake smiled. "Do you want to come with me?"

Mia nodded instantly.

Snake let out his breath. He hadn't been aware he was holding his breath until she answered him. "Well there's this fucking amazing attorney who owes me a huge favor . . ."

****

Not ten minutes later, all hell broke loose. Jax was hollering to Snake to get his ass in there.

Snake jumped up and grabbed his gun. He turned to Mia. "Please stay with me, okay?"

Mia nodded. They ran from the room and everybody grabbed their weapons and extra ammunition. Even the ladies grabbed guns.

"Shorty, can you blow their vehicles once they're safely past the gate?"

Shorty was standing at the window with a makeshift control panel. "Already on it, Snake."

The gate was opened and three Suburbans entered. As the last Suburban pulled away from the gate, Shorty flipped a switch and the second Suburban exploded, sending metal scraps flying everywhere.

The other two Suburbans stopped and the men got out and stayed behind the vehicles.

"Head count?" Snake hollered.

"Sixteen soldiers," Jax hollered.

A rain of bullets commenced from both inside the compound and outside behind the vehicles.

****

At least two hours passed, and it was clear that this would go on until they all ran out of bullets. And Snake had no patience for that shit.

"Jax, get Betty!" Snake hollered to his friend at the next window.

"Fuck yeah," Mac hollered as he slid another sleeve of bullets into his assault weapon.

Jax crawled on the floor until he retrieved the rocket launcher affectionately named Big Betty.

"Cover me, now!" Jax hollered as he stood.

All those in the compound sprayed bullets all over the Suburbans so Jax could fire the rocket. A big *whoosh* sounded and one of the two Suburbans exploded.

A bullet caught Jax in the right leg and he went down.

Snake got down and crawled to Jax and began to pull him out of the room. Santiago was just outside the den and he helped Snake get Jax standing.

Snake hollered to the rest of them to come to him. They all crawled to him and stood just outside the room. Mia, who, true to her word had been his shadow, stood beside him.

"I want you all to get the fuck out of here. I'll catch up. Get in the fucking truck and drive and don't stop until you get to the fucking jet. Am I clear?"

"Not fucking happening, Snake," Mac said.

"This is not a fucking request. I need you to save everybody here. Shorty, when you get in the truck, set the fuses. Do as I fucking say or I will kill you motherfuckers myself when this is done."

There must have been something in his voice to let his crew know that he wasn't fucking around.

Mia shook her head. "I'm staying with you, Jake."

His crew looked at one another. No one had ever called him by his first name, ever.

Snake shook his head. "No, Mia, I'll catch up. Mac, get her in that truck."

In one swift move, Mac had taken her gun and tossed it to Shorty, picking Mia up and putting her over his shoulder. And as he did so, her leopard-print minidress hiked up over her perfect ass to reveal a black lace thong.

Snake scowled but turned back as the front door was kicked in and bullets peppered the interior.

Snake heard the truck barreling around the building. He breathed a little easier for about a second. The bullets kept coming and Snake only had a short amount of time to make it to the roof.

He sprayed bullets of his own and took down three of the four men shooting at him. One man left. He couldn't immediately see where the man was, so he just barrel-assed it to the stairs.

Bullets flew in his direction until they stopped. The fucker was out of ammo. Snake said a quick thank you to the Big Guy and continued up the stairs. He was on the second floor and almost to the rooftop stairs when a knife lodged itself in the back of his thigh and he went down.

Motherfucker!

Snake reached behind him and pulled the knife out of his leg with a loud curse.

That's when he saw Mateo Sanchez standing there with murder in his eyes.

"Who the fuck are you, besides a dead man?" Mateo spat.

"I'm your worst fucking nightmare, asshole. I'm a friend of Sophia Rodriguez Johnson. And you are not going to walk out of here alive."

Mateo looked surprised at the mention of Sophia.

"You are the man who took her away from me. No, amigo, I'm going to kill you with my bare hands," he said, tossing his black tank top over his head.

Snake smiled and hauled his black T-shirt over his head. There was a flicker of fear that ghosted over Mateo's face as he realized just how big Snake was. And the sight of his massive chest and back covered in military and biker tattoos might have been a little intimidating, as well.

But Mateo shook it off and leered at him with murderous contempt. He swung the first punch, which landed squarely in Snake's big hand.

"I don't have time for this chest-beating bullshit," he muttered and put all the force he had into headbutting Mateo square in the face. Snake heard Mateo's nose crunch as it drove into his brain. Mateo fell to the ground, dead.

Snake knocked on his head. "My fucking superpower, asshole. And that's also for Sophia and Mia. I hope you rot in hell."

Snake began to run to the rooftop stairs as he fished the helicopter keys that Santiago had given him out of his pocket.

He made it to Mateo's helicopter and turned the key. Nothing. No fucking way.

He looked down and flipped the safety switch and the engine roared to life.

Snake could feel the building begin to rumble as he started to lift off. As he rose higher in the air, he saw the building begin to light up in sections as strategically placed explosives detonated. Hopefully the one pocket of the compound would remain intact. He had some mercy, but, in reality, those soldiers had probably been as bad as Mateo. So, he'd let the good Lord decide if He wanted them spared.

Snake smiled. He was going to make it to the jet well before the others. He pulled out his phone and dialed Brownie, the pilot, to get ready for them. He told him he had a man injured.

"Roger that. I'll get the first aid ready," Brownie said with authority.

Snake sighed. He began to think of all the ways he was going to spoil Mia. He couldn't have wiped the fucking stupid grin off his face if he tried.

****

It was still dark in the room, but Sophia was awake and smiling. She was cocooned within the warmth of Henry's strong arms and the homemade quilt that made up the bedding in the rustic cabin.

She was smiling because she was remembering the day before that was spent in bed making love. And when they weren't making love or napping, they were having a dance party to the records Henry had found. They danced to Dion's "The Wanderer" and "Runaround Sue."

She had made a beef stew and homemade bread, which was satisfying on a cold fall day. She couldn't remember a time in her life when she has been as blissfully happy and content.

The smile was gone seconds later when the whir of helicopter blades sounded in the distance and became increasingly louder until Sophia was certain the helicopter was going to land on the cabin.

She shook Henry.

"Henry, wake up. I think the helicopter is here for us?"

Henry jerked awake and squeezed her closer to him.

After a moment, he kissed her hair and threw back the covers. He grabbed his jeans and his flannel shirt and went to answer the knock that had just sounded at the front door.

He turned to her before he left the room. "Stay here until I'm sure it's safe."

Sophia pulled her knees to her chest and waited.

She heard voices and then Henry reappeared in the doorway.

"It's the same pilot who brought us here. It's time to go home."

Home. A word that should have made Sophia joyous, but instead she felt sick to her stomach. She had a feeling that home meant Colombia and no Henry. But what if she told Henry she loved him and that they were going to have a baby? Would he demand she stay with him? Did she want to manipulate him into staying married to her? No, she loved Henry too much to do that to him. If he wanted his old life back, she wouldn't beg him to let her stay. Even though that's exactly what she felt like doing. She was shameless when it came to Henry.

Henry put the suitcase on the bed and began to throw their things in it. She picked up items of clothing that had been discarded in a haste to get naked over the last few days.

They both used the bathroom to brush their teeth before giving the room a onceover to make sure they hadn't missed anything.

As they boarded the helicopter, there was a heavy silence that hung between them. Neither wanted to go back to reality, it seemed.

Henry picked up her hand and kissed her knuckles. She had to look out the window so he didn't see the sheen of tears that clouded her eyes.

The trip didn't last long, and before they knew it, they were landing in front of the camp in the very same spot where they had boarded four short days ago.

The camp door opened and three people came jogging out.

Santiago!

Sophia ran to her brother and jumped into his arms. She was overwhelmed by tears of relief that he was safe.

They both just held on to each other and cried until finally Sophia pulled back and cupped his handsome face. The face that looked so much like her own.

"How?" she whispered.

Santiago smiled and nodded his head to the side.

"Mr. Snake saved me. It's over, Sophia. Mateo is dead. He can never hurt us again."

Sophia was speechless as the tears continued to fall.

She stepped to Snake and held up her hands. He had to lean down so she could touch his face. "Thank you, my friend," she said in a thick Spanish accent. "How can I ever repay your kindness?"

Snake had tears in his own eyes as he shook his head. "No thanks necessary, and you can repay me by being happy."

Sophia nodded and hugged him, and when she did, she whispered in Snake's ear, "I haven't told him yet, but I will."

Snake stood back up, looked at her solemnly, and nodded once.

Sophia's eyes shifted to the third person in the group. A beautiful petite woman standing close to Snake.

She looked back at Snake. Snake smiled broadly.

"Sophia, I'd like you to meet Mia."

Sophia could see the love in Snake's eyes and it was wondrous. She smiled and walked to the woman and hugged her tight.

Mia looked surprised but hugged her back.

Sophia pulled back and began to speak rapid Spanish to which Mia rapidly responded. This went on for several minutes as Sophia thanked Mia for helping to save her brother and that she would have a friend in Sophia forever.

The men just stood there gawking at the women speaking animatedly. Santiago just grinned.

Sophia realized that Mia was outside in the cold with just her leopard minidress, thigh-high boots, and Snake's leather vest.

She took Mia's hand and led her into the camp, telling her she would get her some warm clothes.

The men just watched them walk away. All seemed deep in their own thoughts.

****

Once they had all taken showers and dressed, they met in the kitchen. Sophia had started making pancakes and eggs.

Henry clapped his hands together. "Okay. So here's what I suggest. We have breakfast and then debrief and answer any questions."

Snake nodded. "Sounds good. Mia and I will be heading out at first light. We're going to meet up with the crew in Florida," he said, pulling Mia close and kissing the top of her head.

They ate and talked. Henry told Sophia about the deal he had made with the Feds, but it hinged on Santiago being delivered, so to speak, to the Feds.

"But he's not a prisoner, is he?" Sophia asked.

Henry shook his head as he took a sip of coffee. "No, he will be under the government's protection while he deconstructs Mateo's operation. He will be given a permanent visa, and when his work with the Feds is complete, he can do whatever he wants."

"And what about the favor I asked you about?" Snake asked quietly.

Henry sat back and clasped his hands. He steepled his index fingers and pointed to Snake. "Mia has a permanent visa as well. You can pick it up at the immigration office in Miami."

Snake chuckled. "My man. You are one connected motherfucker."

Henry grinned and nodded.

"All charges will be officially dropped tomorrow," Henry said, turning to Sophia.

"Thank you, Henry. You saved my and my brother's life."

Henry picked up Sophia's hand and kissed it, but he didn't say anything. A haunted look crossed his face for the briefest of moments.

Snake stood up. "Okay, the guys will clean up, and then I'm going to walk Mia down to the pond."

Sophia turned to Mia. "How about we make a celebration meal tonight? A real Colombian feast?"

Mia smiled and nodded and threw out some suggestions. Sophia grabbed a paper and pen to write down ingredients she would get at the market.

Sophia, Henry, and Santiago watched out the window as Snake and Mia walked hand in hand down the gravel road leading to the pond.

It was quiet until Santiago said he had work to do on his laptop and Henry agreed that he, too, had a million emails to send.

Sophia stood alone at the window looking out at the red leaves of the maple tree with her hand on her belly. She needed to talk to Henry. Tomorrow. She would sit down with Henry tomorrow and tell him everything that was in her heart.

It wasn't nervous butterflies in her belly; it was angry condors that were whipping their massive wings in her gut, making her want to be sick. Tomorrow. She would lay her soul bare tomorrow, she thought, squaring her shoulders in determination.

****

Sophia and Mia spent the late afternoon cooking the special feast. They shooed everyone out of the kitchen who tried to sneak a peek at what they were cooking.

Santiago just grinned because he could smell it and knew exactly what they were having for dinner, but he wouldn't tell Henry or Snake.

Mia told Sophia about her childhood and being brought to Mateo to be his *puta*. She whispered this part so Snake wouldn't hear.

"You know he used to call me Sophia sometimes," Mia said softly without meeting Sophia's eyes.

"Mateo?"

Mia nodded.

Sophia wiped her hands on her apron and gently held Mia's shoulders. "I'm sorry you have suffered so greatly, Mia. Do you believe in Dios?"

Mia's eyes got wide and she nodded. "Sí, sí."

"Do you believe Dios sent Snake to rescue you and give you a new life?"

Tears welled up in Mia's eyes. She nodded again. "I do believe Dios sent Jake to me. I don't regret anything I have gone through if at the end, I am able to be with Jake."

Sophia smiled through her own tears. "Oh, Mia, Dios has given you a new life. Don't waste a second of it. You deserve all the happiness in the world," she said, hugging Mia tightly.

With the meal on the table, everyone sat down. Sophia asked everyone to join hands while she said grace. Everyone shut their eyes and bowed their heads except Henry. He held hands but—unbeknownst to Sophia—refused to give thanks to God.

"Okay, so we have a special Colombian dish tonight. It's called Lechona and it's delicious. A pork loin stuffed with rice, peas and spices served with *pandebono*, which is cheese bread. Henry, if you would pour the red wine, we can dig in."

Groans were heard around the table as they feasted. Henry and Snake were almost over the top with their praises for the meal.

As they finished their wine, Santiago cleared his throat.

"I would like to thank Mr. Snake and Henry for rescuing me, but mostly I want to thank my big sister for always taking care of me. I love you, Sophia. I know I haven't made life easy for you while I was growing up, but all that changes now. I'm going to take care of you."

Tears leaked from Sophia's eyes. She was so emotional these days. She raised her glass, as did everyone.

"I love you too, Santiago," she said as they all clinked glasses.

"There is one more thing—well, two, actually. First, the Feds are picking me up in the morning and second, as part of deconstructing the cartel's empire, I moved some money around before the Feds even knew it was out there. I have put one million dollars in each of the Four Horsemen's bank accounts . . ."

"Santiago! You can't start your new life being dishonest," Sophia admonished.

Santiago held up his hand. "Sophia, the wealth Mateo accumulated was obscene. It is blood money. The US Government doesn't have any need for that money, but the men who put their lives on the line to bring that cartel down do deserve compensation."

Sophia nodded in acquiescence.

Snake laughed. "My crew went into this knowing this was personal for me. They didn't expect to get paid, say nothing of getting set up for life. Thank you, my friend, and you may call me Jake," Snake raised his glass to Santiago.

Santiago grinned. "I also set aside a million dollars for you, Sophia," he said softly. "You have worked so hard your whole life to take care of me. I wanted to pay you back."

Sophia gasped. "No, Santiago. I won't accept any money for myself, but it would be put to good use if you gave it to the local schools in Colombia."

Santiago laughed and clapped his hands. "See, Snake . . . Jake, I told you that's what she would say! That is exactly what I have done. The school in our village and many others will never have to scrimp to get by again."

"That's wonderful, Santiago. Thank you," she said, wiping away the stray tears.

Henry went to the closet in the kitchen and pulled out an old record player and a stack of LPs. He flipped through them until he held up a Dion record. He started the music, and, as the classic tune, began to play, Henry looked deeply into Sophia's eyes.

****

They all cleaned the kitchen and danced until it was dark and the wine was gone. Snake took Mia's hand and they hugged everybody and told them they would keep in touch. Snake walked Mia to a back bedroom and closed the door.

Santiago said he was also going to bed, but Sophia followed him to his room. They sat on the bed. Sophia took her brother's hands in her own.

"Are you really okay with making a deal with the government?" Sophia asked.

Santiago smiled. "Sí. Because of you putting me through college, I have my computer degree and now a visa and a chance at a new life in America. I will work with the Feds for as long as they'll have me. I've seen firsthand how the drug cartels destroy lives. I am in a position now to give back. I will make you proud."

Sophia cupped his cheek. "I've always been proud of you, *mi amor*."

Santiago clasped her tiny hands in his. "What's wrong, Sophia? I see pain in your eyes. Tell me."

All of Sophia's walls came tumbling down. She collapsed into herself, covered her face, and sobbed.

Santiago held her until her sobs subsided a little.

"You love him," he said.

"Sí, sí. I love him with all my heart."

"John will understand, Sophia."

Sophia smiled and nodded through her tears.

****

Henry walked away from the door that stood ajar. The room that Henry had just heard Sophia crying and telling her brother that she loved her fiancé in Colombia with all her heart. And he'd heard Santiago tell his sister that saintly fucking John would understand what she had to do to save him.

Well, it seemed he had his answer. In his gut he had known all along that she was too good for him. For all his charisma, contacts, money, and smart-assed mouth, none of it could help him now. The woman he loved was in love with another man. Had been engaged to, in fact, before Henry had steamrolled into her life.

He could say he wanted to save her from prison, but he knew what his real motive had always been: he loved her and recognized her goodness instantly. And he made sure he got her. But that didn't do him a fucking bit of good now. The stone-cold truth was she loved another. Period.

His heart was thrashing in his chest. He needed to get away from here, now. He grabbed his jacket and scribbled a note on the counter that he needed to take care of something at work.

He fired up the old camp truck and sped away into the night. He didn't even stop to check the tears that fell from his eyes. He hadn't shed a tear since the day his mother died. He punched the roof of the truck where every Johnson boy had at one time or another lost their temper and taken out their anger as witnessed by the ripples in the truck roof.

As he rolled down the interstate to Portland, he had a steady mantra of how stupid he had been to fall in love. Especially after seeing his father slowly die of heartbreak after losing Henry's mother. No, love was certainly not worth all the pain.

But, even knowing all that, he still couldn't get the sight of Sophia—lying under him, Sophia dancing in her wool socks, Sophia slinging lunch orders at the diner, Sophia with her eyes shut thanking God for all their blessings—out of his mind. And, to be truthful, he didn't want to. He wanted to hold on to those memories.

The little angel on his shoulder nodded sadly. *Fuck me.*

Chapter 36

Sophia sat on her bed and stared at the hastily scribbled note. Why didn't he come find her and tell her? Why leave a note? Maybe he didn't want to disturb her and Santiago's conversation?

Even if he hadn't wanted to interrupt her and her brother, why wasn't he answering his phone or responding to her texts?

It had been four hours and she was worried about him. It was after midnight. She would text him one more time before calling Marcus. He lived in Portland, and as head of the family, he would know how to find Henry. She just wanted to make sure he was okay.

She sent a text and stared at the screen.

Please, Henry, I'm worried about you. Please let me know you're okay.

****

She wasn't sure how much time passed. Ten minutes, twenty, before his return text appeared in front of her.

I'm fine, Sophia. Maybe you should think about returning to Colombia. We both need to get back to our lives. I wish you well.

Sophia stared at the text. Her worst nightmare had come true. Henry didn't love her. He had told her he didn't believe in love. He had stood by her until she was safe and all charges were dropped. He would always be her hero. But he didn't love her and never would.

She lay back and rubbed her belly. Even if he didn't love her, she knew he would love their child. Once the baby was born, she would contact him and set up visitation or whatever people do who share a child. At least her baby would have his love. Of that she was certain.

****

Two days later, she had made all her travel plans and said goodbye to all her friends in Harmony. She dressed warmly in her wool skirt, sweater, and leather boots. She had the small backpack that she had come to the States with on that fateful night she was arrested. It seemed like a lifetime ago.

She zipped her coat up and set her car keys on the counter along with a short note to Henry, telling him how grateful she was for everything he had done for her. She set the cell phone he had gotten her beside the keys and note.

She shut the lights out and closed the camp door. She would always think of this place as home. Actually, she would always think of Henry as her home.

Taking a deep breath, she proceeded to walk to the diner. The walk was just what she needed. It was cold. The customers in the diner said that snow was in the air. They could smell it. She wished she could have stayed until it snowed. She'd never seen snow before.

She smiled as she thought about her baby someday making snowmen and going sledding. She patted her stomach. Yes, her *bebé* was going to have a wonderful life.

The bell chimed as she entered the diner. Sophia stood still in the doorway as she saw all the people she had come to call friends standing there waiting for her.

There was Gracie, Sam, Blue, Lilly, Garrett, Bobby, Ava, Dana, Doug, Officer Josh Lancaster, Chief Keister, and many more whom she had come to know at the diner. They had all come to say goodbye to her.

She thought she had cried all the tears she had in her, but she was wrong. Her heart broke to be leaving this wonderful town and its inhabitants.

When the goodbyes had been said, Doug turned to her and asked her if she was ready.

She nodded. "Sí."

Doug drove her to the Portland International Jetport and, on the way, Sophia told him about her friend Magdalene who was going to be getting out of jail in two days' time. She told Doug that if he gave Magdalene her old job, they wouldn't be sorry.

He told her that if Sophia was vouching for her then of course they would be happy to hire her. Sophia smiled and told him she had gone to see Maggie and given her his and Dana's names and the diner's address. She thanked him for his kindness.

Doug looked at her for a moment. "That's what friends do, Sophia. Dana and I are sure sorry to see you go. I hope you will keep in contact. Baby Tessa is changing every day."

Sophia tried hard to keep herself together. "Sí, I will keep in contact."

The plane rose higher and higher into the air, taking her away from all that she loved. She took out a pad of paper and started making a list of all the things she needed to do when she got back to Colombia. The first on the list was to find an ob-gyn.

****

Henry sat at the piano, pathetically playing the Bryan Adams song "(Everything I Do) I Do It for You" when the camp door opened and every single one of his fucking siblings walked in and sat down. *Fuck me.*

It had been six months since he'd had the difficult conversation with Marcus.

"You can't fucking quit, Henry; you're part owner and a board member."

"I quit as head of the corporate legal department and I am on an extended sabbatical from ownership and board meetings. I give you my proxy for any decisions."

Marcus sighed. "Fine, the legal department will muddle through until you want to come back, but what are you going to do with yourself?"

"I'm going to find myself in Harmony," he sneered.

"So, you're going to camp to drink yourself to death," Marcus said, striding out of Henry's office. He turned around at the door. "Just be prepared for every one of your siblings calling you at all hours of the day and night to check up on you. Be nice to your baby sister when she calls or you'll have me to deal with."

Why the fuck did our parents have to have so many goddamn children?

Henry smiled as he bowed because he knew it would piss Marcus off. "I will be all sweetness and light when conversing with Jack. All twenty times a day."

Marcus glared at him. "See that you are."

As they stood before him now, his siblings stared at him silently as he finished the chorus and then slammed the lid down over the keys. He rested his forearms on the top of the piano.

"So . . . which one of you little bastards sounded the SOS?" he asked, staring at each of his siblings.

"It was me," a very pregnant Lilly said as she sat on Garrett's lap.

"Oh, so there is a traitor in my midst. I thought you wanted me to become your law partner."

"I am not a traitor, Henry. And, yes, of course, I want you to become my law partner. I'm just worried about you."

Garrett rubbed her burgeoning belly. "And we think it's about time you got your head out of your ass," Garrett said, grinning.

Henry tried to hide the smile. It had been less than two years since he had fought, literally, with Garrett and told *him* to get his head out of his ass.

"Touché," Henry said with a nod.

Henry's eyes landed on Caleb and he furrowed his brow. "What the fuck is wrong with you? You look like shit."

Caleb scowled back at him. Very unlike charismatic Caleb. "Bite me. We're not here for me . . . we're here for you."

Marcus stood up and tossed a large envelope on the piano. Henry saw the return address was in Colombia. He just stared at it like it was a bomb. It kinda was.

Minutes ticked by with no one moving or speaking.

"Jesus Christ," Henry said, grabbing the envelope and ripping it open. He took the papers out and began to read.

"Goddamn it!" Henry exclaimed.

Lilly grabbed the papers from his hands. When had she even moved to sit beside him on the piano bench?

"You served Sophia with divorce papers?" she asked with an accusatory tone.

Henry's guts twisted.

"And you offered her a million dollars in marital compensation?" she said way too loudly. She was sitting right beside him.

"Yeah, well, as you can see, she crossed that part out," Henry growled.

Lilly nodded. "Yes, and she initialed it and wrote in: *The Plaintiff petitions this court to allow the parties to leave the marriage with exactly what they brought into it.*"

"I can fucking read. I just wanted to make sure she was well taken care of. So she didn't have to work so hard," he said defensively.

Lilly laid a hand on Henry's arm. He almost flinched with guilt at snapping at her.

"Henry, Sophia doesn't care about money and she loves to teach. It's not just a job to her." Lilly wrinkled her nose. "You stink. What is it about you Johnson men that when your heart gets broken you feel like you don't have to bathe?" she said, walking back to Garrett's lap.

Everyone in the room was grinning—except Henry.

"So noted, Attorney Johnson," Henry said sarcastically.

Lilly nodded. "I also would like to point out that she signed her name as Sophia Johnson. Why do you suppose she would want to keep your last name?"

Henry stared at the signature.

"It doesn't matter, she's probably planning her real wedding as we speak," he said, tossing the papers on the piano.

"Nope, I have it on very good authority that there is going to be no wedding," Bear said smugly.

"How the fuck could you possibly know that?" Henry growled.

Bear clasped his hands together and held them out in front of him, cracking his knuckles. "Well it wasn't friggin' easy, bub. But I leaned on my government contacts until I got Santiago Rodriguez's cell phone number. He wouldn't tell me shit about his sister and I can't say that I blame him. I wouldn't give out any information about Jack . . ."

"AND?" Henry hollered, clearly out of patience.

"But he did say that Sophia was absolutely not going to marry that dickwad named John Williams. You're fucking welcome," Bear said, looking very satisfied with himself.

"But why?" Henry whispered.

"Maybe because she loves you, you big dummy?" Jack said, mimicking her five-year-olds.

Henry shook his head. "No, I heard Sophia tell her brother she loved John Williams with all her heart. And I heard Santiago tell her that John would understand what she'd had to do."

"Are you sure she was talking about this fiancé in Colombia?" Teddy asked.

Henry was silent. Hope began to swell in his gut. Could he have misheard the conversation? Dare he hope that she loved him?

He looked up at his siblings. "I'm scared. I don't think I can recover if she turns me down," he said so softly his siblings had to lean forward to hear him.

"That's how you know it's real, brother. If it doesn't terrify the fuck out of you, then it doesn't mean shit," Marcus said quietly. "I wouldn't survive if Zena was taken from me."

Jack sighed. "Can we all as a family just agree to give Daddy a full pass on any weakness we imagined him to have after Momma died?"

"There was no weakness in him. He was the strongest motherfucker on the planet to get up every damn day and continue to breathe and raise ten fucking kids in the midst of his devastating grief," Bear said with tears in his eyes.

"So, Henry, stop being a pussy and go fight for her. Daddy didn't raise cowards," Ty instructed quietly.

Henry jumped up, toppling the piano bench. He pulled his phone out of his jeans pocket to call the jet.

****

"The jet is waiting for you at the Portland Jetport, bro," Garrett said.

Jack plunked down a suitcase. "You're all packed. You can shave and shower on the jet."

221

Henry grabbed his suitcase and jacket as a police cruiser squealed to a halt in the driveway.

He opened the door to Officer Josh Lancaster standing there.

"I hear you need to get to the airport ASAP?"

Officer Lancaster grabbed Henry's suitcase and tossed it in the trunk. Henry looked shell-shocked but got in the passenger seat.

A voice from the back piped up. "It's about damn time you got your head out of your ass," Magdalene said.

"Yeah, that's what I'm told," Henry said.

Henry looked back at Maggie with furrowed brows. Not only had Henry been her attorney, but he'd also gotten to know Maggie at the diner over the past six months. He'd heard that Sophia got her the job. Which didn't fucking surprise Henry one bit. He'd also heard the entire town had fallen in love with Maggie. Including Officer Josh Lancaster, it seemed.

"So . . . how long have you two been a thing?"

Maggie sighed dramatically and rolled her eyes. "Hey, I warned him I'm not cop-girlfriend material, but he's so pigheaded he wouldn't listen."

Josh was smiling into the rearview mirror. "I eventually wore her down."

"Just keep your eyes on the road, Romeo," Henry warned.

"Damn fool," Maggie said, looking in the rearview mirror and smirking.

Josh smiled back. "Yeah, but I'm your damn fool."

"Am I seriously going to have to listen to this the whole way?" Henry whined.

Maggie leaned over the front seat and flipped the siren and lights on. "It's time for you to haul ass, baby, like I know you can."

Josh grinned. "You buckle up, sweetheart."

"You know I will. I have big plans for you later today."

"Jesus," Henry muttered as Josh punched the accelerator and everything became a blur.

****

Henry was sweating his ass off in his jeans and his white long-sleeve oxford. He'd forgotten it would be hotter than the hinges of hell in Colombia in spring.

He had been all over the damn village until someone finally told him Sophia was teaching at the school.

He walked into the small open school. He stopped at the front desk and asked for Sophia. The lady looked him up and down before she told him she was finishing up for the day. The last classroom on the left.

Henry walked slowly down the hall. He was sweating profusely, and it had nothing to do with the heat. His heart was going to beat right out of his chest. He clutched the envelope that held the divorce papers.

He looked into the small room. It was decorated in happy colors. Henry swallowed as he saw Sophia sitting on a mat on the floor, surrounded by eight rapt faces.

She must have sensed him there because she looked up and his heart friggin' stopped. God, she was so beautiful.

"Henry . . ." she said with a sob.

The children got up and ran out of the room at the sound of the bell. Henry walked over to her.

She held out her hands for him to help her up.

With shaky, sweaty hands he clasped her hands and hauled her up, and as he did, his knees threatened to buckle.

Sophia was very pregnant.

She wore a flowy dress that covered her belly sitting down. She watched him warily as she unconsciously rubbed her bump.

"Please tell me the baby is mine?" Henry whispered with tears in his eyes.

Sophia smiled wanly and nodded. "Sí. I believe we conceived the first time we made love."

Henry swallowed. "Were you going to tell me?" he asked in a voice that wasn't his own. A shaky hand brushed over his clean-shaven face as he tried to keep his shit together and not fall at her feet and beg.

Sophia looked pained. "Oh, sí, I was going to contact you when the baby was born. It would have been too painful for me to have contact with you while I was pregnant. My heart was broken, and the stress wasn't good for the baby. So, I just decided to tell you when the baby was born and we could figure out the visitation schedule together."

Henry couldn't get past one word. "Why was your heart broken?"

Sophia wiped a tear away. "Because I love you, Henry. I was going to tell you the night we had dinner with Snake, Mia, and Santiago, but you left. You told me I should come home so we could get back to our lives. I didn't want to trap you into staying married to me."

"But I heard you tell Santiago that you loved John Williams with all your heart," he said, even though it was killing him to say it. He needed to know the truth.

Sophia looked confused. She shook her head as she tried to remember. "No . . . I told Santiago that I loved *you* with all my heart. He already suspected, anyway, and he told me John would understand that I had fallen in love with you and that I could never marry him."

Henry fell to his knees and oh-so-gently touched her belly with shaking hands. Tears streamed down his face. The baby decided to give a swift kick right at that moment. Henry flinched and looked up at Sophia.

Tears streamed down her face as she smiled. "He or she is going to be a soccer player, I think."

Henry laughed and stood. He cupped her face. "I love you so much. I'm sorry for being such an idiot. Can you ever forgive me?"

Sophia wiped his tears away. "Say it again?"

"I love you. I love you. I love you. I'm going to say it so much you'll beg me to stop."

"Never," she said as he kissed her like the starving man he was.

She tasted like heaven and he couldn't get enough of her.

She giggled and broke the kiss.

"What's the matter?" he asked urgently.

"Nothing, I'm just a little tired. I've been on my feet all day."

"Oh, Jesus. Do you want me to carry you?"

Sophia laughed out loud and it was the single best sound he had ever heard. "No, I just want you to walk with me."

Henry cupped her face. "I'd walk to the ends of the world for you, Soph."

"I love you, Henry."

Henry took her hand and they walked through the small village. People stopped and stared. Henry waved and smiled. His world had just righted itself and nothing could bring him down.

They got to Sophia's little house, which was neat as a pin. He helped her up the stairs and once he was inside, it was a virtual treasure trove of memories. There were photos of Sophia and her family on every available surface.

Henry walked around and studied them. He had a stupid grin on his face as he explored. Every so often he would point to a picture and Sophia would explain what was happening.

"Are you hungry? Can I get you a glass of water or a pop?" she asked.

That seemed to pull him out of his stupor. "No, but let me get you something to eat and drink. You just rest."

Sophia held her hands out to him and he took them and knelt in front of her.

"I just want to look at you. I'm so happy you're here. You shaved off your Balbo," she said, caressing his smooth face. "You look like you're twenty."

He smiled. "I feel like I'm twenty." He rubbed his smooth face. "Yeah, I was a mess. I figured I'd just start from scratch. And now I'm glad I did. I wouldn't want to scratch the baby with my whiskers."

Sophia smiled. "One more month. Can you stay here with me? I really like my doctor."

Henry just stared at Sophia. He cleared his throat. "I'm not sure you understand, Mrs. Johnson, but you are never getting rid of me again. I'll be sticking so close to you that people are going to think I'm your shadow."

Sophia laughed.

"But seriously, I will stay with you until the baby is born and then you and the baby will come back to Harmony with me. How does that sound?"

"I would like that very much. Will we live at camp and you will stay in Portland when you are working?"

Henry looked almost angry and shook his head. "No, I was a coward hiding out in Portland. I was terrified of my feelings for you. No, we will live at camp until our house is built. I thought we could build down by the pond. On the other side of the beach there is a point with lots of trees that we could clear to build a log cabin. Would you like a log cabin?"

Sophia smiled. "Sí, I would love a log cabin. But won't it be a long drive to work for you? We could always live in your condo in Portland so you would be closer to work."

Henry looked sheepish. "No, actually, I quit my job."

Sophia gasped. "You quit?"

"Yeah, after you left, I just didn't have the heart for corporate law or the city any longer. I just hunkered down at camp for the winter. It wasn't pretty."

"Well, maybe I can get a job as a kindergarten teacher and you can be a househusband," she teased.

"Actually, that sounds amazing. But I think, along with nanny and househusband, I can throw in a law partnership with Lilly in downtown Harmony to chip in for expenses," he said, kissing her hands.

"Oh, that's wonderful."

"Sophia . . ."

"Sí, Henry?"

"Can we go to bed now? Not to . . . you know . . . I just want to look at you and hold you," he stammered.

"Sí, we can go to bed, but I think I want to . . . you know."

"Can we do that? Is it safe? Is it possible?" he asked, rubbing her big belly.

Sophia laughed. "Sí to everything."

****

Henry spent hours caressing every square inch of her body as if he had to relearn it. He had never in all his life seen anything so life-changing. Not to mention sexy. He now understood the saying men liking their women barefoot and pregnant, and there wasn't a sexist thing about it as far as Henry was concerned. He would never get enough of touching her pregnant body.

Making love had been interesting. He was terrified of hurting her or the baby so he tried to be extra gentle, but Sophia was hollering in

Spanish for him to go harder and faster. Her neighbors must have been torn between calling the *policía* or an exorcist.

As they lay in bed after they had made love, Sophia asked Henry what the tattoo over his heart meant. He hadn't had it before she left.

The tattoo read *0' 3' 5 N 71° 13' 22' W*.

"It's where my heart was. It's the coordinates for your village."

Sophia traced the tattoo with love, while Henry kept his hand on her belly to feel all the kicks.

"She is active tonight," Henry said, smiling.

"What makes you think it's a girl?' Sophia asked.

"I want a healthy boy or girl, but between you and me, I would love a daughter. And I want her to look just like her *madre*."

Sophia smiled but it didn't last long.

"And, just so you know, no daughter of mine is going to play soccer. In my family, we don't consider that a sport," Henry insisted.

Sophia sucked up all the air in the room. "She most certainly will be playing football. That is the proper term, not soccer. Colombians love their football!"

Henry rubbed her belly and whispered, "Don't listen to her, Garcia. Daddy will buy you a field hockey stick or some cheerleading pom-poms."

Sophia laughed. "Garcia?"

Henry looked up at Sophia. "Yeah, I thought Garcia would be pretty. It's your middle name."

Tears fell unchecked down Sophia's cheeks. "In Colombia, many of the children have both their mother's and father's names. My mother's maiden name was Garcia. How does Garcia Elsie Johnson sound?" Sophia whispered.

Henry tried to swallow the lump in his throat. "That's beautiful."

Chapter 37

Henry soon became known as Mr. Fixit. He would walk Sophia to school in the mornings, and on the way home people would ask him to help them with whatever needed fixing. Sometimes it was an old vehicle, or a clogged sink, and today, it was replacing roof shingles.

He got to know the people who had loved his Sophia since she was a little girl. It was a little like Harmony. They took him in and made him their own. And word traveled fast that he didn't like *football*, so everyone and his brother tried to change his mind. Including making him play in the evenings with the local kids.

He wouldn't tell them, but he did have a newfound respect for the sport now that his legs were covered in bruises. And, if his daughter played football, she would kick ass. He had no doubt from the way she kicked her mother.

Sophia was due any day. It had taken Henry awhile to convince her to let him bring a specialist to the hospital in Colombia. Not because he didn't trust her doctor, but for his own peace of mind. She had refused at first, but it was Sophia's doctor who convinced her to allow Henry to bring in his specialist. How could it hurt to be extra prepared? Sophia had given in and Henry thought that she actually liked the American doctor who specialized in difficult births. Just in case, she had told him.

One day, Henry walked to the school to collect her like he did every day. No matter how much he suggested she stay home and rest, she wouldn't hear of it. She wanted to be with her kids for as long as she could. Especially since she and Henry would be moving back to Maine after the baby was born.

Henry held Sophia's hand as they walked home. The birds and monkeys chattered and screamed in the trees somewhere not too far away.

That night as he held Sophia, his mother visited him in a dream. It was as real as the bed under him.

He was back at camp. He could see her from the porch window. His mother was standing in the exact spot where she died. The field of wildflowers.

She was smiling at him.

He ran out the door and didn't stop until he stood in front of her in case she disappeared.

"Hello, Henry, my precious, precious boy," Elsie said, cupping his face.

"Momma . . ." was all he could say through the lump in his throat and the tears streaming down his face.

With tears in her own eyes, Elsie gathered him close. "Oh, Henry, I've missed you, baby. I'm so proud of the man you've become."

He just sobbed as if a dam had been broken.

Elsie stroked his hair and back until he had cried his tears. She pulled back and wiped his tears away.

"When are you going to let go of your anger and forgive, Henry?"

"I don't know what you mean? I'm not angry at you for leaving."

His mother smiled. "I know it's not me you're angry at, sweetheart. Do you remember when you were little and you used to come to church with me? You loved church so much, your dad and I thought you might become a minister. You would tell all the other boys and girls that Jesus loved them."

Henry did remember.

"But then I was taken from you and you changed. You were so angry at God. You turned your back on him and have never spoken to him since. He's been waiting a long time to talk to you, Henry. He never stopped loving you."

"He took my whole world away from me when he took you."

"I know, sweetheart. But it's time to let go of your anger. Soon

you're going to have a beautiful baby who will need all of your love and guidance. And part of that guidance is teaching her about God. Just like I taught you."

"I'll try, Momma."

Elsie smiled and the whole world brightened. "Now walk with me and tell me all about your beautiful Sophia."

Henry woke with a start. He could feel the dried tears on his face as he tried to calm his racing heart.

Sophia was already up. She had trouble sleeping with the baby being so big and active at night.

He threw some shorts on and padded out to the tiny kitchen where she was pouring coffee.

"Oh, just in time. The coffee is ready." She turned to hand him his coffee, but the cup fell out of her hands and crashed to the floor, spilling hot coffee on their bare feet. He barely had time to register that her feet might be burned when she doubled over in pain and his world exploded.

He picked her up and carried her to the couch. He ran to the counter to grab his cell phone that was charging and ran back to her.

He was dialing the hospital while he asked her if she was still in pain. She nodded and cried out again. The hospital answered and was not surprised to hear Henry's voice because he called every day to make sure he could get through to them and that they were ready to deliver his baby.

They were unprepared, however, at the panic in his voice as he told them that something was terribly wrong with Sophia. They dispatched the ambulance with his specialist on board as he had been sleeping at the hospital while awaiting the birth.

The specialist called Henry as he was on his way and asked a multitude of questions. It seemed like it was hours, but it was only minutes, as they waited for the ambulance. Henry got a cold cloth for Sophia's face. She was sweating and moaning in pain. As he was coming back to her with a fresh cloth, he spied the blood that was saturating her nightgown. His legs buckled as he knelt before her.

His only concern was for her to not see the blood. He cupped her face.

"Look at me, Soph. Just look at me," he repeated over and over.

"Henry . . . promise me," her voice sounding urgent, "promise me that you will save the baby. No matter what . . ."

Henry shook his head. He tried to dislodge the boulder in his throat. The roaring in his ears increased. "Sweetheart, shhh, just breathe. You're going to be fine and so is the baby."

Tears began to fall from Sophia's beautiful, soft brown eyes. The kindest eyes Henry had ever seen. His insides felt like they were being scraped raw.

"Please," she sobbed. "I love you and I trust you. I need to know that you will fight for our little girl."

The tears were freely falling down his face, as well. "Oh, so you agree with me that we're having a girl," he joked with a sob and a laugh.

Sophia cried out in pain but still managed to smile.

Finally, blessedly, the ambulance arrived, and the doctor and attendants burst through the open door. The doctor took one look, then took Henry by the shoulders and shook him. "Henry, I need you to hang in there for me. Sophia needs you, and so does the baby."

Henry shook his head to clear it and nodded.

The doctor gave Sophia a shot and she went right to sleep. They bundled her up and got her into the ambulance along with Henry, who sat in the front seat. The doctor said he needed the space to work, but really he just wanted to be able to talk freely with the hospital and not have Henry freak out.

As soon as they arrived at the hospital, Sophia was whisked away, but the doctor stopped Henry. "Henry, Sophia needs surgery. She's had a placental abruption. I'm not going to lie—it's serious. We could lose them both."

Henry put his arm out to the wall to hold himself up. "If there is any way to save them both, do it. But if there is a choice, you save Sophia. Do you fucking hear me? You save Sophia," he said with a sob.

"God willing, I'm going to save them both, Henry," the doctor said before he sprinted down the hallway to surgery.

Henry sank to the floor in shock. He didn't know how long he sat there until the phrase began to repeat in his brain. *God willing.* Anger blinded him.

Henry jumped up, ran to the ground floor, and burst into the empty, tiny chapel. There were several lit candles that gave off an eerie glow, lighting Jesus as he hung on the cross above the altar.

"Don't you do it! Don't you fucking take her from me!" he screamed as he sprayed spittle.

Henry fell to his knees. "I won't let you take her away from me. Haven't you taken enough? How could you take my mother from me? She was our world. I was fourteen fucking years old! When I needed you the most, you left me and ripped my world apart. Where were you when I cried and begged you just like I'm doing now? I begged you to not let my mother die."

Henry bowed his head and sobbed for a good long while. Miraculously, the anger seemed to have flowed out of him, along with the tears. He was just left with terror.

"I'm so sorry I turned away from you. I was in so much pain. I can't go through that again. Sophia doesn't deserve to die, and our baby is so innocent. Please, if you need to take someone, take me. Don't take them. I promise I will be the best Christian, husband, and father in the world if you just spare my family. Please, Dios, I'm begging you, don't take my family away."

Henry had no idea how long he had been praying and pleading. It could have been one hour or four.

The next thing he knew, the doctor was shaking his arm as he bowed at the altar.

"Henry, Sophia and your daughter are fine. Sophia is in recovery and your daughter is in the nursery. Would you like to meet her?"

The tears began to fall as Henry laughed and nodded. He followed the doctor to the nursery. Henry put on a johnny and a hair cap, stood over the glass bassinet, and cried like the baby he was gazing at. He didn't give two shits if anybody witnessed it.

She was the most perfect human being ever created. She had a full head of wispy, dark hair. She had her mother's perfect tiny nose and ears.

He leaned over the bassinet and put his pinky in her hand, which she grasped tightly. He laughed and cried. She was strong. And perfect.

"Hello, Garcia Elsie Johnson, I'm your papa and I'm going to take good care of you and your momma. I can't wait for you to meet her. You're the luckiest little girl in the world to have her for a madre."

"Mr. Johnson, would you like to hold your daughter?" the nurse asked him in broken English.

He nodded and sat in the rocking chair. The nurse put his daughter in his arms. The very arms that had been created for that moment right there. She fit perfectly in his arms just like her mother.

"When will Sophia wake up?" he whispered.

"As soon as your wife is brought to her room from recovery, you and the baby can sit with her and wait for her to wake up."

Henry nodded and rocked and talked with his daughter. He had so much to tell her. He especially wanted to tell her about her grandmother, Elsie Johnson.

Epilogue

Five years later...

Henry walked Ruby and Dottie down the church aisle to their car after services. It was his turn to be church usher this week. He took his duty very seriously as he shook hands and wished the church members a good day.

He waved to Garrett and Lilly, Bobby and Ava, Sam and Gracie, Doug and Dana. He hadn't rested until everyone he loved, and even those he had just met, agreed to attend their little church in Harmony. He figured he could get them there with his way with words and persuasion, but it would be up to God to keep them there.

He had built a successful law practice with Lilly in Harmony. But not so busy that he couldn't coach his daughter's soccer team. Yes, the very same team that was going to win the championship this year. It was clear that the five-year-olds couldn't care less about winning a championship and thought more about what flavor of ice cream they would get after the game. But the dad coaches cared enough for all of them. It was *game on* in the fall and they would talk smack to each other for the entire season—behind the wives' backs, of course. If they heard, they would shut that shit down. It was all about having fun, they would say. *My ass.*

But Henry didn't have to worry because Garcia was the best soccer player ever. He was pretty sure Colombia would be scouting her in the foreseeable future.

"Papa, look! I got another star for memorizing my Bible verses," his daughter said, pointing to the strip of paper with red and gold stars indicating each week she had successfully recited her Bible verses. The teacher had stapled the thin strip of paper so she was wearing it as a headband.

Henry scooped her up. "Wow. That is super cool! Do you think your teacher will make me one of those?"

Garcia giggled as Henry tickled her.

"No, Papa, it's only for Sunday school students. You're too big."

Henry watched as Sophia, the love of his life, said goodbye to her church friends and family. How was it possible that she became more beautiful every day? She took his breath away.

Sophia had gotten a job at the local elementary school as a kindergarten teacher. Everybody loved Sophia. But no one as much as Henry. She was his world.

And, true to his word, Henry became a part-time househusband and nanny. Garcia would be starting kindergarten in the fall, but for the past five years, she had gone to Little Bear Daycare—less than a mile from their home—on the days that Henry had court. If he didn't have court, she came to the office with him. It wasn't uncommon for Henry to be balancing his daughter trying to burp her while he took notes from potential clients. It was exactly the way he wanted it.

They hurried home to get ready for the barbecue at their house. His best friend, Will, and his wife, Janey, were coming with their twin four-year-old boys.

Henry was tending the grill when he had had enough. He pointed the spatula at Will and then at his boys.

"I mean it, Will. Tell your boys to not play so close to my daughter. Haven't they ever heard of personal space?" Henry groused as he took a swig from his beer.

Will laughed. "Henry, they're just four-year-olds. Chill out."

Henry flipped the burgers and mimicked Will. "Sure, that's how it starts, they're just four-year-olds and then boys will be boys. Don't think I haven't seen how they look at Garcia."

"Henry! Back up! Right now," Sophia hollered as she walked toward them.

Henry flinched and mouthed, "I'm going to get you" to Will.

"Hi, honey, don't you mean, back off?" Henry said, turning and smiling at his beautiful, angry wife.

"Sí, that's what I said. You leave the kids alone. Pretty soon no parents will let their children play with Garcia."

Henry enveloped Sophia in a big hug. "I'm sorry, baby. I'll try harder. I love you," he said as he put his two fingers to his eyes and then pointed to Will's boys and mouthed, "I'm watching you" behind Sophia's back.

Sophia kissed Henry. "I love you too. Now behave."

Henry watched Sophia walk away with a stupid grin on his face.

Will laughed. "Yeah, Henry's Law is dead and gone, never to be resurrected again."

Henry was still grinning as the angel on his shoulder kicked the little devil right over the edge and wiped his hands for good measure.

I hope you've enjoyed Henry and Sophia's journey! I'm always eager to hear from my readers. If you're interested in reading more (This is a ten book series), check out my https://authorcentral.amazon.com/gp/profile - or follow me on social media channels below. Also, be sure to join my Website Mailing List and get a **FREE** novella, plus early-bird offers, news updates, and a ton of other cool, fun and sexy stuff.

www.hollyjmartin.com

Holly J. Martin on **Twitter:**@Princess33Holly
Holly J. Martin on **Facebook**: https://www.facebook.com/hollyj martinauthor
https://www.instagram.com/hollyjmartinauthor/

I look forward to hearing from you! And, thanks again!

Much love and kisses from Maine.

Holly J. Martin

P. S. Please keep scrolling for the preview of *Caleb's Fight*!

Preview of Caleb's Fight

This dog is going to die! Caleb looked around the room that had once been his bedroom and felt his anger spike. He also felt his throat closing and his eyes burn and tear up. Then the sneezing began.

All the while the demon dog barked and tore around the room. And, when she wasn't barking, she was whining and growling.

Every shade and curtain had been torn from the windows or hung limply like some creepy haunted house movie set. All the blankets and sheets had been ripped from his bed. Ripped would be the operative word here. The dog had shredded his down comforter. All over the room tiny feathers floated in the air.

The leather couch in the corner had scratch marks from one end to the other. The bottom drawer of the bureau was pulled out and all his T-shirts were scattered everywhere with one sporting a big dump.

"You are going to fucking die!" Caleb hollered as he stalked towards the dog, hardly able to see out of his tear-soaked eyes.

The dog's ears laid back and a low growl emanated from her. Caleb stopped instantly and had a staredown with his sister's beloved pitbull, Jane Austen.

Neither was giving in but the sneezing began again, which made the dog hunch down as if she was going to attack.

Jesus. There wasn't another person on the planet that could make him as mad as his sister.

Caleb walked backwards out of the room and shut the door. The dog began to go crazy again. He heard a big crash. Was that his bureau? Could a dog thrash a heavy wooden bureau to the ground?

He wouldn't know because he had never had an animal. His siblings, all nine of them, had never let him forget that they couldn't get a dog because Caleb was severely allergic to all animals. It was hardly his fault. He was born that way. He did wish that they could walk in his shoes for one day and be around his sister's spoiled rotten dog. They would see how painful it was not being able to breathe or see.

He didn't need this shit, he thought, as he stalked to the kitchen. Jack, his sister, had written down the name of her veterinarian in case of an emergency. Well, this ranked as an emergency in his book.

His sister had waltzed into his apartment in New York and announced that she and her husband and kids were going to see their brother Henry in Colombia but would not be able to bring Jane, the dog, because they would have to quarantine her and there was no way she could put the dog through that.

Henry and his wife, Sophia, had just had a baby girl, Garcia Elsie Johnson. There had been complications with the birth so Henry and Sophia were going to stay in her home country of Colombia for a few more months before coming home.

He loved his sister but she made him crazy sometimes. Out of all his siblings, he was closest to her but she could also make his temper spike in thirty seconds or less. What made it worse was all of them were scared shitless of his sister. She was formidable.

There was another crash in his bedroom. That sounded like his bedside lamp. He growled as he picked up the paper on his counter and grabbed his phone.

He also grabbed a paper towel to staunch the snot running like a faucet from his nose. Caleb heard the phone ringing as another attack of sneezing gripped him.

"Hello?"

More sneezing.

"Hello?"

"Hi, I'm here," he said, between more sneezing. "I have an emergency. I'm looking for Dr. Walker."

"This is Dr. Walker," the melodic female voice said.

Caleb sniffed.

"I'm Jack Johnson's brother and I'm taking care of her dog."

"I'll be right there. Text me your address," she said and the line went dead.

Caleb looked at the phone in his hand. What had just happened?

Now he had a small attack of guilt forming in his gut. The doctor had acted like his sister's dog was dying. Well, he did say he was going to kill the damn dog. But, was it an emergency, really?

Caleb shook his head. Fuck that. That dog was going insane and may rip his arm off in the night. If that dog killed him in his sleep, his dead body would lay there for a week until his sister was due back. Would the dog eat him?

Caleb shivered and texted the doctor his address and called downstairs to tell the doorman that he could send the vet right up.

Made in the USA
Monee, IL
02 September 2021